A Small War in
a Far-Off Place

A Novel

By

Thomas Hofstedt

It makes no difference what men think of war, said the judge. War endures. As well ask men what they think of stone. War was always here. Before man was, war waited for him. The ultimate trade awaiting its ultimate practitioner."

-Cormac McCarthy, *Blood Meridian*

Table of Contents

The Beginning (1973)   1
A Soldier's View   11
Pasha Khail   17
War & Money   20
The Jihadist Banker   26
Pork Barrels Abroad   29
Nation Building   33
Kaz   35
Camille   40
The Banker's Plan   42
A Meeting - Beirut   45
Liaison in Paris   49
Eve of a Kidnapping   54
A Tipping Point   61
Slater - Day One   68
A Call From Afghanistan   71
Planning the Fix   74
Kaz (London)   77
Not Your Usual Meeting   81
A Special Offer   85
Meeting Recap   89
Recalled Conversations   91
Field Report   97
Family Legacies   99
Doing Business in Dubai   103
Slater - Day Two   107
Slater - Day Four   113
Harlan & Madge   117
Meeting at Achin Adi   121
Slater - Day Seven   125
Slater - Day Twelve   134
The Projects   139
The Meeting Place   146
Kaz and Malik   151
Takhar Province   154
A Walk in the Moonlight   158
Washington D.C.   162
The Absence of Neutrality   164

Kaz and Slater 169
The Patrol 173
Two Old Men 176
Harlan - Kabul 178
The Kaz Wrinkle 184
Camille & Derek (Kabul) 187
Photoshopped 190
Pashtun Options 193
Mujahedeen Reflections 197
Ransom Details 200
A Starring Role for CC 203
Arrangements for a Swap 209
War Games 212
Players in Motion 216
Decisions 220
Tactical Arrangements 224
Loose Ends 230
If You Are Not My Friend 233
Lethal Skirmishes 239
Prelude to an Exchange 244
The Meeting 248
The Conversation 253
Epilog 257

The Beginning (1973)

"So this is what exile is like. We wear tuxedos and go to parties with our enemies."

He said it with a light tone and a slight smile, but Ali knew his father well and was not surprised when he frowned at him and said, "It is not exile. And the British are no longer our enemies. That was a long time ago in a different world."

So he has lost his sense of irony. Not lost, but driven out. There's no room for any emotions except bitterness and regret. The dominant personality traits of a disillusioned revolutionary.

The silent criticism was tinged with real affection. Ali was still young enough – twenty-five – that he could not foresee the possibility that he would become like his father. He was finishing five years of graduate school at Oxford and – although he was committed to returning to Afghanistan – he found himself drawn to Western culture and values. Not enough to emigrate to Europe or the U.S., but enough for him to envision a modern Afghanistan, or at least pieces of it that he could shape.

He felt at home in the current setting. As he looked out across the open expanse of the rooftop garden, it was easy to imagine that he was back in London. But only until he looked beyond the parapet, where the huge Kocatepe mosque occupied his visual field and a sizeable part of Central Ankara.

Just another major diplomatic cocktail party, without the alcohol. A couple of hundred highly civilized and upper class people with fixed smiles in place, constantly circulating while hoping for face time with one of the five or six A-list invitees. A lot of very serious older men in black tie or business suits paired up -- mismatched, really -- with beautiful women in designer dresses.

Then he began to catalog the small and not-so-small differences between what he was seeing and an equivalent venue in London. *Not as many white faces ... all these dusky Arabs and Turks. And so much quieter! One of the nicer side effects of the Muslim's disapproval of alcohol. Makes it so much easier to hear the call to prayer from the minarets. And those designer dresses are not nearly as revealing as they would be in Covent Garden.*

The British ambassador to Turkey was the nominal host, but the guest list included the staff of other embassies -- the ones in tuxedos -- high-ranking members of the Turkish government, and – the reason his father was here -- prominent Afghanis who "happened" to be in Ankara because they were out-of-favor with the ruling party.

The call from his father came just five days ago.

"Your mother and I are going to Ankara. I want you to join us there rather than here in Kabul."

"For how long? Aren't you a new minister in the Khan government?" Ali asked only to test his father's degree of realism. He was pleased by the response.

"I have the title. But, in fact, it's not healthy for me to be in Afghanistan for a while. Khan is putting all of his "modernization" cronies around him. And he's got his pet Russians everywhere. There's no room for those who disagree. Or their families."

Right out of the London Times, except for the 'first person' perspective. Mohammed Douad Khan had just led a military coup, deposing the King and declaring himself to be President of the newly named Republic of Afghanistan. His ruling party – the People's Democratic Party of Afghanistan – was moving quite forcefully to reform and modernize the mostly communist state along mostly secular lines, including an emphasis on women's rights. Khan was strengthening ties with the U.S.S.R., playing on Russia's need to have a strong client-state in the region. To accomplish these changes, he was consolidating power, a strategy being pursued through a ruthless purge of, as Ali's father put it, "those who disagree."

When they met three days later in Ankara, he surprised both himself and his father when he said, "I know you disapprove of Khan, but some of what he's doing needs to be done. It's time."

His father looked at him carefully, perhaps only then seeing that his son had taken on new dimensions. He paused, seeming to weigh Ali's words.

"It can't last," he said, shaking his head. "There are too many powerful factions that think otherwise. The communists, of course. Then there are the nationalists. They're fine with communism, but don't want the Russians in charge. But the real resistance will come from the Islamists. The mullahs and the ethnic tribal chiefs. They cannot stomach Khan's so-called modernization!"

"Those who talk about jihad," Ali said very softly, knowing that his father would count himself as one of those he labeled "Islamist" or "ethnic party chief." *And he expects me to think like he does. I wonder if I can do that?*

Then he asked the important question. "Will you go back?" He did not attempt to analyze whether his anxiety about the response was for himself or his father.

The conflict was evident on his father's face. Before he could answer, Ali said, "We both know that a civil war is coming and that it's going to be long and bloody. If you go back, you – we – will be fighting for a decade or more."

I have never spoken to my father like that. Almost challenging his beliefs. Or my own.

His father looked at him with an immense sadness as if he was also aware of the shift in their relationship. Of the difference between the boy that he had sent off five years ago and the man who stood before him. The tones in his voice reflected that same sadness.

"Yes. I will go back. And there will be fighting, as you say. There always has been fighting in Afghanistan. It's what we do."

That sadness weighed on Ali as he stood looking out over the ancient rooftops of Ankara and the slender minarets rising above them. *Turkey. An Islamic country, but with a secular government. And they're not killing each other ... except for the Kurds, of course.*

Thirty feet from him, a young woman paused, seeing the sadness without knowing its cause. It made what had started out as an act of good manners into something with far more possibility imbedded in it.

One minute ago, her father gestured with his free hand, "Go talk to that young man. He doesn't know anyone here."

She teased, "Do we have a diplomatic interest in 'that young man'? Shall I lobby for a tariff or some such thing?"

He frowned back at her. "It is against State Department policy to use one's beautiful daughter to curry favor with local business interests." Then he smiled and said, "The two of you are the only young – and interesting – people at this entire affair. And all I know about him is that his life is about to become considerably more complicated."

He gave her a slight push. "Just go talk to him."

Maybe it was her father's cryptic comment, but he did look … interesting. He was dressed in grey slacks with a charcoal blazer, looking very English. He walked with a slight limp. Tall and athletic looking, cleanly shaven, with dark skin and black unruly hair. Even in the poor light and from thirty feet away, she knew that – up close – he would be exotic looking, with great eyes.

He turned and caught her looking at him. *So, I'm committed then.* She smiled and quickly closed the distance between them. "I'm Yasmin. I'm the daughter –"

"Of the American Under-Secretary for Trade. I know." He smiled and bowed very slightly. "And I am Ali, son of the newly appointed and soon-to-be exiled Economics Minister of Afghanistan."

Yasmin smiled and said, "Apparently, we are lesser lights, notable only because of our distinguished parents …"

She spoke the words teasingly, partly to make it clear that she did not really believe that to be true but also because he looked so serious, so susceptible to being offended.

He is exotic looking, and he does have great eyes. Twenty-five, maybe? But so terribly serious. Sad. Soft voice, long fingers. And there's something pent-up about him.

Ali had noticed Yasmin as soon as she came into the party about thirty minutes ago on her father's arm. She was hard not to notice. She was half the age of the other women in the space and far more striking. Neither tall nor short, neither stocky nor skinny, with shoulder-length shiny black hair that emphasized her white skin. She was wearing the merest wisp of a headscarf and a long green silk dress that somehow seemed to simultaneously satisfy all of the Islamic conditions for female modesty while leaving little doubt about the gender of the wearer.

She also stood out because her left arm was in a sling.

Very, very pretty. Couple of years younger than me. Nice mouth. Very dark eyes. She would be impressive even with the hijab. But very western. The way she stands, the way she looks at people. She will be self-confident, most likely very assertive, hard to control.

His assessments were objective, lacking any moral outrage. About a year ago, after four years in England, he realized that he was no longer shocked by Western women -- their brazenness, language or the way that they affected him. He also recognized that Islam needed to change, that any culture that condemns half of its people to illiteracy and sexual repression for the sake of patriarchal tribal rituals is doomed.

"I would never refer to you as a lesser light. You're quite beautiful."

"Thank you," she said in an offhand way that told him she was accustomed to the compliment.

She spun completely around in front of him, a nicely balanced pirouette. "Do you like my dress? It's by an Egyptian designer in Paris. He says it is suitable for formal wear in an Islamic culture." Her inflection made it a question rather than a statement.

He smiled. "I would say that it complies with the letter of Islamic law while violating the spirit of the law."

Yasmin laughed out loud. "I think that was his intention."

He gestured at the sling in a way that made it a question.

She shrugged with her good shoulder. "The aftermath of a surgery. Something called a rotator cuff. Smashed in a fall caused entirely by vanity – my insistence on wearing high heeled shoes on cobblestone streets."

Ali could not resist. "So it seems our Islamic culture – at least the dress code -- makes sense. In our world, neither vanity nor high heeled shoes are permitted, so you would have escaped injury."

"Perhaps. But I noticed that you have a limp. I hope you have a more exotic story to tell about how you were injured than I do. And I will note that your religious code of conduct apparently did not shield you from such an injury?"

He looked over at his father and mother standing together talking to the host. *They would be shocked by this conversation ... how far it is from their safety zone, and how quickly it got there.* The thought triggered another, one that had never occurred to him during the last five years.

I wonder if they knew that I would become this halfway-modern creature when they decided to send me to England? Or if they wanted it?

"Alas, no," he said. "A torn calf muscle. Stepping off of a London double-decker bus after a long hard day. No surgery required."

"So. We are both wounded by civilization. I wonder what else we have in common?"

They both paused, each of them struck by how quickly their conversation had become intensely personal; each of them suddenly afraid of breaking the mood, but also wondering if this was going too far, too fast.

Ali reached out and lightly touched her bare forearm, saying, "In common? I think that each of us is bored with this party. Why don't we go somewhere else ... out of the orbit of our famous parents?"

Thirty minutes later, they were naked and in bed in Ali's hotel room.

It was neither predictable nor inevitable, but there were forces in play that made such an outcome unsurprising. Each of them was away from home, both geographically and culturally; in a foreign setting that seemed to both demand and condone new and adventurous behaviors. Each of them was at a stage in their life where major and even dangerous transitions were looming. The sense of "if not now, then when?" was very real.

Simple lust and personal chemistry were at work as well. They were attractive and young. Each of them was a strong-minded and independent person for whom "convention" was something to be avoided. Risk and its consequences were motivators, not deterrents.

The sexual play was incredibly intense, at first awkward and limited by her injury and then strangely enhanced by the constraints it imposed. The need for slowness and deliberation. Her shoulder injury was quite real and her orthopedist would have objected violently if he had been consulted. The act of taking off her sling and then the green silk dress was executed very deliberately with planning and discussion of each movement, including Ali's close inspection of what was exposed at each stage of the unrobing, and a running commentary.

Then the touching began, always with him asking, "Does it hurt here? Or here?" or "Are you OK if I do that? Or this?"

The discipline and restraint required was evident only in their rapid breathing, an occasional low moan, and the exceptional stillness of posture. Even when he lowered her very gently onto the bed, they maintained the same agonizingly slow pace for as long as they could. It ended only when she reached up with her good arm, wrapped her fingers in his hair, pulled his head down to hers and moaned, "Now! Please!"

An Ordinary Afghan Day

Early in 2015

Even in wartime, with all of its chaos, killing and destruction, there are ordinary days. Days filled with events that *seem* independent of one another rather than the product of some master plan, whether divine or secular. This seemed to be one of those days. Only with hindsight would it turn out to be exceptional.

A Predator drone, operated by a civilian contractor near the end of her eight-hour shift in Qatar, fired a Hellfire missile and destroyed an SUV near Kunduz, killing its six occupants. Two of those six were said to be in the leadership structure of al Qaeda. No mention was made of the other four individuals.

A Dutch journalist who had been held hostage for eighty days by a jihadist terror group in the Hindu Kush mountains very near the Pakistan/Afghanistan border was rescued by an elite Afghan commando unit with support from "unnamed American resources."

Photos of a General in the Afghan Army taking cash from a known Taliban warlord were posted on the internet. The pictures were of exceptional clarity and taken from a number of angles. "Informed sources" speculated that they were taken from one of the very small, locally controlled photographic drones that were popular with amateurs.

A girl's boarding school was opened in a remote Northeastern province thought to be under the control of tribal forces. Regional Taliban leaders immediately condemned such an institution as incompatible with Sharia. But the school was under the personal protection of the local tribal chief and his militia, which was unusually large, armed with the latest weaponry, and highly trained.

NATO forces continued to withdraw from combat operations. All across the country, American and British officers were taking down their unit flags and doing the best they could to reassure their Afghan army and police counterparts that they could do the job without them. Both sides knew that to be, if not outright untrue, a necessary fiction.

The leader of a tribal militia force in Farah, one of the provincial capitals, held a lavish banquet to say goodbye to the American officers that had paid him to organize his militia, and then trained and armed his recruits. The day following the banquet, his first official act was to arrest and execute eight men in Farah, claiming that they were al Qaeda allies. In fact, they were his chief business rivals. He confiscated their homes and ordered their families out of the city.

Suicide bombers attacked two Shia mosques in Kandahar Province. One hundred and eighty three worshipers were killed.

But what was "ordinary" can always be redefined. According to the report by the Special Inspector General for Afghan Reconstruction (SIGAR), released in mid-January, the Afghan world would be quite different very soon.

NATO formally lowered its flag this quarter as its 13-year combat mission in Afghanistan came to an end, and the International Security Assistance Force was replaced by Resolute Support Mission, a much smaller NATO mission that will train, advise, and assist the Afghan National Security Forces. At the London Conference in December, the United States and other donor nations emphasized that although combat has ended, reconstruction will continue into the "Decade of Transformation" (2015–2024). They renewed their commitment to provide at least $16 billion through 2015 and maintain support at or near the levels of the past decade through 2017.

Then there are those who get to define what is ordinary; or at least set forces in motion that in their playing out will shape the lives or cause the deaths of Afghans.

A U.S. senator, a member of the counter-terrorism sub-committee of the Senate Intelligence Committee, is in a meeting at the Pentagon with the heads of the CIA and the Defense Intelligence Agency. The subject being discussed is the rise of the so-called Islamic State and what the U.S. response should be.

"The Islamic State crowd is very different than the Taliban or al Qaeda. They're operating in Syria and Iraq and they want territory for their grand caliphate. The Taliban are mainly from Afghanistan and Pakistan.

"One more difference: ISIS really believes that we're in the end times. They want ... need ... to draw us in to make their apocalypse scenario come true. That's why the horrific videos of beheadings and burnings. On the other hand, the Taliban just want us gone."

The alternatives being argued are polar opposites. One option is "Do nothing. Let them fight among themselves." The other is "Send in the troops. The locals need our help or we're going to lose everything we've fought for up to now."

As usual, the meeting degenerated into a series of overlapping monologues and ended with an agreement to set another meeting.

A Soldier's View

It's such a shitty world!

The thought was neither original nor particularly angry. It was a mundane comment, as ordinary in this time and place as a convict's complaint about the poor quality of prison meals. The speaker was standing on a rooftop of a police station in a medium-sized village called Achin Adi in the northeastern part of Afghanistan. He was watching the sun go down, being careful to stay far enough away from the perimeter of the roof to be invisible to a ground-level sniper.

Slater Crosby was an American and a captain in the U.S. Army. Unless one looked closely, however, he looked more like the Afghanis he was advising than he did his blue-blooded American parents. He was lean, dark and intense with deep-set eyes that seemed to be focused on something far away. He looked older than his actual age, the mid-thirties, some of which was surely due to the chronic tiredness that settled on him like a perpetual cloak when he was in the field. He walked with an evident limp, the legacy of a Taliban RPG during his first tour in Afghanistan.

Like many of his military generation, a good bit of the last dozen years had been spent in either Afghanistan or Iraq, and so it was not surprising that he had acquired the characteristic look of someone who spent too much time in war zones. There was the impression of someone incapable of surprise, a guardedness that had become a part of him. Inevitably, his experiences had shaped him in other and more important ways, making him into someone that he had not intended to become and someone that he did not like very much.

He was good at his job, but he no longer valued that job. He was a professional soldier and the third generation of his family to serve in a combat role in the U.S. Army, starting with his grandfather in Korea and his father, whose service began in Vietnam and ended in Iraq. At first, Slater had been proud of that tradition, but by his fourth tour in-country, his main emotions were, first, a deep seated envy of those ancestors and, second, a bone-deep distaste for his daily life.

They had it easy. The people who wanted to kill them wore uniforms and came in bunches. Real armies. Easy to identify and they could fight them with the kinds of weapons that they were trained to use. And they – both sides – had a cause, something to believe in, even if it turned out to be wrong. Here, the kid who you hand a candy bar to may be wearing a suicide vest and the soldier alongside you is as likely to kill you as the enemy that you can't see in any case. And us? We call in an air strike or whistle up a drone and find that we've wiped out a wedding party, including ten kids. Kick a door down and shoot an old man that was reaching for his Koran.

He had long ago stopped believing in their own propaganda. And like most veterans of Afghanistan and Iraq, he had given up on trying to explain what his life was like to civilians. *That woman at the bar in Virginia. Two drinks, some small talk ... some developing chemistry. And then she asked, "So, what do you do?" And I realized that there is nothing in the last fourteen years of my life that would be comprehensible to her. Even if I had the will and the vocabulary to try.*

He thought about his last stateside tour and his conversation with his father. It was awkward, in the same stilted way that it had been for some time. The awkwardness was intensified by the setting. They were sitting in his father's senatorial office. His father had just been elected to the United States Senate and Slater had dropped in before being shipped out on his fourth deployment. It did not go well.

Slater was in his dress uniform, with all the medals showing. He was uncomfortable in the full regalia, but he had just called on the wife of his most recent First Sergeant. His name was Scanlon and he died when a seventeen-year-old Afghan recruit shot him in the face because "he was an infidel." Slater changed the story for Scanlon's wife.

His father was in the usual dark suit and muted tie, with the discreet American flag pin in his lapel, sitting at his desk flanked by American flags. It was not a setup well suited to small talk. To make it worse, Slater could almost feel the leftover accumulated hostility hovering over the two of them from their prior conversations.

His father, Harlan Crosby, had been a three-star general of the U.S. Army. He retired when the U.S. began its pullout from Iraq and immediately became the Director of the CIA. From there, he ran for the U.S. Senate, benefiting from the anti-Washington mood and the incompetence of his opponent. He won in a landslide and was now the single most ardent defender of the U.S. military and the far-flung intelligence community in the Congress, along with his role as the most strident "hawk" in the political establishment.

To Slater's dismay, he himself was often declared to be "a major public relations asset" to his father, given that he was a photogenic and decorated veteran of multiple tours in Afghanistan and Iraq. His father did not play that up, but – in Slater's view – he did not disclaim it either.

What would he say? My son is not really a soldier? He is not a chip off the old military block? He's only doing it to please me? He no longer believes in American exceptionalism?

He was so deep in his own thoughts that he was startled when his father spoke.

"You're a captain, head of an infantry company on the front lines. What's your perspective on the handoff to the Afghan security forces?"

How many misconceptions are there in that question? Where to begin?

He decided to keep it simple, but even then the sarcasm slipped in. "You're a little bit behind. Maybe you didn't hear? According to the President, we've accomplished our combat mission in Afghanistan. The infantry company is gone. I'm now a liaison officer to an Afghan army unit. Or is it training officer? NATO is still working on getting the titles right."

His father waved off the evasion, as though a combat officer without anyone to command was of no consequence.

"You know what I think about that whole idea. But what about the handoff? Do you think the Afghan army and police will be able to take back the countryside?"

Why don't you just tell him what he wants to hear? You know where this will go if you don't!

He had to say it. "They won't even hold on to what they've got. It's going to be a first class disaster."

The reaction was predictable. His father sat up and barked at him, "Bullshit! You're not –"

Slater interrupted what he knew would become an ever-angrier monologue if he let it go on. But he didn't – couldn't – remain silent on this issue, and to agree with his father would be cowardly. It didn't help that the image of Scanlon's wife sitting at her kitchen table was still with him. He used the most conciliatory tone he could come up with, trying to sound reasonable.

"It's degenerating into a playground fight. You've got the government, the Taliban, al Qaeda and now the *real* crazies coming from Iraq and Syria with their so-called Islamic State. Then you throw in the tribal factions and the Sunni vs. Shia hostilities. And just to keep it interesting, every male in the country down to the ten-year olds owns an automatic weapon and maybe a rocket launcher or two! And everybody wants to get even with somebody."

His father was at least listening. "But Karzai is out. We've got a president that is finally paying attention."

"Too little, too late. And I'm betting that Ashraf Ghani will turn out to look a lot like Karzai before he's done."

His father sat still, momentarily depressed by the gap between the two of them. If Slater had stopped there, their meeting might have shifted to a new level. Certainly to a new and less contentious topic. But he couldn't stop.

"And – the way we're doing it, with drones and hired guns -- it's not even close to winnable. All we can do is kill more people, including our own."

This time, his father's face reddened. He stood and leaned forward over his desk, resting on both clenched fists. When he opened his mouth to speak, Slater stood up and walked out of the office.

His last stop before shipping out was to see his mother. He picked a time when his father was out-of-town visiting some defense plant in California.

She was touring Walter Reed Hospital in Maryland. It was a monthly ritual with her, always visiting every new patient transferred in from Afghanistan and Iraq. By now, the press no longer found it newsworthy and she could spend as much time as she liked and say what she pleased without worrying about what

Harlan always called "the optics." But it always ended with a long list of family members to call. And she always went through the list, often in tears.

Slater knew her driver and found him in the cafeteria. He told him, "Take the rest of the day off. I'll be chauffeur from here on."

He saw her coming. As always, he was struck by how beautiful she was. In her sixties, she still exuded a warmth that transmitted itself to anyone with whom she came in contact. It was all the more remarkable because she was so controlled, so – for lack of a better word, "appropriate" -- in all circumstances. In that sense, she was an ideal military and political spouse -- photogenic, loyal, tactful, supportive. The reality that her marriage lacked passion or even affection did not seem important to her.

When she saw Slater leaning on the front fender, she almost ran the last few steps to the car and embraced him fiercely. As always, he felt unworthy of such strong emotion.

She didn't let go, but leaned back and said. "How nice! But you're leaving again, aren't you? Back to …"

He was used to it, but her expression saddened him, as it always did when he told her of another deployment.

He didn't bother to answer, just stroked her arm.

The flash of concern slowly dissolved into sadness, but she flipped her hair back and said briskly, "Harlan's not here. He's in –"

"I know. I saw him two days ago. In his office. Didn't he mention it?"

She looked very closely at him. "No, he didn't. I gather it didn't go well?"

"The usual agreement to disagree. Maybe a little louder than usual."

Yasmin Crosby was Slater's mother, but – more importantly – she had been the model wife of a general officer in the United States military establishment, a role that was honed to an even finer edge by the last few years among the DC political set. It was a role that required at least as much discipline as any master sergeant of an infantry company, or even a first lady.

She knew about, but could not talk about, the "agreement to disagree," and she could have argued either side of the underlying question with both facts and unfeigned passion. Much of her restraint on this matter came from her certainty that her marriage would be forfeit if she spoke out; that her husband would see it as disloyalty to him rather than as a mother worried about her only son or as a citizen tired of seemingly endless wars in obscure places with unpronounceable place names.

As always, the bleak thoughts triggered the same dreary internal monologue in her brain: the question that, over time, had become purely rhetorical.

Would divorce be such a bad thing? You do not love ... you have never loved ... this man. Thirty-five years together and he does not value who I am or care about what I want. He needs me and my son and uses us to further his own ambitions. And, worst of all, he wants our son to be a hero.

The reverie ended as it always did, with yet another unanswerable question.

What if ....?

Pasha Khail

It was a small Afghan village. But it appeared all at once, suddenly before you in its entirety when the dirt track emerged from the great piles of jumbled boulders that were scattered across the floor of the small valley, as if abandoned there in a cosmic game of marbles. The village was typical – a cluster of mud and stone houses that blended into the landscape. It did not even appear on most regional maps.

It was home to perhaps fifteen or twenty families, a tightly knit community where everybody was related to everybody else. Like most Afghan villages in these days, there were very few young men in sight. The population was composed of the non-combatants – the women, old men, and children.

The families and their ancestors had lived there since the middle ages. They had pursued many trades and practiced many forms of worship as generation followed generation, but they always stayed in the same place. For the last hundred years, they were devout Sunni Muslims who devoted themselves and their many sons to opium production and fighting the waves of foreigners and infidels – first the British, then the Russians, and now the Americans.

They were Pashtun, from the Tani tribe, living according to an unwritten code that was as harsh as the land that they inhabited. They were fiercely independent and did not recognize a central government or any other form of authority, although their neutrality and even a temporary allegiance could be purchased with hard currency and respect. They had fought with the Americans against the Taliban and al Qaeda in 2001 and, depending on tribal politics, had gone back and forth since then.

But then those Americans had installed their own form of government in Kabul and created a national army and police force. The central government ignored the tribes; or, even worse, attempted to make them subordinate to the central government. They sent representatives to tell the village elders that *Afghanistan is different now. We are a pluralistic democracy with the rule of law.* But they were corrupt and they violated the most fundamental teachings of Islam and Sharia law and waged war against true believers in Iraq, Syria and Yemen.

So now their village leader was called a "warlord" and he and the young men left their homes and went off to fight with the jihadis, the ones that talked of a new caliphate, one that would span the artificial borders drawn by far-off foreigners and restore a pure form of Islam.

Afghanistan had always been a war without neutral zones, a shifting battlefield where the rule was, *if you are not my friend, then you are my enemy.* So the village elders did not trust the Taliban or al Qaeda either to protect them or to ignore them. They bribed them to leave them in peace, using their poppy fields as their form of currency. As for the government, their soldiers stayed in their cities and fortified towns and let the American and British soldiers do the fighting and dying in the dangerous countryside. The American soldiers occasionally would come through the village with their translators, candy bars for the children, and – of course – their promises. But, even then, the Americans were vastly different from the Russians and the Taliban: you could ignore them or even taunt them without risking your life.

The complete withdrawal of NATO troops and the handoff to the Afghan National Army was a momentous transition for the western governments and the ministers in Kabul, but was largely unnoticed away from the cities, except by the Taliban, who were emboldened. It is unlikely that the villagers of Pasha Khail were even aware of the change. And even less likely that they could do anything to alter what happened because of that change.

There were eight of them that came that day. They were Uzbeks. They all wore the same green uniform, that of the Afghan National Security Forces, and carried the same weapons. But they were not very military. They simply drove into the village in two jeep-like vehicles and parked in the center of the compound. They seemed to have no concern with security, but stood around in the square all in a group, apparently discussing what to do.

They went house-to-house, bringing everyone into the small square in the center; herding them into a tight circle. There were forty-one individuals, more than half of them children. The villagers were used to it, expecting to have their houses searched and to be interrogated about sightings of al Qaeda and the Taliban. But this time was different.

The soldiers took five teenage girls and set them aside from the main group, watched over by a single soldier. Then they began firing. At first, they fired long bursts, their rifle muzzles tracing long arcs from side to side. The arcs became shorter as targets became scarce. A lone boy, perhaps seven or eight years old, stood strangely immune for what seemed a very long time until the streams of bullets converged on him. After that, there were very short bursts or single shots until there was no movement within the untidy mess of bodies lying jumbled together as though they were rag dolls dumped from a giant toy chest.

The five screaming and sobbing girls were stripped naked, thrown on the ground, and raped repeatedly and savagely. It was not long before they were as silent and senseless as their families lying still in the dirt. The single shot to the back of the head was a blessing too long withheld.

The eight men made one more sweep of the houses. Finding no one, they simply got back in their vehicles and drove away.

Behind them, the silence was profound.

War & Money

In the beginning, war was a simple business, easily undertaken and financed. A small and self-contained nomadic and tribal society could easily convene a marauding war party. The cost would be measured in the handful of lives lost. In the Middle Ages, the local warlord would order the blacksmith to step up the production of swords and draft a few dozen serfs to mount a raid on a nearby rival. Such contests would be brief, bloody and cheap.

Inevitably, the local wars became regional and then national and the warlords – now kings and heads of state – were required to finance standing armies for long periods of time. But even the Crusaders paid for it on a pay-as-you-go system, using the gold they carried with them in large chests. Wars became expensive, but the cost was all about getting large numbers of men in the right place at the right time. Once engaged, they still killed each other with clubs, swords and arrows. It was effective, but not efficient.

Beginning in the nineteenth century with the rise of capitalism and the industrial revolution, both the civilian and the military world was changed by the substitution of capital for labor, vastly increasing the efficiency of the worker (or soldier). Repeating rifles, machine guns, tanks, airplanes and missiles enabled one or a few men to kill many times their number. But such advanced weaponry is expensive. A cruise missile costs a million dollars; a B1 Stealth bomber a billion. To simply outfit a single American infantryman costs approximately $25,000 and supporting him or her for a year in Iraq or Afghanistan costs $1.5 million.

But banking and finance has always adapted, as inexorable and indifferent to consequences as water seeking the lowest level.

The politicians, lobbyists and bureaucrats that inhabit Washington DC, the capital city of the richest and most powerful nation in the world, would be dismayed at the idea that what they do could be termed "ordinary." For some, however, the outcome that they feared most was to be "discoverable."

"Black ops" has been an increasingly important part of the interface between the intelligence and the military communities since the horrors of September 11, 2001. The fact that thousands of unsuspecting Americans died unexpectedly seemed to justify various initiatives that required anonymity and deniability as incentives for actions that violated longstanding views of morality and American exceptionalism.

The practical, as opposed to moral, dilemma was financial. Such clandestine operations require exceptional levels of funding, but the usual channels are not available. Congressional appropriations are highly visible and the money comes with the kinds of strings that do not allow for mercenaries with questionable resumes, assassinations, involuntary renditions or commando raids based on probabilities rather than certainties.

So if you're maintaining a clandestine but highly elite military force in Afghanistan, one that is dedicated to the single minded pursuit of American interests, or if you need a few hundred million dollars to buy arms for religious zealots who are delighted to commit genocide for theological reasons, it is important to develop extraordinary funding capabilities.

It was not a major problem in Afghanistan until 2015. Money was easy to come by when there were a hundred thousand troops on the ground and there was enthusiasm for fighting. But when NATO ended its combat mission and switched to "advising" the Afghan forces, the amounts of money plummeted and the controls on its use were increased. It was a new problem without any obvious solution.

But, for some, there was an obvious way to think about the problem. A meeting was convened for the purpose.

The four individuals at the table – three men and a woman -- were familiar with the science of problem-solving and with one another, although they would not acknowledge that in public. Only one of them was on the payroll of the Federal government, but all of them exercised considerable unofficial influence on public policy.

The man at the head of the table was a U.S. Senator and the one that called the meeting. "I want you to think outside the box," he told the three other people in the room. "I have a list. Your job is to brainstorm about each of the possibilities on the list. Tell me how we can get it done. And *nothing* is out of bounds."

The seriousness of the meeting was apparent as soon as he read off the first item.

"How about selling drugs? We are the biggest kid on the block – the block being Afghanistan -- and that block happens to produce major amounts of opium. It's a multi-billion dollar global industry."

A sudden stillness settled over the small group. The only woman cleared her throat and said, more tentatively than she liked, "Well. It's been done. Vietnam, for sure. And the Taliban is doing it in volume."

The man sitting alongside her said, "Talk to the CIA. They won't admit it, but they know how. Hell, they're probably doing it as we speak!" He did not remind the man that he had recently been the head of the CIA.

The man at the head of the table made a note and turned a page. "Selling arms? It's a war zone, after all. Everybody needs more and better. We're on the scene and have the best merchandise. Guaranteed delivery and all that."

The older of the other two men spoke. He was in civilian clothes but still looked every inch the military man that he once was. He gestured at the woman and said, "As she said, it's been done ... Reagan and the contras in Central America, for example. We could be a major broker if we set it up right. The problem isn't finding the goods or doing the deals, it's controlling the buyer. Odds are that the stuff we sell will end up being used against us ... or at any rate against what we call 'the good guys.'"

"Either of these ventures – drugs or arms – has a nice little side benefit as well." Everybody turned to look at the woman. She continued, "The other side is already doing it, and it's a zero-sum game. If we do it, they don't. Our gains are their losses."

Another note, another page turned. "What about donations? Corporate, private, whatever. There's a lot of people out there who approve of what we're doing and might like to support us."

The older man smiled. "Kind of like a Super-Pac for soldiers rather than politicians. I like the concept."

The younger man leaned forward and held up three fingers, folding each one down as he ticked off the points. He looked like what he was – a college professor. He spoke in a careful diction, in whole sentences and without the kinds of verbal pauses one would expect of a person responding to a complex and unexpected question.

"First, the corporates. The obvious ones are the defense contractors. They need the war to maintain revenue growth, so it's clearly in their economic interest to keep the conflict alive and us in the game. They could be tapped, but very carefully and you'd have to be very clear about what they're getting – or not getting – in return. For sure, you'd leave a paper trail and have more people involved than you'd like. It would be a beautiful setup for the whistle-blowers."

"Second, the individuals. For security reasons, you'd want to keep it to a small number. Given the amount of bucks we need, you'd have to be dealing with the whales, probably billionaires. And they'd have to be pretty far right, not the most stable types these days ... lots of prima donnas. Probably too much risk for too little return."

"Third, there are the governments. Forget NATO members, but think about other semi-democratic states in the Middle East that have an interest in us succeeding. Either because they're afraid of their own people if the jihadists win, or because they want a bigger sphere of influence in Afghanistan, Iraq and even Syria. I can think of at least half-a-dozen countries that we could approach, probably through their security services. They can't be seen to be involved, but ..."

He finished with a highly eloquent shrug.

The senator looked around the small group, staring directly into the eyes of each individual for a few seconds. Then he leaned back and asked, "Any other ideas or reactions?"

Everybody looked at everybody else. Then the woman spoke. "Well, as long as we're just brainstorming ..." She looked around at the others as if seeking permission.

"On the question of how to run the operation, there are some models we might look at. Organizations that need – and generate – huge amounts of funds through extra-legal means.

The mafia, for example. Their single most important revenue source is drugs, but we've already talked about that. But they also make lots of money from smuggling, prostitution and protection rackets. Then there are the so-called jihadists that we're trying to get rid of. They start out as religious zealots but wind up as old-fashioned crooks, motivated mostly by money. We could emulate them. That opens up kidnapping for ransom, bank robbery, black market operations … and, I suppose, selling young girls into slavery."

The silence was profound when she finished. The atmosphere resembled a dinner party where an unwelcome guest had just insulted the host. Nobody looked at the man at the head of the table.

He stood up, bringing the other three to their feet, feeling relieved that this particular meeting was ending. Then he said, "Thanks for the input. And this is just a start. Next steps: I want the three of you to think of *concrete* – he emphasized the word – tactics that we could use to raise a large amount of money for special ops in Afghanistan. Think three or four hundred million dollars. And don't be squeamish. Bring me a one page outline of each of these initiatives."

The professor type broke in. "You know, we may be missing the most obvious channel of all. You've seen the most recent SIGAR report on the Afghan mission?"

"I have. Bureaucratic mumbo-jumbo designed to cover up the reality that we pulled out without finishing the job."

No way I'm going there right now, the professor thought. *He's not real flexible on that topic.* "That may be. But it did say that we're ponying up a billion dollars for 'reconstruction.' Given our connections and the level of corruption in that part of the world, we could probably 'divert' a sizeable chunk of that."

The man sat up straight, obviously intrigued by the idea. He nodded slowly. "Look into that. Put it first on your list of personal 'to do's.' Find out how that money gets from the U.S. Treasury to actual projects in Afghanistan. Who do we need to get to?"

They filed out, but just before the first of them reached the door, he called out, "How about white-collar crime? They say it's 'victimless.'"

The Jihadist Banker

Six thousand miles from Washington DC, similar questions were being debated, all centered on the merits of different fund-raising channels. But the debate was entirely within the mind of a single person. Unlike the Washington DC group, this man was a professional within the world of finance. And that world included all of the unconventional financing methods that the Washington quartet was considering.

The man in the Middle East was asking the same kind of questions, but he was quite different than the individuals in Washington. Not just in ethnicity and citizenship, but in far more important ways involving values and the fuzzy boundaries between means and ends.

He was a Sunni Muslim, a devout follower of the Prophet. But he was not one of the apocalyptic madmen that wanted to restore the seventh century Islamic Caliphate. He did feel superior to the Shia Muslims and all of the many other doctrinal variations that existed within Islam, but he did not want to exterminate them.

He was committed to jihad, but only within the Middle East. He did not condone mass killings in New York, Paris or Copenhagen. His vision was a vast Muslim region. Not a caliphate, but a region with modern nation-states that were not at war with one another. A region without Americans, British, Russian or any other armies seeking to protect their "vital national interests." He understood that the thing called "terrorism" was a necessary and useful tactic to achieve that aim, although he was personally repelled by its callous application.

His religion emphasized humility and modesty in all things. Only occasionally and very briefly did he permit himself to reflect on his personal contributions to the cause. But one of his clients had summarized it nicely.

"You are the one who enables jihad. More than Osama bin Laden, Mullah Omar, the Wahabis or any of the thousands of imams shouting in the streets. They are the noisy ones that the

Westerners pay attention to. But we are dependent on you, the one that provides us with what we need to wage our jihad."

What they needed, of course, was money. Not just money, but money in the right place at the right time. The Saudis and the oil-rich sheiks in the Emirates had the money but they needed access to the distribution system. And they needed anonymity. That turned out to be a difficult combination to achieve.

Unless you knew him.

So he had become an expert at converting the proceeds from the sale of opium, stolen antiquities and human beings into the purchase of arms and mercenaries and suicide bombers. He knew how to aggregate the "taxes" assessed by the Taliban on hundreds of scattered small villages and to have that money reappear a thousand miles away as a bribe to a corrupt vice governor of a rural province. He could arrange for the financing of a "pop up" refinery to process stolen oil and make sure that its illicit revenues would wind up in a very private deposit account in Luxembourg or Geneva or Mauritius.

There were limits. There were those that wanted a billion dollars to buy a nuclear warhead or to fund an underground laboratory to cultivate exotic germs. They went elsewhere. But he knew that they were out there and that money was fungible; that it would inevitably flow to the highest bidder.

His greatest achievement, in his own mind, was that he had achieved this while operating as one of *them*, a respected member of the global banking system. It gave him great pleasure when the oh-so-obvious CIA officers approached him about opening a "special account" in his Islamabad banking subsidiary; an account with very large balances, under the name of a Pakistani company that did not exist. He remembered the care with which he arranged his expression so as to convey both disgust and outrage at the request.

I told them, "I am a banker for legitimate businesses and people. I obey the laws and the regulations. And my conscience! Both you and your 'very large balances' are dirty. Get out of my office!"

But when the men left, he was disturbed. *They want me to help them kill people and destroy cultures. I tell them to get out, but they are only asking me to do what I already do for their enemies.*

The disquiet stayed with him, a soft voice that became perceptible in his quiet moments. *You used to help build things -- offices, bridges, ships, companies and homes... Now you collaborate with drug dealers and kidnappers and killers to help them destroy those very institutions that you once helped bring into existence.*

The Sunday *Financial Times* open on his desktop with his morning coffee service seemed to him a sign from Allah. The facing pages featured two different full-page stories, nominally independent of one another but that – for him – showed him a clear path to rebalance his moral scales.

On the left side, the article was headlined "Global Banking Regulators on the Offensive." On the right side, "NATO Countries Commit Billions to Afghan Reconstruction."

For the first time in several years, the man felt a sense of greater purpose, of a possibility worthy of his skills. As if to confirm it, the first call to prayer echoed from the mosque across the street. As he faced Mecca and knelt, he remembered one of his earliest teachings from his madrassa.

'When God closes a door, he opens a window.'

Pork Barrels Abroad

Harlan Crosby was looking at the same *Financial Times* issue and recalling the professor's suggestion about SIGAR and a billion dollars that "could be diverted." He picked up the phone.

It rang in a cluttered office at Georgetown University. When the man saw the caller ID, he reached for a thin file. He punched the speakerphone button and pulled a single sheet from the file, placing it precisely in the center of his desk.

"Good morning Senator."

"You remember what you said about the billion dollars for Afghan reconstruction?"

"Yes. And I've been looking into it. I've got some good sources at Treasury."

"And?"

"Several things. First, we're talking serious money. Did you know that Congress has already spent over $100 billion to rebuild Afghanistan since 2002? And the –"

"Garrison, I'm a member of that very Congress, as you may recall! So skip the civics lecture and get to the goddam point!"

"Sorry. In any case, that's money down the rat hole. No good to us. The important thing is now that we've withdrawn combat forces, the administration has committed to increased funding. They've branded it as a 'Transformation Decade.'"

"Hah! We've already *transformed* the damned country. Into a wasteland!"

The professor kept going. "Second, it's definitely going to happen. A huge CYA maneuver. We get to say 'we're beginning the rebuilding phase' instead of 'we lost the war and are leaving the Afghans in the shitstorm.'

"Third, the good news for us? It's going to happen fast and sloppy. They're more eager for the PR than they are worried about doing it right."

"Sounds promising. How can we get our share?"

"I assume you're still thinking about nine digits?"

"Yep."

"Then we can rule out the usual low risk skims – the so-called consultants and middlemen who rake off fees and commissions –"

"I know those well. Pentagon procurement procedures at their best."

" – and we make sure that we're at the trough when the money is actually disbursed."

"I thought that we'd slapped on all kinds of anti-corruption controls after the Kabul Bank fiasco."

"We did. Before 2010, the United States provided most of its assistance to Afghanistan through 'direct funding' -- contracts, grants, and cooperative agreements that were executed outside the Afghan budget and beyond the reach of Afghan officials –"

"A license to steal! And President Karzai was first in line!"

Garrison permitted himself a cynical smile. *And you were at the CIA, personally approving those thefts that served your own purposes!*

He was careful to keep his voice neutral. "As you say, corruption was widespread. Phantom employees building non-existent water treatment plants. Provincial mayors buying armored limousines and funding private armies. Politicians opening Swiss bank accounts. The usual sort of malfeasance. But since 2010 and the Kabul bank failure, the donor countries have shifted to 'on-budget' assistance. That ratchets up the visibility. And the money is run through the ARTF – the Afghanistan Reconstruction Trust Fund – and administered by the World Bank. Any funding has to get through multiple layers of bureaucratic approval."

"And you think we can game that process?"

"We could, but not in the time frame you have in mind. But there's a really interesting alternative for us. The U.S. is the largest donor country to ARTF and they're fed up with the World Bank bureaucracy. Some of your Republican colleagues think the ARTF is the wrong vehicle. They've insisted on trying out some new methods. The buzzword is 'entrepreneurial.'"

Crosby was derisive. "I know the folks you're talking about. They'd privatize the IRS if they had enough votes!"

Don't get sidetracked into domestic politics, for God's sake! "They've got a program they're calling 'FARD,' standing for 'Funding for Accelerated Rural Development.' The idea is to allocate between one-hundred to two-hundred million of this year's reconstruction funds to selected *non-governmental projects* in the form of fast-tracked grants."

"And just why is that – as you put it – an interesting opportunity for us?"

"Because it's a streamlined approval process. The projects are evaluated by private financial institutions rather than ARTF and World Bank bureaucrats. Treasury is contracting with Global American Bank to oversee the evaluation. The money will be disbursed as soon as a project is approved. And, once the project is on a short list, a single individual can authorize payment – a Global American officer named Kendall Zanker."

"No follow up?"

"ARTF will manage the monitoring and reporting, but they won't even set foot on site for at least six months. By then, the money is long gone."

"What's the time frame?"

Garrison consulted his single sheet of paper. "The grant recipients will be announced by Zanker in Kabul on June first. And the funds will be transmitted instantaneously. It will be a fairly major PR extravaganza. President Ghani will be there. Lots of speeches."

"So what needs to happen?"

"Two major pieces. First, we need to create some actual Afghan reconstruction projects that we control, preferably things that would come under the heading of 'rural development.' And, second, we have to find a way to get them to the head of the FARD list."

"Projects, huh? Like building schools or sewer systems? Running literacy programs for girls? Finding and disarming unexploded munitions?"

"All of that, and more. But the projects have to be real. And each of them will need some kind of formal proposal or plan. Some document that shows how you'll use the millions of dollars you're asking for. And one more thing – there will be a lot of competition for the funds. Once the money is passed out, nobody will care very much about what happens. But – up front -- there will be a lot of people with their hands out. Think beauty contest."

When Garrison stopped talking, the silence continued. He knew the senator was weighing the various alternatives. When he spoke, it was in a thoughtful tone.

"Getting the projects is easy. Between the tribal militias and all of the contractors, we've got enough off-the-books ventures to find a few of them to pretty-up for the money people. I'll get Ollie to draw up a list for us and I've got access to someone who can write slick proposals."

Harlan sat thinking, allowing a long pause to build. The professor waited, knowing that the man was thinking about the second piece of the problem. The more difficult one.

"Beauty contest, huh? And we may not have the prettiest girls in the lineup …"

There was another long pause.

"Maybe we can bribe the judges. What do we know about this banker named Kendall Zanker?"

Nation Building

Harlan ended the call with Garrison and swiveled his chair around to stare out the window. As a first-year Senator, the view from his office was unremarkable, but he wasn't seeing it anyway. His entire focus was inward.

Christ! We've spent a trillion dollars on Afghanistan. And thousands of dead soldiers, mostly just kids. And now we're walking away from it! Gone from a hundred thousand combat troops to maybe a thousand, excluding the so-called "advisors." Walking out in the middle of a bloody civil war with only one ending. Scattering money around to make us feel less guilty. Money that will wind up in the pockets of politicians or – worse – people that will reinvest it to find new ways to kill us here.

The outburst was entirely silent, within his own head. He had learned the hard way that his congressional colleagues, with very few exceptions, were fed up with the war and badly wanted out, even if it meant spouting the contorted logic that *they really don't need our combat presence any longer.* When he was still a general, that kind of delusional thinking and outright hypocrisy disgusted him. But his stint as CIA Director had made him into the ultimate cynic and he had learned the importance of seeming to play along while actively pursuing a private agenda.

That agenda was clear and based on an unshakeable conviction. *We'll have to go back. More boots on the ground than ever. The jihadists will finally kill enough of their own civilians, blow up enough airliners, and behead enough journalists on TV that the world will insist on it.*

The problem that concerned him was how to maintain the war-fighting capacity until that turnabout, so that the military effort could be ramped up quickly with maximum effect. To that end, Harlan and a small group of likeminded friends – they would call themselves "patriots" – were committed to maintaining certain clandestine para-military groups in-country. But that was expensive.

It's always about the goddamned money. The only question is how to get the funding to do what needs to be done.

Three months after 911, we took over the country and chased Osama bin Laden out by buying the tribal militias, paying them with suitcases filled with hundred dollar bills to do the fighting for us. Need money? Just ask for it! Pallets filled with currency flown in on demand! Even later on, the CIA could always come up with funding for some weird black ops stuff if you knew who to call.

Now some accountant asks, "Why do you need this much?" And a clerk insists on triplicate forms explaining how you spent the stuff. And then the auditor shows up and asks you to show him the cost-benefit analysis.

So, we'll have to be creative.

He turned back to his desk and picked up a special cell phone, punching in three digits.

"Ollie. Sorry about the four AM call, but I've got some to-do items for your list."

Kaz

The infant's face was mashed against the limousine's window with such force that he could see the dirt imbedded in the creases on its flattened cheek. The one distorted eye seemed to be looking directly at him, flecked and huge with the effects of malnutrition. The mother's face filled the rest of the window, every pore of her pockmarked skin a silent plea for money. Then the light changed and the limo eased forward across the intersection. The infant's face became three-dimensional once more and the woman faded and became indistinguishable from the dozens of beggars lining the road.

The man in the front seat turned to Kaz and said, "I'm sorry about that. We've tried to keep the beggars away from the center of the city, but the fighting has made them more desperate."

Kendall Avery Zanker didn't respond. He was still seeing the infant's eye pressed against the window.

What does he expect them to do? Sit in their bombed-out villages and die quietly, one by one? She's a mother, using her baby to make their case. She's no different than the Minister of Finance showing us his obsolete computers and rusting derricks to demonstrate that he needs the money. Except for the number of zeros they want on the bills we hand them.

I wonder if she gets more hopeful when a limousine appears rather than the usual overcrowded family car? Whether she somehow knows that it contains a person who has millions of dollars to dispense?

But not to her, or those like her. No, these millions are for "infrastructure." Buildings, equipment, vehicles. Hard assets with real value that can be repossessed. Collateral.

The man was talking, finally bringing Kaz back to the present moment.

"...be there in ten minutes. The Minister has arranged for a suite. At his expense, of course."

I should think so. The prospect of a twenty-five million dollar loan with a World Bank guarantee should call for a little baksheesh.

He sat back in the soft leather seat, feeling – as he often did these days – depressed about what he did for a living.

According to his embossed business card, he was an Executive Vice President for Global American Bank, Inc. and thereby responsible for all of the bank's financial sector relationships in Europe, the Middle East and Africa. Within the top echelons of the bank he was – if they liked him – "Kaz," or – if they didn't like him – "Charles" or even "Mr. Zanker." To his customers and those familiar with bankspeak, he was known as "the GABI EVP for FinSec in EMEA."

Kendall Avery Zanker somehow did not quite look like a man with such an elaborate title on his business card. Perhaps because he had a strong distrust of those who viewed titles as valid indicators of real merit.

He dressed the part – tailored dark suits with fashionable ties, monogrammed shirts and cufflinks, handmade shoes and, every now and then, discreet suspenders. He could easily be mistaken for, say, the Minister of Finance for Switzerland or even a model for one of the Italian fashion megaliths. But he never looked quite comfortable in his clothes. Part of it was his habit of not buttoning the suit coat, or even taking it off at the start of most of the many meetings that he attended. And once that happened, the shirtsleeves were usually rolled up. But even when fully suited up, he somehow gave the impression of a high-school boy at his first formal dance, feeling ever-so-slightly self-conscious and guilty about trying to fool those around him by putting on the fancy clothing.

He was curious about people and places and therefore open to new ideas and projects. He did not deny the existence of social class, but he refused to rely on it in his dealings with individuals, even if they harbored beliefs that he found personally abhorrent. "Why do you think that way?" was the underlying theme in all of his encounters. A long time ago, he had wanted to be a journalist, but gave that up when he accepted that it required him to believe that "the story" was more important than the individuals involved.

The true snobs in his work environment – and they were numerous – would attribute his openness to his working class roots and would use that same rationale to explain other features that they found disagreeable. To their dismay, he would agree with them but fail to see why that was a criticism.

Those roots were genetically complex and both his features and his personality reflected that complexity. His mother was Jewish, a classically Semitic – and, to him, beautiful -- woman with a fiery disposition and an inability to be indifferent about both small and large issues. From her, he got his dark complexion, dark curly hair and an unwavering predisposition for skepticism.

His father was the polar opposite, as though chosen by some ecumenical yenta with a twisted sense of humor. Charles Zanker was thoroughly English; a tall, blond and quiet man who disliked conflict in all its forms and whose degree of introversion was directly related to the number of people in the room. From him, Kaz got his athletic body-type, sense of humor and belief in the power of reconciliation.

His parents met forty-five years ago in New York. They were art students at NYU and encountered one another at the opening of a Greenwich Village art gallery. They stayed in New York City until Kaz was six years old and then moved to Santa Fe, finding the mix of flea markets, opera, high desert light and art galleries to be congenial for refugees from urban American middle-class values. They owned a small boutique gallery specializing in Southwestern art, but paid the bills by building a packaging company; one that specialized in crating and shipping high-end art around the world. They were the "go to" place in Santa Fe for such services.

Kaz figured he might be the highest-ranking international banking executive to come from New Mexico. *Maybe not so surprising, given that I grew up among Latins, Indians – oops, "Native Americans" – and rich white people on vacation. About as multicultural as you can get in the States.*

Another red light stopped them and the crowd of beggars – again, mostly ragged women with infants – surged toward them. But the driver simply ignored the red light and accelerated through the light toward the huge lighted marquee of the hotel a block away.

His cell phone rang. When he saw the caller ID, he had the usual pair of reactions.

Amazing. Nine time zones and seven thousand miles. And it's like I'm down the block. I miss the good old days where I could be out of touch for days at a time.

The other reaction was a reluctance to answer the call. The sensation was new to him, barely perceptible and troubling. *I need to think about this.* The caller ID was "CC," standing for Camille Cailla.

"Hello CC. How's the sunrise in San Francisco?"

"Symmetric, isn't it? You're watching it go down in Qatar while I'm seeing it come up in San Francisco?"

She's a couple of countries behind. Not her fault, given the hush-hush character of what I'm doing these days.

They had been "a couple" for about six weeks now. She had picked him up quite deliberately at mid-morning in a Starbucks in the financial district of San Francisco. He still marveled at, and was flattered by, the way she singled him out and made it clear that he was her target.

He was standing in line with three other men from the local office when she walked in. Kaz – and most of the other men in line – noticed her immediately, an almost improbably attractive woman in a highly tailored business suit. Brad turned to Kaz and captured his sentiment precisely. "If that doesn't shatter the glass ceiling, I don't know what will."

She stood, hands on hips, looking at the line as though deliberating whether it was worth the wait. But it turned out that she wasn't evaluating the wait time.

She walked directly to Kaz and said, "I've tried singles bars, on-line dating, concierge matchmakers and recommendations from my well-meaning friends. Huge waste of time and energy, with a ton of hurt feelings to manage. So I thought, 'the hell with it' and decided to revert to pure instinct. Can I buy you a latte ... or something more masculine, maybe?"

They went from Starbucks to lunch and from there to dinner in Sausalito. They talked continuously until she left to catch a red-eye flight to Chicago. Four days later she showed up at his condo with a small suitcase and stayed for a long weekend. A good bit of that time was spent in bed; enough time to explore lovemaking that went beyond physical need to something far deeper and more important. There was a lot of laughing as well. And the talking continued. Since then, they had met in different cities on three different continents, each rendezvous marked by a mutual and increasing sense of companionship.

So why the reluctance to answer the damned phone?

"Kaz? Are you there?"

He realized that she'd been talking and he hadn't heard a word. "Yes, I'm here."

She laughed. "Sure you are. Tell me what it is that I just said to you."

"Uh. Something about sunsets?"

"That was two sentences back. I was talking about Paris just now."

"CC, I'm sorry. I'm in a street scene that's absorbing most of my attention."

Her voice went down a full octave. "I know how to fix that ... to refocus you ... but it requires proximity."

Then the tone turned serious. "Where are you? What are you doing right now?"

She really wants to know. And I can't tell her.

"I'm about to get out of a limousine and go into a hotel. There's a client who needs money." *And all of that is true, but it's not what she asked.*

Before she could resume, he said, "Look. I'm going to be busy for a while. I'll call you tonight, California time."

There was five seconds of silence, and then she said, "OK. I'm looking forward to that. And Paris."

He ended the call just as the valet opened the car door.

Paris? That's next week. With the thought came an image of CC. She was naked and laughing at something he had just said. Her body was perfect, and the laughter was real.

So what's bothering you? The idea of permanence maybe?

Camille

In fact, the sun was hopelessly shrouded in the fog bank that had crept a few miles inland from the San Francisco Bay. She had gotten used to it, but the dismal sunrises and sunsets still left her feeling disappointed and even slightly defrauded. As a "Chicago girl" – which is how she described herself to the West Coast males that made approaches – she had looked forward to the sun sinking into the Pacific amid a kaleidoscope of color.

Face it! You're a sucker for romantic come-ons! Even when you know they're made for suckers!

She had the proper venue for viewing the promised sunset, one of the higher floors of the Fairmont Hotel looking west over the Golden Gate Bridge. The bridge was visible at the moment only as a pair of red steel spires with dangling cables protruding from the grayness.

She sat looking at the phone still in her hand, as though expecting it to have a message for her. And, as if it was responsive to her mood, it rang. The display told her that it was her boss Derek Williams.

The call was very brief.

"Good morning, Derek."

"CC. How's your calendar?"

"Clear for a week other than finishing up the draft for UNHCR. Then I'm in Paris for three days."

"Hand the UN draft off to Gillespie. You can sign off when you get back."

"From …?"

"Cairo. It's a mess. Needs your magic touch."

"And what do I do when I get there?"

"The usual. But call when you arrive and I'll make sure you have all the detail you need."

"OK."

She said "Goodbye" but realized that he had already gone. A typical Derek Williams phone call.

She mentally rearranged her work plan. *Good riddance to the UNHCR draft, a pure "keep the bureaucrats happy" task.*

"UNHCR" stood for "United Nations High Commissioner for Refugees." Its mandate was to coordinate international efforts to protect the rights and well-being of refugees worldwide. CC's clients were the dozens of large non-governmental organizations focused on the refugees from the war-torn Middle Eastern countries. In that role, she interacted with UNHCR officials in several countries and with several overlapping mandates – notably food, shelter and asylum needs.

Derek had hired her after five minutes of their interview. "It's like you were cloned for the job. You've got a graduate degree in International Law, speak Arabic and Hebrew, and view adventure travel as a plus!"

What he didn't say, but already knew long before their interview was, "And you're also super-smart, ruthless, beautiful, ambitious and resistant to authority." And she had validated his judgment on each of those attributes over-and-over during the three years she had worked for Derek.

Her biggest problem was men. Not the ones that she competed with; they were easy to either intimidate or co-opt. The problem was similar to her need for colorful sunsets, and she knew it. *You're a romantic. You want someone to be "in love" with. But you're also hopelessly egotistical. You want that someone to be your equal.*

She had tried. In the last few years, she had three intensive relationships. Each of them ended badly. Two of them were called off by her when she found herself making excuses for them to justify her interest. The most recent one had walked out on her, saying, "I'm tired of this perpetual audition. You need to make some tradeoffs!"

Kaz was troubling to her. Not because he was inferior to her, but rather because he wasn't. For the first time, she found herself wanting to please a man rather than trying to think up games to inject life into a failing relationship.

And then there's the other problem ... the one I can't fix.

The Banker's Plan

When God closes a door, he opens a window.
The door was not just closing, it was slamming shut.

It was inevitable; a give-and-take dynamic dictated by evolution and vastly accelerated by technology. The phenomena called capitalism and then its cousin, globalization, worked to bring about tremendous good. It enabled shepherds in Mongolia to expand their herds because investment bankers in New York wanted fine cashmere sweaters. Teenage girls in India stayed in school because a private school in France raised hundreds of thousands of Euros through an internet campaign targeted at teachers throughout Europe. Such beneficial interconnectedness was accomplished through a highly efficient and mostly opaque worldwide banking system.

For a long time and to its credit, that banking system worked well for all parties, without discrimination. Vast amounts of money moved around the world, facilitating economic development at all levels. And terrorism, narcotics trafficking, money laundering, arms sales and wholesale tax evasion.

But pendulums swing both ways. First the Americans and then the Europeans began to use the banks to combat the behaviors that they disapproved of. The first angle of attack was, as John LeCarre advised his apprentice spies, "to follow the money." Law enforcement used forensic accountants armed with subpoenas and computers rather than handguns to put names on the depositors, payers and payees associated with certain cash flows. The sources of wealth became visible to law enforcement and "tax evasion" became the indictment of choice for crime lords and narcos.

The second initiative was to control access to the system. New banking regulations made it difficult to transfer a million dollars from A to B unless that money was clearly associated with an "approved" source. That left the criminals with an interesting logistics problem. They could sell tons of illegal drugs or extort billions of dollars but they found it hard to actually take possession of the money or to redeploy it to its highest and best use. The border authorities began to confiscate pallets of cash as often as bales of hashish.

And the *Financial Times* article told him that the third wave of regulation would be the hardest of all for him to work around. It would subject banks – particularly those with substantial business in the Middle East, like his -- to what the article termed *enhanced screening*. The focus would shift from identifying questionable *transactions* to *institutions*. The regulations were complex, but it was immediately clear that his access to the global payments system would be severely restricted.

But then there was the window that Allah had opened.

First, they make war on us. They talk of "nation building" with enthusiasm, but they do the opposite. They destroy our institutions, our buildings, our economy. And then they get bored or disillusioned and they leave. But they feel guilty. Or perhaps they actually believe their press releases -- that they have created a foundation that can support their vision.

So the various NATO countries who were withdrawing from the military effort in Afghanistan would commit more than a billion dollars to its reconstruction. The money would come from both direct grants and from supranational lenders in the form of loans. The World Bank and the IMF would provide guaranties "in those cases where capital markets are insufficiently formed." But the really interesting piece– the "window" that Allah opened – was something called FARD, the "Funding Accelerated Rural Development" program. The primary recipients would be "non-government Afghan-owned agencies engaged in primary industries in rural areas."

The final and most interesting takeaway from the FT article was unremarkable on its face. But for the man concerned with doors and windows, it opened entire new horizons.

Kendall Zanker, with Global American Bank International, said that the first hundred million dollar tranche has been committed, pending the selection of the actual projects. According to Zanker, he is authorized to extend grants for up to five Afghan projects that have been analyzed by Global American Bank and are pre-approved by Afghan authorities and him. Awards will be announced on June 1 in Kabul.

The man walked to the window and looked out at the lights and the way that they so abruptly ended where the desert came to the edge of the city. Another time, he would have thought about the symbolism of light encroaching on darkness. Or was it the other way around? But tonight, the view was just a view. He was formulating a plan.

He turned and went to his phone. He placed three calls.

The first was one of his many staff members – the one with the unorthodox portfolio of projects that extended far beyond commercial banking. "I need you to look at yesterday's Financial Times, pages three and four. Then find out everything you can about Kendall Zanker and his hundred million dollar tranche."

The second call was to Kabul. It was answered with a simple "Yes?" The man asked, "Do you still have access to the ARTF files? And do we have any of our people fairly high up in their organization?"

He listened for thirty seconds. Then he said, "Durani, We need to meet. Beirut, in two days."

The third call required a change in tone. After all, he was talking to a respected colleague, not one of his subordinates, even if only to his voice mail. "Kaz. This is Abdul-Karim. Can you call me please? I have some banking puzzles that I'd like your advice on. Thank you."

A Meeting - Beirut

The banker was always saddened by his trip from the Beirut airport to the hotel. Part of it was that the city reminded him that he was once young and believed that everything was possible. Also, he could not help remembering what the city used to be like before 1975 and the start of the Lebanese civil war. Much of the city was destroyed by that and the interminable conflict between the Israelis and the rest of the Arab world.

"The most beautiful city in the world," he had called it. And even though much of it had been rebuilt and Beirut regained its stature as a cultural and banking center, the man wished these last forty years could be expunged from history.

You're old, and you want to be among other old things. A city that is sixteen-hundred years old is appropriate. An old city for an old man.

The broad boulevard lined with sidewalk cafes and boutiques, with its strolling tourists and locals, sharpened his nostalgia and made him sad. But then the car passed the cordoned off site of last week's car bombing. The blackened pavement, shattered windows and pockmarked walls were signs he was all too familiar with. He could quite easily picture the other signs that had been taken away -- the shattered bodies and bloodstains that always accompanied such events. Not for the first time, he wondered at his massive hypocrisy, his abhorrence for the destruction even as he worked to sustain the very forces that brought it about.

This is what you're too old for – the killing, plotting and scheming ... the sense that it will never end ... the fear.

He went immediately to the hotel conference room and was surprised to see that he was the last to arrive. As always, the feeling of inadequacy came over him. Not because of any professional or class-based differences between him and the other men in the room, but because he was aware of the extraordinary effort and outright risk required for these four men here with him. For him, it involved a short flight on a private jet with leather upholstery and then an armored limousine for him and the special bag that he carried, all carefully arranged by his personal travel agent.

The feeling passed quickly, succeeded – as it always was – by worry. *They sent a Navy Seal team into Pakistan to kill Bin Laden. What would they do if they knew of these men gathered in a single room in Lebanon? A 'who's who' list of what they called the terrorist chain of command ....*

The four men were in everyday Arab dress and – at first -- seemed indistinguishable from the many hundreds of men he had driven past on the streets from the airport. But, up close, there was an intensity, a seriousness, about them that was disconcerting. They seemed wary of their surroundings and one another as well, like they were here only because of some overriding mutual interest that transcended their mistrust and dislike for one another. What they had in common was a desire for a pure Islamic world and a reluctant adherence to the belief that *the enemy of my enemy is my friend,* but other than that, their ideological differences made them enemies as often as allies. It was an atmosphere that did not allow for the usual elaborate courtesies.

Such exquisite irony. We believe in the same things and seek the same outcomes. But these men risk their lives every day. And cause others, both friends and enemies, to do so as well. They endure physical hardship and live apart from their families. I live in air-conditioned comfort and risk only my reputation. Yet they are dependent on me.

They were not the CEO's of their respective organizations, but they were high up in the hierarchy, sufficiently so that their capture or death would rate headlines in the Western newspapers. These particular men were more like CFO's than CEO's; their value was in managing the finances. Their skills were in revenue generation and cash management, essential elements of asymmetric warfare.

The four men all watched him take his seat in the only remaining chair at the head of the table and enact the silent ritual that was the purpose for their gathering.

He carefully lifted his roller bag – an overlarge lawyer's case for documents -- onto the table in front of him, opened it and poured varying sized stacks of U.S. dollars and Euros on to the glossy surface. Once the case was empty, he closed it and put it on the floor alongside his chair. He took a thin sheaf of folded papers from the inside pocket of his suit coat and placed it in front of him on the mahogany table, being very careful about its alignment. The top sheet was filled with numbers and coded phrases.

Looking at the top sheet, a bit like a child assembling Legos from an instruction sheet, he rearranged the currencies into four distinct piles, again of varying sizes, and arrayed them in front of him spanning the table from edge to edge. Then he folded his hands on top of the paper and looked intently at each of the men in turn. Peering out from behind his stacks of money, he looked like a poker player who had busted the casino.

He glanced down at the top sheet of paper in front of him. Still without speaking, he pushed each of the piles of money to a new position in front of each man. None of them spoke or made any move to count the money.

He began speaking. "The usual amount in the usual denominations. Sufficient for payroll for a month."

He handed each of the men a single sheet of paper, keeping only the top sheet filled with notations.

"Here is your account summary for the time since our last meeting. In all cases, your balances are higher. This will be true even after the courier runs that are scheduled for the next few days. The details about routes and schedules are included on the sheet I just gave you."

Withdrawals from special deposit accounts accomplished by mules and even camels on obscure mountain passes; by women concealing hundreds of thousands of dollars beneath their burkhas! What a strange kind of banking world I inhabit!

"We've increased the withdrawal rates. But your organizations are generating significant inflows, so the balances grow. This is not necessarily good news."

He was pleased to see them look at him with a mixture of concern and hostility.

I say "significant inflows," but do not mention the sources – opium sales, trafficking in young girls, extortion, illegal oil sales, kidnapping, bank robbery! We once thought of these as necessary means to achieve a higher end, but now we pay more attention to our account balances than we do to our original Islamic objectives!

He sighed inwardly. *Another few weeks and I can stop worrying about it. Time to give them the news.*

He spoke slowly, careful to make eye contact with each of them as he spoke. "There are new banking regulations. It is mixed news. The bad news: Our present arrangement will have to be dissolved. The good news: It can be dissolved in a way that will provide our cause with a hundred million dollars."

Liaison in Paris

"You don't look much like any of the bankers that I know."

Camille looked up at Kaz and smiled. "That's only because I'm not dressed properly." She emphasized the fact by letting the silken sheet slip a few inches more, exposing both breasts.

"You *are* sending mixed signals though, given your reading material." He leaned forward and gently kissed each of her nipples.

She wriggled, a kind of full-body shudder that he had come to know well. But she picked up the booklet from alongside her and found her place. "Let me be. I'm just getting to the good part … the one on 'streamlined and functional conditionality in project financing.' God! Who writes this stuff?"

"Nobody that looks like you."

"You're being sexist. But you know that, don't you?"

I am. But I'm learning fast. It helps when you keep demonstrating that behind those perfect features there's a brain that's way ahead of most of us.

"What if I said, 'Nobody as smart as you?' Would it be OK if I discriminated based on intelligence? Or the lack of it?"

It was their second morning at the Le Bristol Hotel in the heart of Paris. CC had flown in from Cairo and Kaz had picked his British Airways flight so that they could meet at Charles DeGaulle. That gave them three days sandwiched around his daily meetings with the dozen or so individuals working out the details of the Afghan contract. They spent most of their discretionary time in bed.

"This is what you're working on, isn't it?" She held up the glossy book titled "The World Bank: Credit Enhancement Products for Developing Markets."

"That's a part of it, yes. For the better part of the last three months."

"I didn't think that banks like yours were interested in taking credit risk in Afghanistan these days. Not since 2010."

"2010" was shorthand for the economic crisis that was precipitated by the collapse of Kabul Bank due to rampant corruption. Mahmood Karzai, the President's brother, was directly involved and international lenders shut off funds as the scandal deepened.

"We've been on the sidelines since then, along with everybody else. But some of us are thinking it's time to restart. And that's the vehicle." He pointed at the stack of papers on the spindly-looking desk. "There's no credit risk involved. But it's complicated."

Complicated? It's a three-ring circus!

When they convened this morning, they barely fit around the conference table. He counted twelve individuals. All were men, every one of them at least ten years older than he was. At a glance, they were about equally divided between Northern European and Semitic types. Kaz knew all but one of them and easily divided them into three approximately equal groups.

The most important and the best-dressed ones were the bankers, Kaz and three others. Each of them was an expert in some aspect of infrastructure lending in developing markets. The second and most nervous subset was the trio representing the potential grant recipients. They were all Afghani. Their leader was an Assistant Secretary in the Afghan Finance Ministry. He was unknown to Kaz. He noted the name – Mohamad Durani – and made a note to himself to find out more. The other two Afghanis were an owner of a Kabul-based construction company and an executive of some kind of agricultural processing operation in the south of the country.

The third and most pompous looking subset was the bureaucrats, although Kaz had alternative and more colorful labels for them. They were from the world of supranational banks. They had different employers, but each of those was affiliated with the World Bank or the International Monetary Fund.

We've got the International Financing Corporation (IFC), the International Development Association (IDA), the Afghanistan Reconstruction Trust Fund (ARTF), and – for some reason I don't quite understand – the European Bank for Reconstruction and Development (EBRD).

There were two others there, sitting apart from the table and making everybody else nervous. They were journalists; one from the Times and the other from The Economist. Kaz had invited them and made it a point to let everyone know they were there as interested parties.

"That's outright brilliant, having those guys watching," CC exclaimed when he described his plan. "All those civil servants sitting around the table will fall all over themselves to demonstrate their commitment to the developing world."

Kaz chaired the meeting, in keeping with his position. The U.S. Treasury had contracted with Global American to evaluate the projects and disburse the funds, and he was the executive within GABI charged with making the deal come true. As he looked around the table, he thought again about how much he thrived on this strange combination that characterized his professional life. Almost everything he did endowed him with lots of responsibility but very little real authority.

Like deciding who gets a hundred million dollars!

But what happens if you pick the wrong people? The thought jarred him, enough that he stopped listening to the IFC suit who was droning on about the need for public-private partnerships in international capital markets.

"Mr. Zanker?"

Damn it! Pay attention! You're supposed to be the one person who knows what's going on.

"Sorry. What was the question again?"

The speaker was Mohamad Durani. It was the first time he had spoken in a day and a half. "Your syndicate. Is there any room for more funding?"

Incredible! Does he not know how much time and effort we've put into this proposal? How hard it was to get the U.S Treasury and the Afghan government to agree on what's in front of him? And he wants to change the single most important clause in the one hundred and forty page document?

Kaz's expression did not change. To the other men sitting at the table, he seemed to be actually thinking about the possibility. Slowly and with a feigned reluctance, he shook his head.

"Regrettably, no. We are flexible on some elements of the package. But not that. We offer up to one hundred million U.S. dollars, to be divided among four or five preapproved infrastructure projects in the rural development sector. The only other absolute for us is that the grants must be supported by endorsements from one or more of the supranational banks represented in this room."

"But you want us to provide those endorsements with – as you Americans say – 'no strings attached.'" This came from the IFC Director and Kaz was surprised that it had taken so long for one of them to bring up what he knew to be the single most important obstacle to the deal getting done. He was pleased to see the two journalists perk up noticeably.

CC had picked up on it right away.

She waved the booklet at him. "I've been on the fringes of some World Bank financings. They bury you in paper and drive you nuts with their codicils and conditions. Half the time, by the time they've signed off, the need has disappeared."

The IFC guy was looking expectantly at him, and the rest of the acronyms were abnormally still. This was why they were here. He said the same thing he had told CC, even recalling the image of her sitting naked in bed with legal documents strewn around her as he recited his set speech.

"Not so. You can attach all of the strings that you like." He laid his palm on the two-inch-high stack of documents in front of him. "You already have. But we want that done *now*, so that the actual money can be advanced immediately on June First. We have thirteen preapproved and eligible projects, subject to the known risk factors and terms. The only uncertainties are which four or five projects will be selected and the exact dollar amount. And that is for me to decide."

He looked directly at the two journalists who were clearly paying close attention. He had invited them precisely because he knew of their interest in – and criticism of – the IMF and World Bank programs that were run through the ARTF. A recent lead article in The Economist said, "They don't mind red tape … as long as they can cut it lengthwise."

He went on while the IFC spokesperson was looking around the table for support. "We've all spent a lot of time getting all the paperwork in order precisely so that we can fund as soon as a *prequalified* project is selected."

Then he said, very clearly, exactly the words that CC had suggested to him as he was leaving their hotel room that morning. She said, "Tell them what they want to hear."

She sat up in bed and said in ringing tones, "This will show the world that your institutions are more serious about getting things done than in generating legal fees and paper."

The fact that she was naked, with perfect breasts and tousled blond hair, and that she would be there when he returned from this meeting, made it difficult for him to repeat her words without breaking into an outright grin.

When he returned just as it was getting dark, she was sitting at the desk reading his copy of the two-inch-thick legal document. She was wearing the monogrammed white bathrobe provided by the hotel and – as far as he could tell -- was actually taking notes; an entire page was filled with numbers and short phrases.

He tried to look shocked. "A whole free day in the City of Light … and you study infrastructure financing agreements?"

"I look on it as improving my vocabulary. Just in case I'm stranded on a desert island with an octogenarian economist."

He stood behind her, letting his hands slip into the gap left in the loosely clasped robe. He bent forward and kissed her very gently at the point where her neck merged into her shoulder.

"I can help with that. Let me show you an interesting variation on 'streamlined and functional conditionality.'"

"Oh good! But not too streamlined, I hope …"

Eve of a Kidnapping

Typically, life is lived in a straight-line fashion. Progress is incremental, predictable and taken for granted; so gradual that a person looks back and wonders *how did I get to this point* without being able to point to any particular date or event where things changed. One's personal history is described as an "arc" or a "trajectory," as smooth as the path of an inanimate object falling through space.

There are, of course, exceptions to this generalization, differing mainly according to scope. There are the tectonic shifts, so dramatic that they define a "before" and an "after;" a bright line in a nation's collective memory. For Americans of a certain age, the JFK assassination and September 11, 2001 will always evoke an exact recall of where they were and what they were doing at that precise time when it became apparent that the world was going to be different.

At the individual level, where real people lead real lives, such inflection points in time are associated with real changes in experience, not just a perception of larger forces at work. There is pain, sadness, and personal danger to be endured. *Their* life will be altered.

Beirut, Lebanon

A Middle Eastern bank executive placed a series of phone calls. The call to Kabul was very satisfying.

The man who answered the phone spoke in the bureaucratic prose common to government ministers. "My department has completed their report. We shall 'recommend' a total of thirteen projects for the FARD program. Of those, I have five projects that we can use. Each is a legitimate business enterprise that we can control. But there are some problems."

The executive was silent, knowing that the man's nervousness would overcome his silence.

"The projects are small and two of them are barely out of the startup phase. A sensible banker – one such as Mr. Kendall

Zanker -- would advance a few million dollars and then wait to see if more is needed."

"That is a problem that we can solve. Leave Mr. Zanker's motivation to me. Anything else?"

He could almost feel the man's fear through the telephone lines. It was even more evident in his voice. *I wonder if he's more afraid of me than he is of the government's counter-intelligence service?*

Again, he allowed the silence to continue.

"It may not be a problem …"

"A problem that is not a problem?" This time, he let his impatience show in his voice.

"Our managers … for our projects … Some of them may resent paying taxes to the government … or using the funds to buy trucks and irrigation pipe rather than mortars and rifles."

The executive spoke, trying to keep the impatience from taking over. "They will learn that we need to govern once the fighting is over… that we will need factories and highways … that drought and famine are as much our enemies as the government forces. And, for those that cannot adapt, …"

Achin Adi, Afghanistan

A U.S. Army captain assigned to the NATO training mission sat talking to an elderly Pashtun man named Ali. An Apple iPhone was lying between them on the table. There was a long time when nothing was said.

Finally, the Captain nudged the phone toward the Afghan. "You should take this. It belonged to Gholam."

"No. It is an evil thing. It holds infidel music and pictures of unveiled women. Such things are forbidden by Sharia. You keep it."

It is merely a highly sophisticated man-made gadget. But it does indeed hold evil sounds and pictures. Of soldiers firing automatic weapons into a crowd of children, women and old men. Of young girls being raped.

"Ali, I –"

"These were your men. You gave them uniforms and weapons. You taught them how to shoot and kill. You command them."

They are not my men. And I do not command them. But this is not the time or place to lecture Ali on the fine points of the NATO training mission.

Ali pointed at the iPhone. "What will you do about … this?"

The captain had been thinking about the same question for most of the preceding night. *In my army, the soldiers would be court martialed and almost certainly sentenced to imprisonment for life. Perhaps a death sentence. If I was a reporter, I would saturate the web with Gholam's video. But it is not my army and I am not a reporter. I am an "advisor," one who has been in Afghanistan far too long.*

The silence went on long enough that Ali knew that no answer – no *satisfactory* answer – would be forthcoming. So he asked another question.

"You know of Pashtunwali?"

The captain shuddered inwardly, knowing where this discussion was going. "Of course. It is an ancient and unwritten code of honor for Pashtuns. It governs every aspect of tribal life."

"Then you know what is required?"

Vengeance. Revenge. An eye for an eye. Blood. Going on and on. Stupid, mindless back-and-forth killing.

He knew that his words were futile, but he said them anyway. "Ali. Let me deal with this. I promise you that the people that did this will be punished."

London

Kaz looked at the stack of documents on his desk with pride mixed with amusement. *So much paper! And almost all of it was boilerplate, there to satisfy the lawyers and politicians. The part that matters – thirteen standardized project evaluations – is on my laptop.*

The deal was essentially done. Durani in the Afghan Finance Ministry had selected the thirteen projects from the flood of proposals received when FARD was announced. Analysts from the Infrastructure and Project Finance Group at Global American had visited the thirteen projects and completed their analysis. The only remaining piece was to select which four or five of the projects would be funded, and that was up to him.

The money was appropriated and wired into a single account at GABI under his control.

The World Bank endorsement was in place, to be automatically triggered when the funds were advanced. *Thanks more to the shaming power of the press. The Economist and Financial Times did more than anything that I did.*

Prior to June 1, Kaz had the option of visiting a subset of the thirteen. Part of the site visits would be to determine how much to advance to each of the projects and to settle on the specific terms of repayment for each of the projects.

All that was left to do was to disburse a hundred million dollars. That would happen on June 1 in Kabul and was being planned with all of the care and attention to appearances that would ordinarily be associated with the Academy Awards or, these days, the selection of the winner on American Idol.

Cairo

Camille felt strange talking to Derek Williams in person. She had become so accustomed to the staccato phone calls and terse emails that she was slightly nervous to have him sitting across from her in the hotel lobby.

Some of that nervousness was the expression of self-doubt, experienced as the rash of second thoughts that were now part of her waking life.

Kaz thinks I'm ... He doesn't know what I'm doing to him. This is not what I thought would happen ...

Derek could read the signs. Betrayal was as natural to him as the act of brushing his teeth, but he understood quite well its corrosive effects on the betrayer. Camille might as well have been waving a sign saying, "I quit! I don't want to do this any more!"

But we need her for a little bit longer.

"Our client is very pleased with what you've done. And you don't think Zanker has any suspicions?"

"No. He's clueless."

Even that simple three-word response was tinged with bitterness directed at herself. But even in the midst of despising herself and Williams and everything they were doing, she could not help but wonder about the apparent needlessness of whatever grand plan was driving them.

"Derek, this still doesn't make any sense. The grant has been preordained. The money is there; it's going to be disbursed on schedule. Why all this cloak-and-dagger stuff? None of this sneaky bit you've had me play out with Kaz ... Zanker ... has ... made a bit of difference."

That's a very good question, CC. But you don't need to know the answer. And you wouldn't like the answer very much either.

He played it to perfection, rolling his eyes and holding his hands out in the classic "Who knows?" gesture. "It's what the client wants ... an excess of caution."

The question you should have asked is, "Who is the client?"

Georgetown, Washington DC

The woman sitting in her living room in the semi-dark is like the others, in that her life is about to be changed dramatically. However, unlike those others, she is the least aware of the forces that are in motion and she has no power to influence the outcomes. Despite that factor, she, perhaps more than any of the other actors, will be the victim.

In a sense, she has been practicing for that role for more than three decades, living with secrets and ambitions and festering enmities and a husband that – if she had shared them – would have shrugged and told her to "get over it."

She no longer thought very much about her husband. He was like the weather; an indifferent but powerful presence to be taken into account, to plan around. Their marriage had long ago and without any discussion or negotiation settled into a routine that would be dispiriting except each of them discovered that they had neither expectations nor remedies. All of the alternatives were worse. For a long time, she thought it was her fault.

She did think about the other two men. Her son, so much like his father and yet different. Like him, a committed soldier, but with many more dimensions to him. She wondered what he'd be like if there were no wars, no more deployments to a place that slowly and surely wore away what he was, as well as his possibilities. She could not stop regretting the absence of a daughter-in-law that she could talk to or grandchildren that she could play with, but she no longer daydreamed about them. Such thoughts had become casualties of war.

The other man was a much more infrequent visitor in her thoughts. Not surprisingly so, since she had not seen him for more than thirty years and then only for a few days. She had come to realize that she thought of him only during what she thought of as her "sad times," those nights when she was more alone than usual and prone to dwell on what might have been.

She no longer trusted her memory, so she felt even freer to reconstruct their time in Istanbul and Ankara. By now, the images were more imagined than actual, but a green silk dress was always involved. It still hung in her closet. Not because she intended to ever wear it again, but because it reminded her of the man she had been with the last time she had worn it.

Her thought-pictures went far beyond mere recall as she tried to imagine what he would be like today and what he might be doing. She wondered what he called himself now and whether he might be one of those trying to kill her son. She wondered if he knew.

The Afghan Countryside

For the man – the one in the woman's head and the one who would be the primary cause of the event that was about to change the arc of these several lives – the sun was just rising and he had just finished his early morning prayers. Two other men were waiting for him to brief them on today's raid. If informed that he was about to transform several lives, he would not have been impressed. "En'shallah," he would say. "Allah has ordained everything, whether good or evil."

So when the messenger arrived from Ali, he did not question its deeper meaning. But he knew that what he had to do would change him as well as the others.

Ali's message was brief and to the point. "A patrol tomorrow night. Uzbeks and Crosby. Allahu Akbar."

After he briefed Sahid, there was nothing left to do except wait. Inevitably, he thought of the Crosby's. It was hard for him not to feel that some strange sort of fate was at work. How else could it be that three individuals from a single family of infidels, acting independently of one another and over a forty year period, were dropped into his life, each time causing him to question who he really was?

He sat in the darkening shadows and thought about the thing the westerners called "fate."

A Tipping Point

It was early in 1980. A dark time for both him and Afghanistan. He went to the meeting in Istanbul filled with grim premonitions .

The meeting was entirely unofficial. The six individuals met in the Old City in an ornate 19th century Ottoman palace almost in the shadow of the Blue Mosque. The three Americans did not wear their uniforms and the three Afghanis had done their best to look like standard European tourists. All of them stayed in separate hotels on the European side of the Bosporus, arriving each morning in taxis or on foot at staggered intervals. Security – a squad of American MPs in civilian clothes -- was tight but quite invisible.

The Russian war against the Afghan insurgents -- the mujahedeen -- had settled into a bloody routine that showed no sign of ending. Some said that its very viciousness signaled a lack of patience on the part of the Russians, a trait they would sorely need against the intractable insurgents. They had added to their army and were using counter-terrorism tactics that exacted a terrible price from the civilian populace.

The Americans, made wiser by their Vietnamese experience, saw it as a chance to thwart Russian influence in the region. American aid to the insurgents in the form of hundreds of millions of dollars and tons of munitions was being negotiated, very quietly.

The Istanbul meeting was strictly business. The Afghanis brought their shopping lists of arms, topographical maps and on-the-ground assessments of Russian capabilities. The Americans brought their satellite photos, intelligence reports and – most prized of all – their catalogs of weaponry. The ranking American was Colonel Harlan Crosby, a fast-rising officer currently assigned to the staff of the JCS at the Pentagon.

The three members of the Afghan contingent were barely tolerant of one another, united only by their desire for American arms and dollars. They reflected the fractious diversity of the mujahedeen insurgency, composed of several different ethnic groups, each of which had shifting priorities and loyalties. One of the six – a relatively young man known to Harley only as "Khalid" – was spokesperson for the Pashtuns. His personal history was obscure, but American intelligence believed him to be the number two or three person in the vague and constantly shifting hierarchy with all of its tribal factions.

At first glance, Khalid and Crosby seemed to have nothing in common other than their casual western dress. Even out of uniform, Crosby was unalterably a soldier. He stood ramrod straight and spoke in a clipped fashion with no room for ambiguity or dissent. He looked and was physically fit and did not smile. Khalid spoke softly, using impeccable English with an accent that was a blend of BBC and Pashtun. He preferred to ask questions rather than make assertions, emphasizing his words with his expressive eyes. He was of average height with broad shoulders and a carefully trimmed and very short beard. He was economical in his motions and gave off a sense of stillness, of waiting. He managed to look comfortable even in the unfamiliar clothes.

What the two men had in common was hard to detect but far more important to the outcome of the meeting. They shared a deep and abiding patriotism for their respective countries; a belief in the rightness of their cause and the ultimate certainty that they would prevail over their enemies. In short, they were inclined to fanaticism. They were also leaders of men, although their personal styles were quite different. And they were warriors. Their natural milieu was war and – although they would deny it and it was a long time before they themselves acknowledged it – they had become at home with the destruction and dying that war brought about. They were about the same age and, although their experience with war was different – Afghan vs. Vietnam – they recognized in each other the same obsessions.

Crosby's wife was with him in Istanbul. She was the daughter of a past U.S. State Department official posted to Turkey during the 1970's and had lived there as a young girl. For most of that time, she was cooped up in Ankara. So when she heard that her husband was going to spend several days in Istanbul, a much more interesting city than Ankara, she asked to go along.

At first, he dismissed the idea. "It's sixteen hours a day of meetings, maybe more. No fun for you."

"I won't bother you. I've got friends there I can stay with until your meetings are over. Then we can spend some time together. Just a few days."

He finally agreed, mainly because she wore him out with her pleading. They had been married only three years, but he had long ago decided he needed a wife to help with his promotion plans. An ambassador's daughter was ideal. To him, all of the rest of what came with the marriage contract was a bother.

He arranged for one of the MP's assigned to his security detail to pick her up at the airport and bring her to the meeting site. She was sipping Turkish coffee on the veranda, trying to count the minarets that studded the landscape between her and the Bosporus when her husband came downstairs, talking with a small group of Afghans. The Afghans looked like they were clearly done for the day. Two of them carrying briefcases headed for the taxi rank across the street.

Crosby was exceedingly correct when he saw her. A very discreet kiss on the cheek, actually a near miss. Yasmin's expression remained unchanged, slightly matronly, but she thought, *the height of passion, for Harlan!*

She paid no attention to the Afghan man standing next to her husband. He, however, was frozen in place, his mind racing, unable to stop a series of images from the past that made it impossible for him to move or speak for a few brief seconds.

This is not possible!

Crosby turned to the Afghan. "Khalid, this is my wife Yasmin. We're going to spend a couple of vacation days as tourists in Istanbul, starting when our meetings are over."

Khalid recovered enough to smile and make a very slight bow. "Yasmin? In the Persian language, you are a flower." He stopped himself just in time. *I could add, 'very appropriately, too.' But Americans are so unpredictable about their women ... especially if they are as pretty as Yasmin.*

She looked closely at the man. He was still smiling but seemed strangely serious. *That's probably a pretty good combination for a diplomat. Be nice if that rubbed off on Harlan.*

"I don't feel much like a flower, but I do like the name," she said. "My father learned Arabic in graduate school and was insistent. My mother wanted 'Jennifer' but never had a chance."

Her voice trailed off and she almost dropped the cup she was holding. *Harlan called him Khalid? But it's Ali. That smile. And the seriousness. He's thinner and has some gray hair. But it's him.*

The two of them looked at each other with helpless expressions, not knowing what to say or do. To cover up their mutual and increasingly obvious awkwardness, she turned to her husband and asked, "So. Are you done for the day? Can we start to explore what is in this wonderful city?"

For once, she was glad for Harlan's inattentiveness. His primary concern was to conceal his mounting resentment that she was here, in Istanbul, and badgering him to act like a tourist. Caught up in his own immediate needs, he failed to notice that both she and Khalid were intensely nervous. He smiled in a way that made his resentment even more apparent.

"Actually, we have a couple of supply issues that we need to check out with Washington. Given the time difference, I'm afraid I'm going to be chained to a phone for the next few hours at least."

He glanced at Khalid who was smiling strangely. But Khalid's thoughts were not so bland. *Supply issues! Five hundred American Stinger missiles that kill Russian gunships but have to be approved by a congressman that goes home to his suburban house with a green lawn and swimming pool!*

Later, when she had learned and practiced all of the diplomatic protocols associated with being the wife of a high-ranking officer in the U.S. military culture, Yasmin would have covered up her disappointment. But at that point in time, she was still a civilian at heart, so she sighed quite audibly and said "Oh!" in a particular way.

Khalid had moved a couple of steps away, observing the discomfort building between husband and wife. He cleared his throat and said very tentatively, "I would be pleased to serve as escort for Mrs. Crosby. It *is* one of the world's great cities and a few days is too little time to absorb its wonders."

Both of the Crosby's spoke at the same time. "That's very nice of you, but –"

He interrupted. "Turkey is secular, but it is still an Islamic culture. A culture that takes itself very seriously about hospitality for our guests. I would be honored to serve as guide for a few hours."

Harlan looked confused. She, on the other hand, was beginning to smile. Then she looked at her husband and the smile faded.

Khalid tried once more, still speaking softly but now directly to Harlan. "And some of our more devout Islamists might be offended by an unattended woman walking through the Old City, especially at night."

What an incredible understatement that is! And what an incredible hypocrite I am! But she wants to keep our secret. I have no claim on this woman. But she is so beautiful. And I have been far too long in a place where killing and dying is the main expression of Islam!

For the first time in a long time, an image of his wife and son came to him. It was the image that he thought he had suppressed, showing them eating ice cream on the plaza just before the Russian Hind gunship made its strafing run and turned them into bundles of bloody rags. And leaving him with a sense of guilt that would reappear whenever he saw a young boy with his mother.

He felt a hand touch his forearm. Both of them were looking at him strangely. Crosby asked, "Khalid? Did you hear me?"

"I'm sorry. I was thinking of something else." He was faintly surprised that his voice sounded normal.

She spoke with real concern, repeating what her husband had just said. "It's very kind of you, but I do know it's been a stressful day and you have much to do. So if you'd rather not …" She kept her hand on his forearm and he thought – or imagined – a slight tension in her fingers, as though urging him to some action. *But which one?*

"Nonsense. I'm delighted." He looked at his watch. "I think Hagah Sofia is still possible. But we must hurry."

They walked three blocks without speaking and then sat at a tiny table in the courtyard of an old Ottoman palace. Only after the tea had been served did she break the silence.

"Is it Ali? Or Khalid?"

So we ended with a lie ... and now we begin again with another one.

"Please. You must forget Ali. Both the name and the person. He was ... is ... in the past. Now I am Khalid."

He looked incredibly sad and she remembered her first sighting of him on the Ankara rooftop. But today's sadness seemed ingrained in the lines of his face, not just a momentary emotion. And there was more. His eyes were different. There was less curiosity and humor, as though he expected less from the world. It was as if far more than seven years had elapsed.

She spoke softly, but wondered at the cruelty in her words. "It is hard for me to forget this Ali from the past. The past that lasted only those three magical days. The past where Ali and I talked about marriage."

"Yasmin ... We were young. And the world was different."

"Yes, we were, but ..." The wistfulness in those few words made Ali feel like crying. *I thought I would never cry again. This woman will make me unfit for what I do!*

He spoke huskily, feeling a coward for what he was saying. "And you are married now. To Harlan Crosby. And I am a ..."

When it was apparent he was not continuing, she said, "And you? Are a what? Are you married?"

All of the softness faded from his features. Even his voice hardened. "I had a wife and son. He was three years old. They were killed by a Russian helicopter gunship while they were eating ice cream in a village square."

She could think of nothing to say. She just looked at him, seeing him come back to the present, to a world in late afternoon sunshine where two people sat and talked about ordinary things in an ancient courtyard.

"Do you and Harlan have children? Somehow, I don't think so."

"No. We've tried ... are trying. But ..."

She could not stop herself. She leaned forward across the table and looked into his eyes. "Why did you leave without saying anything? That was the hardest part, that you said nothing. Were just gone."

"I couldn't stay. And you couldn't go where I was going. But I was a coward not to tell you. I am sorry about that."

She whispered, "So tell me now." Even though she knew that she didn't want to know. That he left for reasons that had nothing to do with her or their three days together. It would be about dubious concepts involving honor, duty and Islam.

He was silent for a long time, but she knew that he would tell her; that he was silent not because of reticence, but because the memory itself was painful.

"Our last night? When we talked about a crazy impossible future for us? When you left, I called my father. But he was gone. He flew to Herat, thinking that he could escape notice if he stayed away from Kabul. Khan's intelligence service – our secret police – met his plane. They delivered his body to his brother three days later."

She reached out and put her hand over his on the tabletop. "So, you went back to Afghanistan … and became Khalid." It was not a question.

They sat quietly, thinking there was nothing left to say. But they were wrong.

She stirred, shook herself as one with a sudden premonition. Then she smiled in a way that was as old as the city around them and the world seemed to tilt slightly.

"Do you remember that green silk dress? How hard it was to take it off?"

Slater - Day One

The shooting was over in seconds. The five Afghan army soldiers in his patrol were dead, strewn around him like so much trash, and the dozen or so Taliban fighters circled him. He placed his M4 rifle down very carefully and stood very still.

They stripped the bodies of their Kevlar vests, boots, night vision goggles, communications gear, and weapons. They also collected the ID tags and personal items from the pockets. They did the same with him, but when one of them gestured for him to take off his boots, the leader – or at least a man significantly older than the others -- stopped him, saying, "Let him keep them. He has a limp and we need him to keep up."

They moved quickly and efficiently. He estimated that no more than six or seven minutes had elapsed between the time the firing started and when they were forming up to leave, with the bodies neatly lined up in the middle of the road like so many mannequins awaiting disposal.

Abad was gone, taken somewhere into the reeds on the far side of the bridge.

When they were ready to leave, the man came up to him and said only, "You do not speak. That is the first and only rule for now."

He spoke Pashto, slowly. So they already know who I am.

They walked for six hours, on ancient worn paths that seemed to go no particular place other than further into the Afghan countryside. There were a dozen men, dressed in the usual Afghan manner. They did not seem particularly military in their bearing and, in the dark, they all seemed the same. One of them – indistinguishable in dress and manner – was the leader, but that was apparent only because he spoke once, saying only, "We go now. This way." The others called him Sahid.

Because of the narrow paths, they generally moved in a single column, keeping him approximately in the middle and always closely watched by the same two men. They stopped only once to confer about how to bypass a farmhouse that dominated the small valley they were traversing.

They pay no attention to security. No point. No flankers. They carry their weapons comfortably, not in the way soldiers would in hostile territory. They are the insurgents fighting against the government, but they are so sure of themselves that they move across the land as confidently as I would stroll down the main street of my home town. I envy them.

Their complacency in a war zone depressed him. A dozen years, billions of dollars … how many lives? And they still control most of the land and the people!

These are the same people that I've been training. They are natural warriors. Guerrillas who have perfected their tactics over decades, first against the British, then the Russians, now us. These men – probably some of them boys – have known nothing else except guerrilla warfare over their entire lifetime. How can you negotiate "peace" with someone who has never experienced that very concept?

He thought of the many patrols he had led over the last ten years in this country and the way that the fear was always with him. The way that it shaped everything about him, both mind and body, turning him into a person he did not want to become. It altered his very posture. He no longer stood up quite straight, but pulled his shoulders in and tucked his chin. He took smaller steps, staying more on his toes, and his eyes were always moving, scanning a one-eighty arc along his path, even if that path was only from his tent to the briefing room at their outpost. He was suspicious of the people, whether they were men or women, civilians or soldiers.

I've lost the ability to see, really see, the world I travel through. I wish I could be like the Englishwoman on the flight from Frankfurt to New York. She was a travel writer for some website or other. She went on and on about the quality of the early morning light in Kabul, the elegant simplicity of the mosques, the way the women used the rooftops as an integral part of the Afghan home, the dignity of the people and the way the children marveled at her blond hair.

She could have been describing life on Mars. In the Afghanistan that I know, rooftops are where the snipers are. And the children? They are afraid of you. Except the ones that hate you and show it in every way that they can, including the occasional grenade. The mosques are sanctuaries for killers, armories stocked with weapons, and speaking platforms for imams who advocate an Islam based on a Koran that I do not recognize.

The path changed direction frequently, dictated by the terrain. But they were almost always climbing and moving generally in an easterly direction, marked now by a predawn lightening. They had long ago moved beyond the area he was familiar with; what the NATO liaison referred to with a straight face as the "daylight influence zone" of their Achin Adi outpost.

We must be close to wherever it is that they are going. They know who I am, so they also know what will happen when I turn up missing. They are tribesmen ... herdsmen or farmers who have never farmed because of the perpetual war. But they have learned about satellites and drones and the way that the movement of groups of men stands out against this landscape. Daylight is their enemy.

He gauged the very faint grayness of the eastern horizon and thought, *"... within the next half hour."*

Ten minutes later, they entered a narrow gorge and walked into the center of a small group of buildings. *Not a village... more like a large family farm. Visible only from directly overhead. The gorge runs north-south, so won't get much sunlight. A good spot for people that don't like cameras in satellites.* The men headed off in pairs and triplets, each small group heading for a particular building. His two minders stayed standing with him.

The leader Sahid faced him.

"Do you remember the first rule?"

"I do not speak."

"Excellent. Here is rule two. You do not leave the building where we put you unless you are told. Do you understand?"

"Yes."

The first thin slash of sunlight appeared high on the rocks above them as he ducked his head to pass through the low door.

An omen? Of what, I wonder?

A Call From Afghanistan

Funny how you can be surprised by something that you always knew was going to happen.

A more introspective man might have been curious about the apparent contradiction. But Harlan Crosby was very much of the "Shit Happens" school of thought. He had bootstrapped himself from childhood poverty to the U.S. Senate by not worrying very much about murky cause-and-effect relationships. Much better to define the problem, develop alternative responses, pick the best one, and then execute.

There were two phones on his desk. The one that rang was the important one; the line that very few people knew of. Madge picked it up, saying only "Senator Crosby's office."

She listened for about five seconds and then handed him the phone. "It's a Major Dalkie. Sounds Scottish. He's asking for you."

"Do we know a Major Dalkie?"

"No. But he's got the right number. That's a very short list."

Harlan took the phone, putting it on speakerphone so that Madge could listen. Later, he would recall a very slight premonition.

"This is Harlan Crosby."

The Scottish burr was quite pronounced. "Senator. I'm the head of the NATO training mission in Achin Adi. I'm calling to report that your son Slater is missing in action."

OK. You've imagined this call hundreds of times, with all of the variations. Deal with it. You can think about the other stuff later.

"What happened?"

"A routine night recon. Three miles out and back. There was an ambush. Five ANSF killed. Your son and the Afghan commander – a Captain Abad – are missing."

"No survivors? Witnesses?"

"No sir. They got hit about six hours ago. We've got people on the ground out looking, and I'm requesting some air assets, but ..."

"What's your assessment?"

There was a four or five second pause. Long enough to telegraph that a carefully rehearsed answer was coming.

"Sir. Our patrols get hit all the time. The Taliban just got lucky this time."

Harlan used his military voice. The one for subordinate officers. "Major Dalkie. I asked for your assessment, not a press release."

The response was instantaneous and one could almost imagine Dalkie snapping to attention on the other end of the line. "Sir. Slater -- your son – was – is -- an excellent combat officer. The ambush scene is inconsistent with what I know about his tactics. And those of the Taliban. It's –"

"Dalkie. Have you told anyone else about this?"

The Scottish burr became even more pronounced and the man's unease came through very clearly. "No sir. I thought that ... given his connections ... and you being ... well, I thought I should check with you first."

"Good. Don't say anything to anybody. I'm sending a personal representative of mine – his name is Oliver. He's already in-country and can be at Achin Adi within the next few hours. Write up the usual report, but don't share it yet. And call me – this number – if you learn anything new."

"Sir?" The single syllable was reeking with nervousness. "I'm obligated to report –"

"Dalkie, when I hang up, I'm calling the Chairman of the Joint Chiefs of Staff at the Pentagon, the President of the United States and then the commander of NATO forces in Afghanistan. In that order. I think that should satisfy the requirements to report up the chain of command! I appreciate your discretion so far and hope that I can count on it as this unfolds. Do we understand one another?"

He replaced the receiver without waiting for a reply.

He and Madge looked at one another. Their twenty years of shared history made the silent exchange as eloquent and emotional as any outpouring of words or embraces.

She stood. "I'll get to Ollie. You make your calls to JCS and the President."

"Yasmin first. God! This will be hard!"

Madge stood, obviously wanting to say something. Finally, she sighed and said what they were both thinking about.

"They'll know who he is."

"Yes."

"We can expect a ransom demand. That's their usual pattern in that sector. A very, very large ransom demand ..."

"Yes. One that we can't pay, unless ..."

Neither of them could bring themselves to say out loud what they were envisioning as the alternative if they could not pay.

Planning the Fix

"Zanker may be a problem."

Harlan looked blankly at the man with the decidedly unhappy expression standing in front of his desk. Then he remembered the name.

"The banker who gets to allocate $100 million among the prettiest girls?"

When Garrison nodded but continued to look unhappy, Harlan asked, "What's the problem?"

"First, the good news. We're set to go for the June 1 show. We've got five of Ollie's projects included in the final set of thirteen. They present well and – I think – impressed, or fooled, the GABI account officers who did site visits."

Harlan leaned back in his chair and put his feet up on his desk. It was his favorite position for thinking. "Thirteen, huh? And five are ours. Which brings us back to Mr. Zanker…"

"I've run a Level V scan on him. Everything from his college essays through tax returns. Interviewed people he works with, plays with. Talked to ex-girl friends, customers, teachers. Read his emails, both business and personal."

"So. Now that we know all of the details of Mr. Zanker's life, how do we get him to make the right choices?"

"That's the problem. There's no evidence that he would be receptive to an appeal to his patriotism. In fact, he's fairly outspoken – and critical -- about our foreign policies, particularly since Bush came up with the idea of preemptive warfare."

"Can he be bribed?"

"It would be risky to try. As far as we can tell, it hasn't been tried in the past. Or, if it has, it hasn't worked. And several people who have worked for him commented on his integrity in the face of pressure. Apparently, there are several cases where he lost a large commission because he wouldn't cut certain corners for one of his corporate customers."

"Blackmail?"

"He's like an adult Eagle Scout. Nothing to work with that I can find. He spends a lot of time in bed with a very good-looking and fairly prominent woman. But they're both single and transparent about what's going on. These days, that's not a scandal. He'd be envied."

"Can't we manufacture a scandal of some sort and then threaten him with exposure?"

"We could. But I think it would backfire."

"That's the other part of the problem. This Afghan deal that he's running is his baby. He's spent months putting all the parts in place and is strongly committed to making it work. If we ask him to deliberately screw it up ..."

"Worth a try, isn't it? Keep it low profile ... a covert approach by a highly deniable and anonymous agent. He says 'no,' we're no worse off."

"We might be. Zanker has one more potentially troublesome feature."

Harlan leaned back and looked at Garrison through his steepled fingers.

Garrison said, "He used to be a reporter – St. Louis Post Dispatch. Emphasis on international stuff. Spent time as an imbedded journalist during Desert Storm."

"Used to be?"

"Never went back to it after grad school. Joined the World Bank and then Global American. But my reading is that he could revert to form at any time. Especially if some shady character squeezed him to divert a hundred million dollars to a bunch of CIA fronts in Afghanistan."

"Can we threaten him?"

"Sure, maybe even get him to go along and disburse the funds like we want him to. But two weeks later, he blows the whistle and shows up on Face the Nation on Sunday morning!"

Both men were silent, thinking. Then Garrison said, "There is one wrinkle, but I can't see how to use it."

"Let's hear it."

Garrison hesitated, then blurted out, "Well, there is Slater! Your son in Afghanistan ..."

Neither Harlan's expression or his posture changed, but every sense went on high alert. *Slater! Nobody knows about him being missing but me and four other people!*

Garrison picked up the faint atmospheric change and went on quickly, hoping to forestall whatever reaction he'd triggered. "Zanker and Slater know each other. They were at Berkeley at the same time and we know they spent some time together – an Arabic language class and some social time as well. Drove across country together at least once."

Harlan relaxed. "That was a long time ago. Do we know anything about their relationship? Any subsequent meetings?"

"Nothing that I can find."

Harlan stood up. "Forget about the Slater connection. Keep digging into Zanker's history. There must be some hook we can use."

As soon as Garrison left, Harlan called Madge into the office.

"Madge. There may be a way that we can pay that very, very large ransom demand that we anticipate…. Get Ollie for me, will you?"

Kaz (London)

The Dubai flight to London touched down thirty minutes ahead of schedule, but the Heathrow tarmac was its usual mess. Even traveling first class and with carryon luggage, it took almost another hour before he got to the taxi rank. But it felt like he was home, as much as one could be "home" while traveling two-hundred thousand miles a year on airplanes. Kaz spent most of his in-office time in London and owned a flat in the city's Mayfair district. He also maintained a condo in San Francisco; not for professional reasons but just because he loved the city.

Exiting Heathrow, he thought, *Another day, another major city!* For Kaz, the thought was a positive one, although tempered by his realization of the blind luck that had brought him to this point in his career.

I was going to be a "journalist." Ever since eighth grade. Write for the New York Times. Win Pulitzer Prizes. Turned out to be the St. Louis Post Dispatch, but that was OK. I'd work my way to New York. Then came the chance to be one of those "imbedded" reporters with the troops in Desert Storm. A very short war without much real drama. But it made me want to be a "war correspondent" and – God knows – there are plenty of wars to go around. But first the Graduate School of Journalism at Berkeley. Laying track for that Pulitzer.

Then the randomness. The World Bank sent a recruiter to Berkeley. *He was German. Spoke six languages and talked about "the post-Soviet world" and the endless possibilities for a truly international man. And my first year would be spent living in London, Prague and Budapest!*

The post-Soviet world turned out to be depressing and resistant to change. And the promised "London, Prague and Budapest" turned out to be Frankfurt, Helsinki and Cairo. Even worse, the World Bank was an old man's institution – an elephant's graveyard for economists and bureaucrats. He lasted three years.

But all of Eastern Europe was seeking massive amounts of reconstruction capital. And all those ex-communists wanted to be capitalists and thought I could tell them how. They needed me. I learned about real banks and how they work. Or don't work. And I met real bankers, Ministers of Finance, Secretaries of the Treasury, managers of sovereign wealth funds with billions of dollars.

One of the bankers he met was Dieter Mundt, a Vice Chairman of Global American Bank and responsible for all of EMEA. They met when Kaz made a pitch to Mundt on behalf of the World Bank, seeking GABI's participation in rebuilding the Bulgarian banking system. Mundt looked bored from the instant he came into the room. He stopped him three slides into his Powerpoint presentation.

"Do you know how long it takes to clear a check in Sofia?"

"Approximately twelve days."

"Do you know why there are no ATMs in Plovdiv?"

"Because there is a Soviet-era law against deposits or withdrawals unless done through a teller."

"Do you know how many signatures it takes for the World Bank to approve a ten million dollar loan to a state agency for an infrastructure project in Bulgaria?"

"Six. Unless the term is five years or less. Then it's five."

"How many privately owned Russian banks – not government banks – are there in Russia today?"

"Nobody knows for sure. But there will be fewer next week. And the term 'Russian bank' is an oxymoron."

Mundt sat back and looked closely at Kaz.

"Are you really from New Mexico?"

"Yes."

Mundt sat back in his chair, saying, "Please finish your presentation, but I'm not sure that our shareholders think that GABI has a role to play in the reconstruction of Eastern Europe."

Mundt invited him to dinner. During the meal, he questioned Kaz about his personal and professional history. Once the dishes were cleared, the subject matter shifted.

Mundt started. "As Vice Chair for EMEA, I'm responsible for a dozen or so industry sectors – health, technology, automotive – you know the labels. But the one that worries me the most is our financial sector."

Where is this going? This guy's about eight rungs above me in the business world. And he's confiding in me about his professional life?

"Uh, Mr. Mundt, I'm –"

"Call me Dieter, please. As I was saying, the financial sector … I've got maybe a dozen or so relationship managers for the segment, but all of them are from the old school. Making an actual decision scares the hell out of them. More worried about using the right fork at dinner than understanding the customer. That worked for a while, but banking – especially in EMEA – is changing very fast."

What the hell? He seems to value forthrightness.

"So why don't you just fire the lot of them?"

Mundt grinned. "I'd like to. But I'd lose all my customers. It is a relationship business, after all."

He leaned forward over the table. "I'd like you to join the team. Middle East and Africa is open at the moment and your Arabic would come in handy."

"But –"

"I will double your World Bank salary and give you a generous housing allowance for a city of your choice, anywhere in EMEA. In the old days, I would recommend Beirut … but times have changed."

That was fifteen years ago. Now Dieter Mundt was six months away from retirement and Kaz ran the entire financial sector with his own team in place. And the last six of those fifteen years had featured more change and the largest banking crisis since the Great Depression. It left even the old-timers shaking their heads.

No Pulitzers, but I wouldn't trade the experience even if they offered me one.

The current deal that he was working was his favorite so far. His office desk and part of the floor was covered with stacks of paper, mostly legal-size sheets with impressive looking logos on the cover pages. If it all came together, it would be a one-hundred million dollar grant to Afghanistan to help with reconstruction. GABI was contracting with the U.S. Treasury to manage the project evaluation and disbursement process and Kaz was the primary person leading the entire project on their behalf.

He looked at his desk calendar. June 1 was circled prominently. *Two weeks away. Almost there. All we need is the paperwork for that World Bank endorsement.*

The phone rang, the line from Dieter's office.

"Kaz. Can you step down to my office please?"

That's a tad formal for him. Must have either his boss or a major customer in there. And he sounds like he isn't very happy.

"Thirty seconds. Anything I should be pondering while I'm on the way?"

"Yes, but I have no idea what that is."

Kaz was there in under the promised thirty seconds, driven partly by a need to know what had caused his boss – for the first time in Kaz's memory – to admit he did not know what was going on in his domain.

Not Your Usual Meeting

Mundt looked decidedly unhappy, but it was not the kind of unhappiness that Kaz associated with a loan gone bad or a customer departure. And whatever the source, Mundt seemed to view Kaz as somehow responsible. *This is anger mixed with helplessness. But what's it got to do with me?*

There were two men with Mundt and to Kaz's surprise, neither of them stood up when he walked in. And no one offered to introduce himself. He knew neither of them, but they struck him as Americans. He looked questioningly at Dieter.

The anger came through quite clearly when Dieter stood up and said, "I don't know who they are either. And neither of them will tell me."

He went on, clearly giving a rehearsed speech. "I've been told – by some very important people – to tell you that if you do what they ask you to do, the Bank and our various minders will be most grateful. I am to assure you that this … this … venture takes precedence over all of your other duties and that it will in no way diminish your standing within the Bank."

He headed for the door, saying, "And I am not permitted to answer any of the many questions I'm sure you have." He closed the door behind him, leaving Kaz standing in the middle of the room and looking slightly dazed.

One of the men gestured at the empty chair. He was dressed appropriately for Executive Row of a major financial institution, but didn't seem quite comfortable in the pin-striped suit. He impressed Kaz as someone that would be more comfortable outdoors. He was older, perhaps mid-50's, but undistinguished in every other way. Except maybe his eyes. They seemed more intense. The other man was about ten years younger, dressed a little more carefully than his companion, and seemed at least faintly hostile.

Kaz did not sit down. *Maybe a little offensive ploy?* He said, "FBI? CIA? Interpol? Maybe Treasury?"

The older man said, "We're so obscure, we don't even have an acronym. And I know this whole process is objectionable to you and Mr. Mundt, but I assure you it's justified."

Kaz sat down, still studying the two men. It was crazy, but he flashed back to his time at Berkeley. *This is the conspiracy fantasy we all had. That Big Brother is going to show up and say something like "It's for the good of your country."*

"We could tell you our names, but you wouldn't believe us, and we'd lie. Same for ID's ... they're easier to fake than the names."

They got past Dieter, which takes some doing. Indignation on my part is a waste of time. They're going to tell me whatever it is they want to tell me. So there's really only two questions.

"Why me?"

It threw the man slightly. Maybe because of the lack of outrage at the breach of protocol or perhaps because it usually was not the first question. But he recovered quickly and spoke without hesitation.

"The qualifications for the job we have in mind are quite narrow. Very few people meet our conditions and we have little time for an exhaustive search. Fortunately, or unfortunately depending on your perspective, you look like a good fit."

"You'd make a good politician. You answered my question and told me nothing."

The man smiled.

So, the second question then.

"Exactly what is it you want me to do?" Kaz tried for a disinterested tone, but suspected that the intrigue was getting him hooked. Or at least curious.

"Mr. Zanker. Believe it or not, you have the right to decline to participate in what we are about to discuss. If you tell us to leave the room right now, we will. But it is essential for you to understand that, from this point forward, none of what is said here can be shared with anyone. Now or ever. With anyone. Whether you accept or decline our offer. Regardless of the outcome. This is non-negotiable and there are extreme sanctions if you violate this agreement."

"This is beginning to sound glamorous. And dangerous."

"I assure you it is *not* glamorous. It is almost certainly at least a little bit dangerous."

"So, again: What is it that –"

"Do you accept the condition?"

They've certainly set the hook. I wonder if any one has ever walked out at this stage?

"I presume you have some serious looking document for me to sign?"

The man opened the black leather folio in front of him and slid a document across the table. It was a single page, untitled, with the date and a line for his signature at the bottom. He read it quickly. The language was both unambiguous and daunting. *It refers to "legislative and judicial authority" but fails to indicate which country's legislature or judiciary. Quite clear about the nasty things they can do to me.*

He signed the document and slid it back across the table. "Enough foreplay. Tell me what it is that you want me to do."

The two men looked at each other. To Kaz's surprise, the other man spoke for the first time. "Did you see the Times this morning?"

"With my Corn Flakes. What's that got to do –"

"Front page, center, above the fold. The beheading?"

Christ! The photojournalist from France! Horrible!

A sudden surge of pure anger welled up within him, driving out every other sensation. He stood up and walked to the windows, looking out at all of Canary Wharf stretched along the Thames but seeing only the young man in the orange jumpsuit with the thousand-yard stare kneeling before his black-clad executioner.

He said, "Yes, I saw it."

He returned to his chair. Somehow, during the course of his transit to the window and back, the room turned darker, the two men more sinister.

The tall man took over again. "He is … was … one of a dozen or more hostages being held somewhere in the Middle East by some group or other. One of those people is a friend of ours and we'd like you to help us get him back."

He looked at them incredulously. *Is there another Kendall Zanker? Some Rambo type that they've got me mixed up with?*

"Yes, it does seem absurd, doesn't it?"

The man seemed to sympathize with his reaction, but the seriousness of his expression did not lessen in the slightest.

Kaz waved his arms. "It's beyond absurd! It's .. it's … off-the-scale lunacy!"

"So are beheadings. But they're quite real."

A Special Offer

"We'd like you to help us get him back." Such an innocent sentence! *But they are not lunatics. They are deadly serious and they think I can actually help them.*

"OK. Let's keep it really simple. The same two questions: What is it you think I can do for you and why me? And I warn you that I think – however you answer those questions – that you're wrong!"

The younger man was sitting back in his chair watching Kaz closely. He clearly was going to be an observer. The other man with the intense eyes also sat back, looking as though he was composing his thoughts.

He said, "It may be that you're right. I don't think that you are, but before we're done here, we have to decide that question."

He stood up. "Look. We've come a long way in ten minutes. Can we get some coffee? This next bit may take a while."

Kaz picked up the phone on Dieter's desk and asked his assistant to bring in a large carafe of coffee. When she had arranged the cups and left the room, the man stood and poured three cups. He handed one of them to Kaz and sat back down.

"Your questions – what you can do and why you instead of somebody else – are not simple ones. I will try to answer them, but those answers will lead to more questions. I will try to answer those as well. But many of them I cannot – or will not – answer. This will be unsatisfactory to you, but there is nothing I can do about it."

Kaz nodded. "You said that – at any time – I can refuse to participate and walk away. Is that actually true?"

"Yes. Although I hope you won't. And, if you do, this document remains in force." He tapped his index finger on the paper that Kaz had just signed.

The other man picked up his coffee cup and walked over to the windows. He stood looking out, seemingly uninterested in the now two-way conversation.

"This is awkward… this no-names bit. Why don't you call me Ollie … short for Oliver?"

Kaz almost smiled. *So they care enough to try to soften me up a bit. Coffee and now first names. Surely they must know that I spend most of my time in rooms with people who are pretending to be nice to me because I have something they want.*

"OK ... Ollie. Now can we take on some of those not-so-simple questions you referred to?"

"Sure, let's start with the easy ones. First, what we want you to do. Specifically, we want you to negotiate the release of our friend."

"With what?"

"Money, of course. We expect a significant ransom demand."

"He's American?"

Ollie turned to look at the man gazing out the window. He made no indication of being aware of their dialogue. Ollie hesitated and then simply said, "Yes."

America does not negotiate with terrorists. The U.S. government does not pay ransom. At least, that's the official position. But I guess they may send a couple of spooks to develop a behind-the-scenes approach. Let's see if we can push a little.

"So any negotiation has to be both unofficial and covert?"

Ollie smiled and gave an expressive shrug, as if to signal his gratitude for being spared long and complicated explanations.

"But why me? I have zero experience at negotiating ransoms. With terrorists on anybody else for that matter! Surely you know that?"

Ollie held up four fingers.

"But you are an experienced negotiator. One of the very best, according to our sources. Especially where significant amounts of money are involved."

"Second, you know and respect the culture. You speak Arabic. You have gained respect from tribal elders ... the kind of people that will be on the other side of the table."

"Third, you know the history, who the mujahedeen are and what they want. You've been on the ground with troops."

"Right! In 1991. And I was a reporter. Not a grunt."

He went on, as though Kaz had not spoken, folding down the fourth and last finger. "And you travel throughout the

Middle East. There's nothing implausible about you being on the scene."

Kaz stood up abruptly, his impatience finally getting the better of him.

"I can personally name ten other individuals who meet all of those conditions and are far more involved with the politics of the Middle East than I am. Why not them? Where's that famous diplomatic 'back-channel' that always gets credited for the really groundbreaking negotiations?"

Ollie started shaking his head while Kaz was still talking. "Back channels are great. But if your official position is 'No negotiation with terrorists,' it's still much too public an option."

"And you underrate yourself. Even with that back-channel option, there are maybe only two or three other candidates. But you have some very special qualities that they don't have."

Kaz spread his hands, the classic "show me" gesture.

Again, the man turned toward the other man, who turned away from the view and stared back. He nodded his head once and turned away again.

Ollie said, "There are two very important attributes that you possess. First – and I need to be a little vague at this point -- but I can say that our representative ... negotiator ... needs to have some expertise in international money transfers. In short, we need a banker."

Crazier and crazier. "What kind of a kidnapper wants me to write a check? What the hell happened to good old-fashioned kidnapping protocol? You know? Where you get a ransom note with all block capital letters and get told to cram a lot of used hundred dollar bills into suitcases and drop it at a prearranged place late at night?"

He was struck by a sudden thought. "How much are they asking for?"

Ollie grimaced as if sensing an oncoming headache. "We don't know. Actually, they haven't made any demands at all."

"They?"

When Ollie just looked at him, Kaz said, "You said 'they.' Who are 'they'?

The grimace turned into embarrassment. "Actually, we don't know that either."

Kaz no longer tried to disguise his sarcasm. "How about 'where' and 'when'? Are those unknowns too?"

Ollie's silence was an eloquent answer. But Kaz was thinking of another variable. *The Times ran through the list of known hostages. There were no Americans on the list.*

"How about 'who'? What's the name of 'your friend' who's waiting for his head to be lopped off?"

"I can't tell you that unless you'll agree to participate."

Kaz stood up and looked down at him. "Well, why don't you call me when you have more detail? Then we can revisit the question of my involvement."

The other man spoke as though reciting a script, still looking out the window. "We anticipate a demand for an unknown but significant amount of money, to be distributed instantly to different recipients in different countries in different currencies, all of whom are currently unknown to us. The negotiation will take place somewhere in rural Afghanistan over the course of one or two days. We want you to negotiate the deal. It is imperative that we get him back, but we don't want to pay more than we have to. And once the deal is done, you will oversee the distribution of funds, which will require considerable expertise with international banking regulations."

He walked back to where the other man was standing. He picked up the document on the tabletop, put it back in his leather folio, and both of them turned toward the door.

Kaz let them get almost to the door before he said, "You said that I have two very important attributes that make me the one to try to get your man back. I'm a banker. What's the second one?"

That stopped them. Neither of the men turned around, but Ollie said, "You know him."

Meeting Recap

Ollie took off his suit coat and stripped off his tie, throwing both items into the back seat of the rented Mercedes. "I hate dressing up in these monkey suits!"

Derek Williams laughed at him. "You're the big believer in camouflage. Fit in with the terrain. Blend in with the background. All that stuff. And believe me, with that suit you really do look like a general purpose federal bureaucrat a few years from retirement."

They were silent until out of the garage. Once out on Westferry Road and crawling along in concert with what seemed to be most of London, Ollie said, "What do you think?"

"He's smart. But we already knew that."

Ollie nodded. "And he's not impressed by authority. Or maybe I really didn't impress him as an ominous federal agent with the power to destroy his life if he failed to cooperate?"

"You did fine. What surprised me was the absence of indignation. How many overpaid bankers do you know who wouldn't be shouting about their rights and calling for a lawyer within the first two minutes of that conversation?"

Ollie nodded. "There's something else too. He didn't ask enough questions. Especially for someone that once wanted to be a global correspondent for the Times."

"Yeah. I noticed that. I think at least part of the reason is that he knew we wouldn't answer them."

"And just maybe it was because he thinks he's going to get them answered somewhere else?"

"Could be. Should we worry about that? Maybe a bug or two?"

Ollie was silent, clearly thinking about the question. "I don't think so. Not yet. We already have some surveillance set up. Enough for now, I think."

"Change of subject?"

"Sure. We're done with Mr. Zanker for now."

Williams shrugged, "This concerns him, but indirectly. I think CC may be a problem."

"CC? I thought that was all good. The stuff she's been funneling us about Zanker is right on. She's gotten close to him."

"That's just it. She may be getting a little too close ... Maybe losing her objectivity, if you know what I mean."

Ollie smiled, not in a particularly pleasant way. "Relax, Derek. The closer she gets, the better."

They crawled along in the traffic, momentarily silent. Then Ollie spoke, as though talking to himself. "I think that maybe, just maybe, our man is focusing on the wrong problem."

Williams just looked at him. After a few seconds passed, he said tentatively, "Our man? Exactly which man is that?"

"The honorable senator. We started out a couple of months ago with this elaborate scheme to divert a hundred million bucks to us, so that we could fight a war properly. We've got all the pieces in place except the last one – how to ensure that Zanker chooses our projects. Then the senator's son gets captured and Zanker becomes the means for paying a huge ransom. He cooperates with us to save the good captain."

"So? Happy endings all around."

"Two nasty little uncovered contingencies. One: What if there is no ransom demand? Just a really nasty beheading on YouTube? Then what's Zanker's incentive to do what we tell him to do? Second, what if some really important people still want the hundred million dollars to finance their private little war rather than to keep the family intact?"

"Oliver, I don't –"

"In fact, those same important people might think that a public beheading would be just the thing to keep their private little war going ..."

For the briefest of times, Derek Williams experienced a mere flicker of a long-dormant conscience. He was reminded that he served truly evil people.

Recalled Conversations

The two men left Kaz sitting in Deiter Mundt's corner office, still trying to digest what he had just been told.

Slater Crosby!

That explains a lot – the hush-hush style, the spooks, how they were able to co-opt Dieter (and probably the CEO above him). Everything but why they think I'm the right person to help them.

The son of a U.S. senator goes missing in a combat zone!

His next reaction would bother him for a long time in the future, but it was quite real. *Now there's a Pulitzer Prize quality story. It's too bad I signed that non-disclosure agreement!*

They said, "You know him." I guess that's true if you define knowing someone as spending six days together a dozen or more years ago.

Actually, it was late August in 2000. Kaz was finishing his second year of journalism graduate school at Berkeley. His first encounter with Slater Crosby was in an advanced Arabic language class. They were both ethnic misfits within the class, so it was probably both natural and inevitable that they gravitated toward one another. After class one night, they wound up in a bar on Shattuck Avenue.

Kaz asked the obvious question. "OK. What's a white middle-class American undergraduate student doing in an advanced Arabic class?"

"Doing what Mommy always wanted me to do would be the best answer at the moment," was the quite serious response.

When Kaz frowned, he went on. "She – Mommy -- is the only daughter of a former Ambassador to Turkey. She grew up in Ankara and it affected her. She loves everything about the Middle East – the food, art, history, culture. She's fluent herself and has always tried to inoculate me with the same value system."

"Is she a Muslim?"

Slater laughed. "Mommy! No way! She's married to a very upcoming American military hero, the fearless warrior that spearheaded Operation Desert Storm. Mustn't muddy the waters where Daddy's career is involved!"

They met for a beer a couple of times after class. Kaz learned that Slater had just finished his sophomore year and – from the stories that he told about his collegiate history – had spent most of his time at Berkeley acting out the stereotypical role of a firebrand dissident. He attended more anti-war rallies than classes and was a figurehead at most of the anti-establishment theatre that UCal Berkeley was famous for. It repelled Kaz, who found the life-style to be both boring and juvenile. His emerging friendship with Slater quickly plateued.

The real involvement with one another was the result of a car trip. When Kaz learned that Slater was planning on driving back to Washington for a visit to his parents, Kaz negotiated a ride in exchange for sharing the driving and gas expenses. At the time, his parents were still in New York.

It was a leisurely trip. Neither of them was particularly anxious to get to the East Coast, so they meandered through the western states seeing the major national parks along the way. They quickly discovered they had much in common. One of those overlaps involved the military.

They had barely cleared Sacramento when Kaz said, "So your father's a general or something?"

"One star. They call him a 'brigadier general.'"

"That's pretty far up the ladder. I only saw a couple of those types when I was a reporter in Iraq."

"It's like the top half-percent for the Army. The trouble is, he wants to be in the top one-tenth of one-percent. Three more stars to go."

"Those last couple of promotions are tough to get. I recall names like Eisenhower and Pershing."

Slater's sarcasm came through quite strongly. "It helps if you're a war hero ... and a mean son-of-a-bitch! And he's both of those. And he's got the right genealogy! I wouldn't bet against him."

"Genealogy?"

"His father – my grandfather -- won a Medal of Honor. Got it the hard way. He was a Major with the 7th Infantry Division in Korea. He died at the Chosin Reservoir."

There was something in Slater's tone that told Kaz this was a topic to be careful with. Nevertheless, he asked, "And you're the only son, right? Sounds to me like you're saddled with a legacy …"

That remark caused an abrupt change in Slater. His expression turned stony and Kaz could see the veins on the back of his hands stand out as he tightened his grip on the wheel.

"Enough family history. Why don't you take a nap or something?"

The topic stayed dormant until they stopped to tour the Little Big Horn battlefield in Montana. It was a warm sunlit day and the regimental flags of the 7th Cavalry snapped in the wind.

"What a colossal idiot he was!" It was Slater's first comment in their hour-long walk around the monument.

"Custer?"

"Who else? You like statistics about army generals: Did you know that Custer was promoted to Brigadier General at age 23, the youngest ever?"

"A prodigy?"

"Hardly, he graduated last in his class at West Point. But he had what war heroes need above all else."

Kaz said, "And that was …?

" A war, and it was a dandy. Our so-called 'Civil War' was a breeding ground for dead heroes, a lot of them generals."

As they were getting back in the car, Slater said, as though talking to himself, "His father was a farmer, so he at least had a choice."

It was a curious comment and Kaz couldn't let it slide by. "You mean George Armstrong Custer?"

"Yes. They say his father wanted him to be a clergyman and we know he taught school for a while. Why did he go to West Point if he didn't have to?"

"Maybe to spite his father?"

Slater looked at him sharply as if expecting to find an expression in contrast to the comment. Kaz simply said, "It's what kids do … spite their fathers. Maybe that's why you *didn't* go to West Point?"

When he looked back on it, it was as if his comment gave Slater permission to talk about issues that are usually reserved for posthumously published biographies. They sat in the parking lot for the next hour, with Slater doing most of the talking.

"I was always supposed to go to West Point. Become the third-generation career military man and war hero. My father always assumed I would go there and – I think – I myself believed that too."

"What changed?"

Slater was silent long enough that Kaz thought he'd opted out of the conversation. But then he said, very thoughtfully, "Two things, I think."

He shook his head. "The first one is the usual psychoanalytical crap. About boys needing to test their fathers. About late-adolescent males trying to show that they're grown up and can make their own decisions. We fought about almost everything my last year of high school. Who my friends were, who I dated, what courses I took. It was funny, I did everything he told me not to! And that's why I did it. Because he told me not to."

He smiled. "It's funny. He was … is … so uptight … so binary about right and wrong … so military … that almost anything I did was guaranteed to set him off.

"The other thing that changed? The Gulf War – the first one, Operation Desert Storm and everything that came after that. It turned me off. I was almost twelve years old and like most twelve year old boys, I was envisioning being a soldier as something like being a knight at King Arthur's Round Table. I would slay dragons, fight man-to-man against real villains. Fairy tale stuff. But then, thanks to TV, Mom and I watched as Colin Powell patiently assembled massive amounts of weaponry and manpower and then methodically flattened everything in his path. The ground assault lasted one-hundred hours and the U.S. suffered exactly one-hundred and forty-eight combat casualties. Saddam wasn't even a real dragon, just stupid. The idea of me being a professional soldier in that kind of world seemed just about the same kind of stupid."

Kaz was only halfway present. The mention of Operation Desert Storm sent him deep into his own head, dealing with an image of a press "briefing" against a backdrop of a Saudi dust storm that was enveloping a column of armored vehicles posed for the benefit of the dozen or so "imbedded journalists." At the time, it seemed an ill omen.

When he realized that Slater had stopped talking and was waiting for some kind of response, he asked, "Where was your mother on this topic? Of West Point?"

"That was another change. Until then, she always sided with my dad. Basically, she views her role in their marriage more or less as her being the good top sergeant for the company commander. She has been, in every sense of the word, a good military wife. And she's responsible, I think, for a lot of his rapid advancement; particularly in the last couple of promotions where they start to look more closely at the spouse as well as the officer."

"So, what changed?"

"The world. When the Soviet system collapsed, our military strategies became instantly outdated. We were prepared to fight large-scale ground wars in Europe and Asia using tactics and weaponry in 'conventional' ways. Now the wars would be nasty little wars, the kind that kill women, children, journalists, tribal elders, doctors and teachers, and anyone else that offends you simply because they have not taken up arms in your cause. And my mother saw that – in this post-Soviet era, and particularly after Kuwait -- those wars were going to be fought in the Middle East, in the places where she had grown up and within a culture that she loved."

Slater was looking inward. "She and I watched Desert Storm on TV. We knew Dad was in the first unit over the Iraqi border and that thought hung over us while we watched and read all the news accounts. But each of us became a little bit anti-war during that time. Me because it offended my knightly fantasies about soldiering. Her because she could not stop identifying with the Iraqi people and what was coming at them. I think she knew that the entire region was going to become a gigantic killing zone."

"Did she outright tell you that she didn't want you to become the third-generation professional soldier that your father had in mind?"

Slater smiled again. "Not a chance. Didn't I tell you that she was a good military wife? But she was the one who encouraged me to apply to UC Berkeley ... 'just in case something goes wrong with the West Point approval process.'"

A lone bugler was silhouetted against the setting sun, playing "Taps" as they drove out of the parking lot.

Field Report

Ollie's black leather folio held one other document. It was contained in a buff-colored folder that had "Security Level VII" stamped on its face in very large, very bright red letters. The document itself was all text and fifteen pages in length, double-spaced. Numerous phrases and sometimes entire paragraphs were blacked-out.

Captain Crosby left the (deleted) Outpost in (deleted) Province at 22:20 hours on (date deleted). The mission was a live training exercise involving night reconnaissance. Captain Crosby's role was as Advisor and Liaison to the six Afghan National Security Forces (ANSF) members that were part of the recon team. They were, in order of rank, (deleted), led by (deleted). The equipment they carried was normal for this type of patrol—light infantry weapons and night vision capabilities. They were on foot and had radio contact with the outpost. Drone coverage was available but was not requested except for "standby" support needs. A (deleted) man ANFS swift reaction team was also on standby for support, if needed.

Captain Crosby briefed Major (deleted), NATO liaison, on his intentions prior to the mission. The briefing was necessarily open-ended due to the nature of nighttime recon operations and the need for improvisation. He intended to walk through the village, staying on the main street and then conduct a sweep of a ten-kilometer stretch of the (deleted) Road between the (deleted) bridge and the entry into the village square.

It was Captain Crosby's practice to convene such training patrols two to three times a week, always with a different contingent of ANSF personnel and always on a different route. According to his reports, contacts with the Taliban had been infrequent and limited to brief skirmishes during the past four weeks. That was consistent with the overall experience in the region during that same time period.

The first and only radio contact was at 23:05, reporting that the team was leaving the village limits and that the recon was free of incidents at that point. Attempts to establish radio contact were initiated from (deleted) Outpost, beginning at 02:23, but were unsuccessful.

The ANSF standby support team left (deleted) Outpost in two armored Humvees at 05:10. The delay was due to (several lines of deleted text). They found the five enlisted ANSF members of the recon team at the (deleted) bridge. Each of them was killed by multiple gunshot wounds to the head and upper torso and the bodies stripped of weapons armor, communication devices and boots. Other than the dead soldiers, there was no evidence that a firefight had taken place and interviews with villagers who lived nearby failed to add any useable information.

Neither Captain Crosby nor Captain (deleted) was found and has not been heard from since. Both NATO and ANSF ground teams, with extensive satellite and drone support, have conducted area-wide sweeps but so far have yielded no information as to his whereabouts or the events that led to his disappearance.

There has been no change in the level or nature of Taliban movements or communication during the time since the incident.

Family Legacies

Who is Slater Crosby?

Kaz typed the four words into the Google "Search" box and hit "return." He was no longer amazed to observe that he got 754,000 hits in 0.37 seconds. It took him considerably longer than that – about forty minutes – to sift through the first layer of that deluge of information and draw some early conclusions.

First and most important, there were no news flashes whatsoever about him being missing. It impressed Kaz. *I didn't believe that news like that could still be suppressed. Either Ollie and his tightlipped friend are lying to me or somebody with heavy-duty clout is able to keep this contained. Like a U.S. senator maybe?*

Second, about half of the items he looked at were about Slater Crosby himself, mostly focused on his military history and his three tours in Afghanistan and Iraq. For the other half, he was important because he was the son of a newly elected Senator. The three Crosbys – father, mother and son – were a highly photogenic, made-for-TV trio in the media circus that swirled within and around election-year politics.

Even then, Slater is mostly in the background. He smiles, recites some platitudes about his Father's major talking points, and says all the right things. But he ducked a lot of the major events and always shied away from the policy questions, citing the American tradition whereby military officers did not openly campaign. It helped that for much of the time he was completely out-of-reach in remote parts of Afghanistan and Iraq. I wonder if volunteering for a war zone was merely a way to get away from his father?

He found one lengthy feature article from a Sunday news magazine that used Slater as a case study of how a officer's career path is limited if he or she enters the service other than through a service academy. The general conclusion was that the West Pointers advanced further and faster than those officers coming from ROTC, the National Guard, the Reserve, or Officer

Candidate School. Interestingly, Slater was an exception to the rule.

The author cynically suggested that the promotions had a lot to do with being the son of a charismatic active-duty general on a fast track to Joint Chiefs of Staff.

But that's not what I remember.

June 1999 – Somewhere in Montana

It was if the plaintive drawn-out notes of "Taps" required the silence that had settled between them to be maintained for a respectful interval.

Kaz and Slater had just finished a tour of "Custer's Last Stand" in South Dakota, better known as the Battle of the Little Big Horn. Twenty miles away by now, they picked up their conversation. Kaz admitted to himself that he was hooked on the unfolding story.

He's what? Twenty? And he's grown up on army posts, with a domineering father and the kind of expectations that tend to go with what they call "legacy." And whatever else he is, he's one of the more introspective kids I've seen. An unhappy combination, I think.

"So, not only did you not go to West Point, but you decided to attend the most obviously anti-military campus in the entire country? I'll bet Daddy didn't approve of either choice."

"'Decided' is too strong a term. You'd need a highly skilled psychoanalyst to sort out my logic, but – like I said -- I think it was just an only son's classic rejection of his parent's 'my way or the highway' style. It was the scariest thing I'd done up till then."

He smiled, obviously envisioning a scene from his past. "And, no, Daddy did not approve."

"That was two years ago. How do you feel about your decision now, with hindsight and all its advantages?"

There was a long silence, then, "Do you know that the term 'snafu' is really a military acronym? From World War II, I think."

"'Situation Normal, All Fucked Up' ... A very useful description for a lot of situations I've been in."

"It pretty well captures my view of the last couple of years. I've done the anti-war bit, written petitions, set up rallies, distributed leaflets, sat in at recruiting offices. Everything but throw rocks at the occasional uniform on campus."

"And...?"

Slater answered casually, but the sadness came through quite clearly. "It hasn't worked. It was a 'fake it until you make it' strategy that never had a chance."

The words were matter-of-fact, somehow making them into an unchallengeable and incredibly sad self-indictment. For the first time, Kaz began to wonder if Slater had ever talked with anyone else about what he really wanted. *Not daddy. That's for sure.*

"I tried. I really did. But once I made the grand gesture – not going to the Point – it felt like playacting ... me being someone I really didn't want to be ... all the time watching myself pretending.

"I can't stop comparing Berkeley with the military posts where I grew up. These kids are ... well, kids. They've got IQ's that are off-the-scale; most of them worked their ass off to get into Berkeley, and now they think they know what the rest of the world needs."

"Pretty standard stuff for college campuses..."

Slater looked over at him in a way that suggested he had missed a critical point. "But I grew up on bases where a lot of the kids had mothers and fathers actually in war zones. It made you think pretty hard about the choices they made ... and the way they did what they had to do even if they disagreed.

"Especially when they didn't come back."

He got real quiet. "You always knew. The women – it was always the women – would visit one particular house, usually carrying food of some sort. Your parents would whisper a lot when the kids were around. A couple of small kids might move in with us for a couple of days."

Kaz cleared his throat. "Kinda makes you think about what's really important, I guess."

"It's funny. I didn't think about it very much until Berkeley. I thought I was just sending a message to dear old dad. It turned out I was self-exiling myself from an entire culture."

"So, after two years of exile ...?" Kaz asked the question casually. It turned out that he had failed to understand the cathartic nature of the last few hours.

"That's why I'm going home. I want to tell my Dad that I'm entering the ROTC program at Berkeley. I'm going to be what he's always wanted me to be."

Doing Business in Dubai

Kaz was due in London but had scheduled a half-day stopover in Dubai. As always, he marveled at the architecture and opulence that lined the boulevard from the airport to the offices of United Commercial Bank of the Emirates. *If you're an Arab, Dubai is like an oasis of forbidden pleasures. And if you're doing banking business in the Middle East, you'll be spending a lot of time in Dubai ... and Abu Dhabi.*

UCBE was arguably the single most important private commercial bank in the Middle East. Not for its size, but for the range of its contacts and access to the people that mattered. And the man who stood to shake Kaz's hand when he entered his office was the single person responsible.

Abdul-Karim was seventy years old. He started at Citibank and stayed for thirty years, finally leaving when Citi – in his opinion – made a series of blunders in Europe and the Middle East. He spun his Rolodex and raised enough capital to start UCBE. For the last fifteen years, he had worked tirelessly (and ruthlessly, many claimed) to build its reputation. Along the way, UCBE became one of GABI's single most important relationships.

So when Abdul-Karim called him two days ago, Kaz answered promptly. The call lasted ten seconds.

"Kaz. I have some odds and ends that I'd like your help with. We could probably do it on the phone, but I'd appreciate it if you could stop by. And I always enjoy seeing you."

"No problem at all. I've also got something that I want to run by you. Would Tuesday morning be a convenient time? Say eleven o'clock?"

"Excellent. I look forward to it."

For today, Abdul-Karim was in western business attire. He gestured to the low coffee table in the corner of his office and waited for Kaz to choose one of the two leather chairs.

The next ten minutes were a ritual as old as the dunes that they could see in the distance from their fortieth floor perch. As soon as Abdul-Karim sat down, a young man in the classic Arab dishdasha entered from a side door pushing a tea service cart. He poured tea and left, leaving the two men to ask about each other's well-being and gossip about common acquaintances that were of current interest in the banking world.

As usual, they spoke in English. Kaz's Arabic language skills were sufficient for the street, but were inadequate – and inappropriate – for the executive suites he frequented. The small talk ended when Abdul-Karim leaned back in his chair, steepled his fingers together, and looked serious.

"I have some business to discuss."

Kaz held up his hand, palm outward. "Me first. Do you remember our discussion about my role in the Afghan Transformation Fund, the part that is called FARD?"

"Yes, of course. It is a tremendous endorsement of your reputation in Middle Eastern banking circles."

Kaz bowed slightly. "Thank you. But I need your help. GABI has very limited disbursement capacity in Afghanistan itself. I want to route the funds – a hundred million dollars – through your Kabul subsidiary."

"A short term deposit account?"

"Yes. Just until the selected projects can open accounts and start drawing down the money."

Abdul-Karim smiled. "Obviously, I'm delighted to help. You'll be our largest single depositor in that branch."

"Since the Kabul Bank failure, your personal reputation for integrity has made your bank the 'go-to' choice for transactions such as this one. And this will go a long way toward restoring confidence in Afghan financial markets."

"Thank you, both for the business and the compliments. It makes my requests seem almost ungrateful."

Kaz smiled. "Never. What can I do?"

"I'm bothered by some rules."

Kaz waited. When the silence continued, he said, "Yes. Rules can be a nuisance. But they usually serve a purpose."

"For Americans, perhaps. Your Foreign Corrupt Practices Act, your money laundering requirements, your sanctions against so many countries for so many reasons! It makes it very hard for an old-fashioned banker like me. I was wondering if there was any way that you could make it easier for us?"

Kaz almost smiled at the reference to "old-fashioned." Abdul-Karim knew and used every trick in the book and was often the innovator. However, it was easy not to smile. The "rules" that he was talking about were no laughing matter. He spent a good bit of his time ensuring that they were abided by.

This is not like him. He knows me better than that.

"I'm sympathetic, Abdul-Karim. I really am. But there is nothing that I can do to make these rules go away. Both of us have to live with those rules if we're going to be in the business."

Abdul-Karim smiled and went on, as though uninterested in Kaz's response. "Yes, I suppose so. So let me ask about two other matters.

"First, as you well know, GABI provides us with a backup credit line for our trade finance business. We have a very large transaction in process – construction equipment for the modernization of Dubai's harbor– where there is some substantial uncertainty about both the amount and the timing. We may well bump up against our limit and I'm wondering if you could arrange a temporary increase. Say a few million dollars for a few days?"

Before Kaz could reply, he went on. "And we've finally decided to close down our Syrian and Yemeni branches. There's just too much risk. We'll manage the relationships from here. I know that will affect several of the GABI products that we use and that country limits will have to be adjusted, among other things.

"I'm hoping that all of these adjustments can be managed without a lot of fuss? Even if they run into all those "rules" that seem so essential to people in Washington and London ..."

This time, Kaz did smile. "That's easy. Those rules are just internal guidelines. I have lots of discretion to interpret them in ways that make life easier for the customer. You do what's called for in Syria and Yemen and I'll make sure the bank goes along."

GABI is sensible that way. I have substantial lending authority to increase limits on the spot for just these kinds of situations. It has to be justified back home, but for UCBE, that shouldn't be a problem. We could easily have done this on the phone.

As if reading his mind, Abdul-Karim took a small package from his desk drawer and handed it to Kaz. "Actually, the reason I asked you to come is to give this to you."

"Abdul-Karim, I –"

"I know. Another "rule." But this is a personal gift, nothing to do with business. This comes from friendship, not commerce. And it has no value for an accountant. It is only a book of Persian poetry. Rare but of little value."

He handed the package across the desk to Kaz, but held on to it briefly, saying, "You have been a good friend to us. This is to indicate how much we value your friendship."

A bit over the top for Abdul-Karim ...

"Thank you. I shall use it to improve my Arabic."

Abdul-Karim stood and extended his hand. "Thank you for coming. And for your flexibility."

He watched Kaz leave, feeling sorry for him.

Slater - Day Two

How did I get here?

The silent question had so many dimensions to it that he immediately felt embarrassed for himself when it unexpectedly popped into his mind. That first reaction was based on an image of himself that stemmed directly from a hardheaded practicality; a "quit whining and deal with it" approach to problems that did not allow for either self-pity or a regret for what might have been. It was a soldier's philosophy, well-suited for life in a war zone.

But then he had never been in this situation before, one with a complete absence of choices. He felt like a drunk awaking from a blackout, not knowing where he was or how he got there, but also knowing full well that he alone was accountable for the fact that he was lying face down on the pavement in a puddle of vomit.

The first and most practical version was to try to reconstruct where he was in the physical world.

I know where I started. That damned bridge with the five bodies neatly aligned in the middle of the road. And I know we walked generally uphill and generally in an easterly direction for six hours. That puts us within a couple of days hiking to either Tajikistan or Pakistan. New country for me. But I know it's not good. Everybody within a hundred miles is Taliban, al Qaeda or some combination of the two. And they all hate outsiders – that's me – and the central government about equally.

He filed the information away, roughly classified as "interesting but of little use at the moment."

The much more difficult version of "how did I get here" stemmed from his awareness that he was here – wherever "here" was – because of a series of choices, each of which seemed right at the time and even independent of one another, but now appeared to him as a preordained chain that led him to this particular place.

Obviously, joining ROTC ... volunteering for another tour, staying on as part of the NATO training cadre even though

I knew the futility factor. But each of those was the result of prior conditioning ... learning Arabic, growing up on military posts ...

He winced at the pretentiousness of his thinking, recognizing it as a never-ending tracing of cause and effect, capable of being twisted to suit any ending that he liked.

Let's stay with the concrete. A step at a time, backwards in time. How did I get to that damned bridge?

It began three days ago.

Something's up with Abad.

Captain Ahmed Abad was Slater's "shadow." The term defined a complex relationship, one where the formal and informal rules were still evolving. Their formal relationship was as trainer/advisor (Slater) and trainee/advisee (Abad) and was intended to achieve a transfer of military tactics from the American to the Afghani. The informal part was the means of achieving the transfer of knowledge: Abad would "shadow" – i.e., follow Slater around – and learn by watching.

It was an awkward relationship. Abad was a proud man and very sensitive to any suggestion that he *needed* advice, particularly if any of his Afghani subordinates were watching. Much worse, Slater was unsure of Abad's commitment to the mission.

NATO troops pulled out a month ago, leaving the Afghan army and police force to take over the work of the highly professional and modern NATO forces, mostly American and British. They were badly trained, lacking critical equipment and arms – particularly communication gear, helicopters and drones – and hampered by corruption and poor leadership. But the most serious problem was the cultural mismatch between the troops and the civilian population. Afghanistan was a patchwork of fiercely independent tribes, many of them hostile to the others. Often, the hostility arose from religious differences. Cooperation, let alone loyalty, was hard to come by.

Abad was the commander of the Afghan National Army forces – about five hundred soldiers – responsible for the security of the countryside surrounding the village where they were stationed. They were mostly Uzbeks, operating in a region populated mostly by Tajiks and Pashtuns. One of the consequences was that Abad's forces stayed close to home, leaving the countryside to what they called "the insurgents."

Slater pressed Abad to establish a presence, advising a series of "recon in force" daylight outings to gradually extend the reach of the central government and to begin to build some level of trust within the close-in civilian population.

They go out in the morning and come back at dusk. But what do they do out there?

He asked Abad for daily debriefings, but they were useless; a tracing of dotted lines on topographical maps with bland stories of meetings with elders and time spent talking with villagers. There had been one firefight, with five ANFS soldiers killed by an ambush in a village about twenty kilometers out. He tasked a drone to circle the village for the next three days, but all it detected was normal village life.

Then he saw the video.

He was observing his usual routine, walking the length of the three major streets that defined the heart of Achin Adi. As usual, he stopped to visit with Ali. It was a chance to sit in the sunshine and amuse Ali with his attempts to speak the local Pashto dialect. Ali himself seemed as ancient as the stone wall that he sat alongside every morning, selling tiny cups of tea or a thick sludge that he called "coffee." His customers were mostly the soldiers. Occasionally, one of the many old men in the village would stop and join Ali at the three-legged table where he sat throughout the day.

This morning, Ali was curt, strangely serious when he sat down across from him. He looked at Slater in a way that made him feel guilty, like a ten-year-old boy being called into the principal's office for some unknown transgression.

He said, "Good morning, Ali. You seem quite serious."

Ali said nothing. Instead, he reached inside his tunic and pulled out a small dark object. He kept it covered with his hand and slid it across the table toward Slater, still with that accusing look.

Slater sat down, not knowing what was expected of him.

"This belonged to my nephew's son. His name was Gholam." Ali spoke in Pashto, very slowly for Slater's sake. That and his use of the past tense signaled that this conversation was to be a serious one.

He said nothing, but looked at Ali's gnarled hand covering the object on the tabletop, then raised his left hand in the classic "please continue" gesture.

Ali lifted his hand to reveal a totally unexpected object. An Apple iPhone, the screen partly covered with dried mud. It was as out-of-place in this rural province as a bright-red Lamborghini or a surfboard. Slater's first reaction was to smile, but that quickly faded under Ali's unchanging glare.

"I told him it was vanity, but Gholam was from Kabul and wanted Western toys. He told me that it plays music and tells the weather and does many useful things."

Slater started to speak, but Ali's voice changed. He spoke even more softly, but the tones were those of sadness and anger combined.

"He showed it to me two days ago. He stopped to see me on his way to see his aunt, his mother's sister. She lives in Pasha Khail."

This is not good. Pasha Khail is where Abad's five men were killed last week. I don't think I want to hear this story.

But Ali was still talking. "A man brought it to me yesterday. He said to turn on the pictures."

With that, Ali stood up and walked away, leaving the iPhone on the table. Its blank ebony face seemed to be examining Slater with the same accusative stare as Ali's.

He picked up the phone and pushed the "on" button. The Apple logo blinked once at him and the screen went dark immediately. *No battery left.* He took it to his room and dug out his charger. He waited five minutes and, while waiting, he took a wet cloth to wipe the dried mud away; but as soon he started, the cloth turned red. It wasn't mud that encased the phone. He remembered Ali's use of the past tense in referring to his nephew.

After wiping the screen, he pushed the "on" button once more. The first thing that appeared was the "no reception" emblem. *No surprise there. We're a hundred miles from an antenna.*

Then he touched the "photos" icon, knowing that this was why Ali had given him the phone. He also knew that he did not want to know what was on the phone.

There were hundreds of pictures in the iPhoto albums, but he immediately scrolled to the bottom row of thumbnail squares.

The last one was a video. The caption indicated it ran forty-six minutes. *There's the reason for the dead battery.* There were four jpegs just before the video, all dated as of two days ago. Each of them was a young man posing with two young girls, taken from "selfie" range. All of them were wearing everyday tribal dress and smiling in ways that signaled "family reunion."

The first thirty seconds of the video were apparently shot from a window of a house. It panned across two sides of a typical village square; about half an acre of bare dirt with a well and a pair of goats in the center. It then focused on a pair of jeeps with ANSF soldiers that entered the square. From then on, the video was chaotic, never focused on any single thing for long. The camera was always on but was jerking around erratically and often pointed at the ground or the sky. But the iPhone microphone picked up the sound throughout the filming and Slater could reconstruct the story.

Gholam and the family were forced out of the house and pushed into the center of the square, along with other occupants of the other houses. He wound up near the perimeter of the tight little group and kept the camera pointed outward from what seemed to be about waist level. Much of the video was obscured as the constantly shuffling bodies blocked the camera, but there were numerous clear shots of the soldiers from about thirty feet. They were smoking and laughing, holding their weapons casually.

At first, the villagers' voices were angry or sarcastic, either mocking the soldiers or urging them to finish searching so that they could go back to work. That changed when they separated the girls and put them to the side. Gholam's video had a clear ten-second view of one of the girls being pulled apart from the group. She was one of the smiling cousins from the selfies.

Slater knew what was coming, but he could not stop himself from watching. *Did Gholam know what he was filming? Did this young boy from Kabul with an expensive toy know that he was documenting his own death?*

It started with a sharp command that brought the guns to bear, followed by a shrill scream of pure rage from a woman who must have been very close to the iPhone. The firing of what sounded like several M-16's on full automatic lasted for about twenty seconds, tapering off to short bursts and – finally – to isolated single shots.

When the shooting started, the video jerked around violently. Then it was still, and for about ten seconds, it was focused on a bright light filtered through some kind of fabric very close to the lens. Slater guessed that it was inside the boy's tunic and facing the sun. Then the picture began to darken, as though successive layers of a bright red cloth were being laid across the lens. *Gholam's blood.*

The last thirty-five minutes of the video were the same – an unchanging darkness marked only by the advancing time indicator and, finally, the "low battery" warning. But the microphone continued to pick up sounds … the screams of the girls, the laughing men, and the ugly bestial sounds of rape. The last sounds were five single, spaced shots and the engine noise as the soldiers left.

Then there was only silence.

Slater - Day Four

It was a small perfectly square structure, one of three identical sand-colored cubes in a row. It measured six paces each way, with adobe-like walls that were seven feet high. The only entry or exit was a single door, three vertical planks reinforced by a diagonal strip of metal. It opened outward. The roof was made up of overlapping sheets of green corrugated plastic lying on top of two rough wooden beams that stretched from wall to wall. The simple construction left a six-inch gap running around the entire perimeter along the top of the wall. The floor was packed dirt.

The translucent roof and the horizontal gap at the roofline enabled light to penetrate the room, but only enough to maintain a constant greenish dusk during daylight hours.

A very simple building. Some kind of storage shed. Probably for grains. If the ANSF raided this place, the first thing they would do is to dig up the floor looking for – and probably finding – weapons and ammunition.

There were five items of furniture in the room. A small table with rickety legs, a three-legged stool, a mattress – burlap sacking stuffed with straw, a single blanket, and a metal bucket. There were three more items on the table, a Koran, a crude candle – wax in a tin cup, and a book of matches.

Three men came twice a day, morning and afternoon. The routine did not vary. One of them, armed with an AK47, stood outside. Another unarmed man stood at the door while the third carried in a tin plate with meat, rice and bread and a half-liter of water and placed them on the table. They left and came back in exactly twenty-five minutes. In the mornings, they took the bucket away and brought it back in the afternoon.

They spoke among themselves, but not to him. But by the morning of day three he had begun to carry on imaginary dialogues with them for his own amusement. From listening, he knew their names -- Abdul, Badi and Cyrus. Easy to remember because of the "ABC" sequence and because they increased in height by about six inches as you went from 'A' to 'C.' He imputed entire personality profiles to them based on the smallest of clues. Abdul had the gun and was the smallest of the three, so he deemed him to be insecure and in need of flattery. Badi was badly scarred in a way that left a perpetual scowl, so he was mean and sensitive to criticism. Cyrus, because he was the one who actually carried the food and waste in and out, was classified as unintelligent and from a poor rural family. Each time they came and went, he would add to their stories and personal histories. They became, in his mind, complex men with problems at home and mixed feelings about their own little war.

The only variation was in the morning of the second day, after his first long night in the small square building. The three men came in together at about noon. He was told to sit on his stool against the wall and to hold a newspaper across his chest while Badi took several pictures with a pocket camera.

So they're going to tell somebody that I'm alive and they have me. I wonder who?

Later that same day, he was sitting at the table reading the Koran. A man came in by himself. He was carrying a stool like the one that Slater was sitting on and he placed it directly opposite him and sat down. He was older, but his exact age was difficult to assess. If forced to guess, he would say "between fifty and seventy."

Slater's first impression was *this is how Hollywood would cast a tribal leader for a remake of Lawrence of Arabia.*

He was about six feet tall, probably 180 pounds. Like most Afghans from outside the cities, he was lean; sinewy rather than muscular. Whether sitting or standing, he had a stillness about him, as if poised for some imminent and unexpected movement. His once-dark hair was long, with grey, almost white streaks woven in, seeming to frame intense and very dark eyes, the sort where "piercing" is the descriptive word of choice. The greyness dominated his beard, which was short. His skin was dark for an Afghani, partly because of his tribal genes, but also weathered by a life largely lived outdoors in sun and wind. His facial features were regular, although Slater was somehow sure that a western woman would call him "intriguing." He exuded a quiet authority and had an aura about him that was hard to define. He seemed troubled.

They looked at one another for at least a minute, the Koran lying open between them. Finally, the man took his hand from within his robe and placed Slater's ID card on the table alongside the Koran.

"My name is Malik. We can speak in English if you prefer."

A very slight accent, probably English. Definitely different than the bunch that brought me here. A significant leader, I think. A respected elder. Not an imam; he does not have the look of a fanatic. His eyes are curious, not hostile.

He answered in Pashto. "I have been told I am not to speak. Rule One."

The man smiled and seemed genuinely pleased by this mild form of resistance disguised as compliance. "This rule is for the others. We shall set it aside for the moment. For now, you are my guest."

"Then we shall speak English. You are far better at that than I am with my Pashto."

The man let his eyes rest on the Koran. "But you are practicing. Surely your language courses at the University of California gave you a good start."

It startled him. *Damn Google and Facebook! So he's done his homework. And very fast. I thought I would have more time to prepare.*

"My name is Slater Crosby. I am a Captain in the U.S. Army. My service number is —"

The man raised his hand. "Yes, yes. I know all that. Your service number is RA17522573, date of birth December 26, 1982, son of Yasmin and Harlan Crosby, resident of Northern Virginia, on your fourth tour in Iraq. You read literary mysteries, study languages and drink your coffee black. And I know that — in your world of Geneva Protocols and *humane war* — that you believe you are not *required* to tell me more."

For an instant, the man's contempt and anger was so evident that Slater knew that the civility was a very thin veneer and that the softer qualities of respect or even mercy would be many layers deeper, perhaps unreachable by either of them.

He struggled for a response, but the man shrugged and went on. "We have a dossier on each of the NATO officers in our province, from Captain on up. It is quite easy to compile, especially for the younger Americans who use the social media. Or for the only sons of congressmen."

He emphasized the last phrase in a way that made his contempt quite clear.

"And we update the dossier with periodic data from our field commanders and … shall we say, *sympathizers*, from within your camps. Information that is far more useful than college transcripts."

"I am flattered by your efforts. So who are you?"

The man frowned slightly at the abruptness.

He would cut off my head but is offended if we get serious before tea is served!

But then the man said something totally unexpected. "I do not care about troop movements or tactics. We have already won the war and are just waiting for it to end. What I want to know is why you killed your own soldiers."

Harlan & Madge

Harlan Crosby kept his smile in place until the junior senator from Oklahoma had closed the door behind him. Only then did he look at the woman sitting across from him and grimace.

"The man has never stood up for anything!"

The woman smiled in a knowing way. "Maybe he needs an extra-large dose of Viagra? Might stiffen his spine rather than … "

The imagery amused him, until it reminded him of his own dependence on the little blue pills … and this woman.

Marjorie Prentis – "Madge" when they were alone together – was a retired U.S. Army Lieutenant Colonel. She was forty-five years old and had been associated with Harlan for twenty of those years, beginning in the military, then the CIA and now the Senate. The titles varied but she was always in the role of "chief of staff," his primary gatekeeper and advisor.

Her other role had no official title, but she had been his mistress for much of that time as well, although "mistress" was not a term that seemed to apply to Madge. She was a formidable woman, both physically and intellectually. Coal black, mannish and tall, with broad shoulders, more regal than she was pretty. She had a Master's Degree in Electrical Engineering and had parlayed that into an in-depth knowledge of the uses of technology for intelligence gathering. She demanded and earned respect from her superiors, peers and subordinates. The single word often used to describe her was "intimidating." Inevitably, she was known (not to her face) as "the iron lady." Part of the reason that their long-running affair stayed under the radar was that – for the outsiders -- it was difficult to think of Marjorie Prentis as a sexual being.

Each of them would have been puzzled if asked whether they loved each other. It was a relationship without extraordinary language or passion, a second level of existence that they had kept hidden for so long that they became incapable of expressing it. It was mostly about companionship, although their sexual play was infrequent but intense, varying along every dimension that they could control.

Given their long tenure together and the proximity that went with it, scandal – either real or imputed – would seem inevitable. But they were untainted.

Some of it was pure image. Each of them was a career military officer, with the kind of quiet patriotism that is apparent to everyone around them. They had no outside interests outside of serving their country. They radiated integrity and self-discipline, the very quality that enabled them to keep their carnal appetites caged until they could be safely exercised. She was the widow of an army officer, one of the very few soldiers killed during the first Gulf War. And Harlan appeared to the outside world to have the perfect marriage. Yasmin was a model officer's wife.

Her reference to Viagra also induced in Harlan a very slight ripple of pleasure. One of the oddities imbedded in their relationship was that she had always dictated the timing of their sexual encounters, as if that was part of her "gatekeeping" duties. During the last year, she had adopted the practice of placing one of the blue pills on the "Senator's Daily Schedule" that she prepared for him as Chief of Staff, located precisely on the day and hour that she had chosen. The mere sight of the pill never failed to arouse him.

The pills, however, appeared infrequently and most days were like this one – meetings and phone calls with self-important people that wanted something from him. More and more, he missed the clarity of his military life, where organizational boundaries were sharply drawn and influence could be exercised directly with predictable cause-and-effect. In the CIA and now the Senate, he was continually exasperated at the murkiness of power: who had it, who didn't, how it was used, and – most of all – how to acquire more of it.

"We've got about forty minutes before your cyber-security sub-committee. We should review –"

He interrupted her, knowing that his question was superfluous. "Madge. Anything come in about Slater? Anything at all?"

It had been six days since he'd received the "missing" report. So far, the story was contained. Only the President, about three people at CIA, and a Major Dalkie in Afghanistan knew of Slater's disappearance. And whoever had him, of course. So far, they had been silent.

He had not told Yasmin. Their regular weekly call to Slater was tomorrow, so he knew that he was running out of time. Every evening for six days now when he walked in the door, he had the same monologue run through his head.

You're a coward. Tell her. She's his mother. We need to get through this together. She's got the right to know. You're a coward!

He knew that Madge was working both the CIA and the Pentagon angles and that she would tell him of any change. His question displayed an uncharacteristic emotion; one that he was unfamiliar with and thought of as a weakness.

She recognized the symptoms, and said, "Nothing. They're looking, very hard. But there's been no sign. The only thing …"

The hesitation was unlike her. He waited, knowing that she would overcome whatever made her pause.

"His Afghan liaison – A Captain Abad – is turning out to be a question mark. He's an Uzbek and Dalkie has speculated that he might have engineered one or more atrocities on the locals. They're mostly Pashtun."

"Are the Special Ops people –"

"I've got two separate teams – Seals and Rangers – on standby. And we've got CIA assets on alert as well. And we've got Ollie's off-the-books people if we need them. Any or all of them can be in the air within ten minutes of a sighting … once you say 'Go' …"

No need to finish that sentence. He knows as well as I do what the odds are of a successful hostage rescue.

"What does CIA think, given that six days have gone by?"

"The same. That he's been captured, probably by Taliban, and that they know who they've got. They think the delay is them trying to figure how to use him for maximum advantage."

Nice language – "maximum advantage" – like staging a public beheading for millions of people to watch.

"Do they expect a ransom demand?"

"Fifty-fifty. But if there is one, it will be for a very large number and probably offered very quietly through some back channel. Whoever it is will know that they won't get any payoff if this gets to CNN."

"So. We wait."

"For the moment."

Prentis's cell phone rang. Both of them recognized the special ring tone that she had assigned to a very special CIA source. Later, Harlan would marvel at the timing of the call. It was as if some master playwright was waiting for their conversation about Slater to get to that precise point in the script.

She answered "Yes," listened for about fifteen seconds, and then took her laptop from her briefcase and set it on the corner of his desk. She hunched her shoulder to keep the phone in place and began typing commands. She ended the call, with a curt "Got it. Run it through the techies and let me know what they see."

Harlan watched her closely. He knew her body language well enough to know that he did not want to know what the call was about.

She hesitated only a second or two.

"They found our missing Captain Abad."

"Where?"

"On YouTube. Where else?" The bitterness in her voice was profound.

She pivoted the laptop and he found himself looking at an arid landscape with an Afghan man kneeling in front of his black-clad and hooded executioner.

Meeting at Achin Adi

The man Kaz knew as Ollie felt and looked much more at home in his clothing than when he had called on Kaz in his London office. He could have been either a sloppily dressed soldier or a very outdoorsy sort of civilian. The hiking boots were thoroughly scuffed, with the bottoms of his cargo pants stuffed into them. He had on an olive-drab T-shirt and an unbuttoned and very faded fatigue jacket with darker swatches where insignia had once existed.

He was tired. He had flown for sixteen hours to get here, the last two of those hours in a helicopter. The copter sat one-hundred yards from where he sat talking to a very nervous-looking Major Dalkie.

Dalkie definitely did not want to be there. Part of it was simple arrogance. He was a major in the British Royal Marines, 3 Commando Brigade, with the last seven years in Afghanistan. Not only did he find himself away from his unit, but he was reporting to an American who headed the multinational NATO training mission. Worse, he had been told by that American to show up for a civilian, almost certainly a spook, and to "answer his questions about this incident, even if you don't want to."

The other and much larger part of his reluctance stemmed from his certainty that this "incident" would not, could not, have a happy ending. And that he and his career had an excellent chance of becoming road kill on the way to that ending. The fact that none of it was his fault was irrelevant to everyone except him.

There were no introductions or handshakes. The man said, "Call me Oliver. I've read your Field Report, but I still have some questions."

Some of the questions were easy to answer.

"Your opinion of Crosby...?"

"He was a first-rate officer. One of the best of that rank that I've come across in twenty-two years of service. In any army that I've been a part of."

"Did the men like him?"

"Was he popular? Yes. To a point that I disapprove of. Officers should maintain some distance, particularly when you're on a training mission, as we are. His men – both the Americans and the Afghani's that he liaised with – liked him and trusted him. They would try hard to do what he asked them to do."

"Did he ... drop names?"

"Do you mean did he use his father's name to get ahead or to get out of something? He did not. Categorically, emphatically *not*. If anything, he went out of his way to dissociate himself from his father's position. Personally, I think he put himself in front of his troops too many times, just to make the point that he was no more privileged than they were."

Other questions were harder, because they were simply too complex for simple answers.

"Did he approve of your mission?"

"He was a good officer. He followed orders. But – like many others who have been in-country for a while – he didn't believe that we were doing much good." *Like most of us who have been here for more than ten days.*

He hated the war. What it was doing to the people and the culture. The way that it had brought back all of the all tribal feuds and turned the country into a perpetual killing zone.

"Did this attitude come before or after the withdrawal of NATO forces?"

"Both. I didn't know him then, but from the stories he's told me I think that he was quite gung-ho on his first tour, when the Americans were chasing Bin Laden, all fired up about 911. Then when all the attention turned to Iraq and the Taliban quietly began taking back the countryside and Karzai didn't turn out to be George Washington, I think he lost faith. By the time I met him two years ago, his main commitment was to his men, trying to keep as many of them alive as he could. When we became a pure training mission with just a few of us working with the ANFS, he was pretty cynical about what we were tasked with."

Pretty cynical! Now there's a bloody understatement! We'd tried our first company-level operation. An all-Afghan sweep of a village thirty clicks out ... a known hangout for the "insurgents." Three of us as "observers." We took fire – small arms fire, maybe four or five shooters – on the outskirts. The Afghani's sat down and said, "Call in the airstrikes." We said,

"Those were the old days. This is your operation now." The commander sat there drinking tea until dark and then we went home. Crosby and I came back and got drunk together.

"What was his attitude toward the local tribes?"

The simple answer? He wanted to be the next Lawrence of Arabia. But this asshole named 'Oliver' wouldn't understand that!

"He knew a lot about the culture and he respected it. He knew Arabic when he got here, good enough that he spoke their language when he worked with AFNS troops and their officers. He was even learning some of the local dialects and variations in his off-time, mostly Pashto and Dari. Some Uzbek because of the troops he was working with. He spent a lot of his time in the village, just talking with the shopkeepers and everyday people."

Then there were the questions that he couldn't answer.

"What do you think happened to him?"

"I don't know."

"Do you know of other cases like this? Where a British or American officer goes missing?"

"No I don't. If they go outside the base and don't come back, we find them close by and dead." *Although, sometimes they're hard to identify.*

"Anything unusual about that patrol, that night he turned up missing?"

"A couple of things, but I have to speculate."

"Speculate."

"He took the misfits."

Oliver looked at him, waiting patiently.

"I found this out the next day. He picked – by name – the five men that he wanted to take out that night. They were among the five worst soldiers in the whole Afghani contingent. Two of them were criminals who'd enlisted to stay out of jail and all of them were rated by their NCO's as 'likely to desert.'"

"Why would he do that?"

"According to his Captain Abad – his Afghani counterpart -- Crosby told him, 'If we can train this lot, we can train anybody.' Apparently he viewed them as a demonstration project."

"You said there were 'a couple of things' unusual about that patrol. What else?"

"Nothing happened out there."

Oliver showed his first emotion, a strong annoyance. "Other than five dead Afghanis and two missing officers, one of whom is a very high-profile American individual."

"That, yes. But not what should have happened."

Oliver started to speak, but he stopped him. "We get patrols ambushed all the time. Everybody's trigger happy, on both sides. This time, there was no firefight, no IED's, no apparent resistance. The five dead guys were standing in a bunch when they were shot. At close range, from head on. You've seen the terrain. It's open country all around until you cross that bridge. These guys were in radio contact and had night vision equipment. Crosby's too good an officer to walk into an obvious trap and he sure as hell would have fought back. What the hell happened out there?"

Ollie stood up to leave. "If you figure that out, let me know. And remember, this conversation never happened."

He thought about the other question that he had, but decided not to ask it.

"Why do you keep using the past tense when you're talking about our missing Captain Crosby?"

Slater - Day Seven

The man came back for three straight days, always carrying his stool and always with questions about Slater. He told him nothing about himself other than his name. "Malik," an honorific for "chief." He did not ask about troop deployments, infantry tactics, fellow officers, ANSF morale factors or any of the other 'conventional' topics for interrogation. He was curious about Slater's boyhood, family, college courses and girl friends. Only once, when the talk ventured into politics, did Slater have misgivings about his duty to be silent.

The man said, "Your father was on the TV show you call 'Nightline' yesterday. He spoke quite strongly about NATO's withdrawal of troops from Afghanistan. He called it 'a major mistake.' "

His favorite phrase when I was growing up was "Stay the course." Still works for him, I guess.

He said nothing, just sat there with his hands folded on the table between them.

"He was on for five minutes of the hour. The rest of the time – fifty-five minutes – was devoted to analyzing the salary structures of football coaches in your major universities."

So you object to our fixation on pop culture? You think of us as shallow and self-absorbed? And we are, of course. Ninety eight percent of them cannot spell 'Afghanistan' or locate it on a map. It's not their fault. Unlike you, we can choose sides – or not -- without risking our lives.

He wanted to ask, "Did he say anything about me?" Not for ego reasons, but because he needed to know if word was out yet. *How long can they suppress the fact that I'm missing?*

I wonder how they're dealing with it… me being missing? Not Dad. He'll compartmentalize the hell out of it. But Mom? It was probably the thought of her that caused him to blurt out the question.

"What are you going to do with me?" He was surprised that he spoke the question aloud, and he silently cursed himself for his weakness.

The man was equally startled. He sat back with his arms crossed and seemed to be thinking about how to answer. Finally, he said simply, "I don't know."

The guard he had named "Abdul" opened the door and said, "They're here."

The man stood and picked up his stool. "Would you like to go outside for a short time? I have something I want to show you." After a brief hesitation, he added, "It might have something to do with the question you just asked."

The full daylight was at first overwhelming. He had been living in perpetual twilight or by the light of a single candle for a full week and it was a full minute before he could fully open his eyes.

The scene was one that, by now, was familiar to hundreds of millions of YouTube viewers. His first reaction was nausea, and he barely kept from vomiting. Then came the horror of knowing what was coming, so strong that he turned away to go back into his now-familiar semi-darkness. But his two minders – Badi and Cyrus – had moved in closely behind him and each of them clasped an arm and turned him back to face the tableau in front of them. Malik had set his stool down and Badi and Cyrus guided Slater to a stool alongside him.

The sense of horror became much worse. *They've staged this for my benefit!*

He and Malik were seated immediately behind a fixed video camera mounted on a tripod. The camera was aimed at a pair of men. One, in the uniform of an officer of the Afghan National Army, was kneeling with his hands bound behind him, facing the camera with his head bowed. The other was standing to his left side and slightly behind him. He was masked with a black hood, clad in an all black tribal costume, and was holding a broad, long and curved knife. They were framed between two ranks of what Slater took to be village elders, four or five men in each row. They were arrayed as spectators, far enough to the side to be out of the camera's field of view.

There was an absolute silence that filled the space within the rock walls, reinforced by the physical stillness of the dozen men so carefully placed. All eyes were on the kneeling man who slowly raised his head and looked directly at Slater.

It was Captain Abad, his Afghan liaison from the outpost.

"No. Not that. Please!" Slater did not realize he had spoken aloud, until all the eyes turned toward him. As they did, he felt the sheer volume of hate that they transmitted. It was almost tangible in its intensity.

Malik nodded at the black-clad executioner. The man pointed at Abad and spoke. Slater could not tell if he was addressing him or the watching elders, but he easily translated the short sentences.

"You know this man and what he has done. He is a representative of the government and a tool for the foreigners. He is a coward who has slaughtered our families and raped our daughters.

"He deserves to die."

The executioner took two steps forward, wrapped his left hand in the thick hair of the kneeling man, pulled his head back and made quick chopping strokes with the heavy knife. The headless corpse toppled forward and his killer held the head out at shoulder level and slowly turned in a complete circle to display his gory work to the camera and the two rows of watchers.

Cyrus left his side and went to the camera. He turned it off, dismounted it, and carried it and the tripod into a building on the far side of the compound. Badi walked to the corpse, spat on it, and then he and the executioner – still carrying the head -- followed Cyrus. The two ranks of tribesmen went off in groups of two and three to reform near a stand of small trees where a very large and colorful rug was spread on the ground and a long table held a large samovar.

The three of them --Malik, Slater, and the headless corpse of Abad -- were left alone in the middle of the compound. Slater slowly became aware of the usual afternoon sounds – insects, a very slight breeze through the overhead rocks, the faint voices of the tribesmen. Malik was watching him closely, in a way that made Slater think of his question just before they brought him outdoors --"What are you going to do with me?" And of his response: "I don't know."

Neither of them spoke. Malik stared at him expectantly, as though waiting for him to respond to a question so obvious that it did not have to be asked out loud. Finally, Slater turned and walked back into his cell and its now-comforting semi-darkness, pulling the door closed behind him.

War by Media

Harlan did not get home until nine that night. Such hours were common for the last several years and Yasmin had adapted her schedule to match. They usually had a late and simple dinner before watching the late evening newscasts. Those dinners had become very quiet affairs lately. Conversation was limited to a review of the day's events and gossip about old acquaintances. It pained Yasmin that their marriage seemed to have settled into a routine that was satisfying to neither or them, but she did not know how to change that. Other than by leaving. Even worse, she did not know if she wanted it to change.

That night was different. The house was dark and the table was not set. Harlan found Yasmin sitting at her desk in the extra bedroom that she had converted into her personal office. She was staring at her desktop computer screen, which was displaying her screen saver – a photo of the Blue Mosque in Istanbul that she had taken at sunset.

Something about her posture told him that she knew even before she spoke. And when she did talk, there was an edge to her voice that he had not heard before, something that hinted at barely contained feelings.

She pointed at the screen. "This – and something else – came two hours ago. To my personal email account. You knew about this, of course. Why wouldn't you tell me?"

She reached out and touched a single button on the keyboard. The screen was suddenly filled with a color photo of Slater. He was sitting on a simple stool before a blank sandy-colored background, holding an Arabic newspaper with the front page facing the camera. He was expressionless, as if posing for a driver's license or passport photo.

"They also sent this."

Another click of a button and the photo faded, replaced by the opening scene of the video of the beheading of Captain Abad. She did not push the "play" icon to start the video.

"Yasmin, I –"

"You knew! But you didn't tell me! About our son! How he's sitting in some dark rathole in that misbegotten country, waiting to have his head cut off! You didn't tell me!

His mother!" She began slowly, each word bitten off. By the time she was finished, she was standing, screaming at him, her fists clenched.

He stood without moving, his head down, knowing that he deserved this.

"I'm sorry. I should have –"

"You should have told me is what you should have done!" The hysteria was gone as quickly as it came, replaced by an ominous calm.

"How long have you known?"

"He's been missing for six days. We know almost nothing about the circumstances. That photo you received? You're the only one. It's the first contact from whoever's got him. I need --"

"Get him back!"

"We are –"

"And don't give me your press conference bullshit about 'negotiating with terrorists' or 'all options are on the table' or 'those responsible will be hunted down.' He's my son and I want him back!"

She turned and walked out of the room.

It took less than six hours for the Langley analysts to get back to him. It helped to be the ex-CIA Director and a U.S. Senator.

The caller was Arthur Denison, his replacement at the CIA. He was a long time professional within the Agency and at one time had run the counter-terrorism division. He was the country's leading expert on terrorist media releases.

"Good news, relatively speaking. They've been unusually sloppy."

"Tell me," said Harlan.

"First of all, the photo. It's authentic. Nothing tricked up. And they left some clues."

"Arthur. Just tell me. Does it tell us where he is?"

"Almost. It's all about the light."

"Arthur! Goddammit—"

"OK, OK! It's obviously taken indoors in dim light. But there are two other telltales. The light is general, not coming from a single source, and it has a greenish hue. The whiz kids say that it's because it's being filtered through green plexiglass roofing material, the sort of cheap corrugated stuff that is used on farm buildings around that part of the world."

"They can tell that?"

"Believe it or not, they actually replicated the conditions. And there's a lot of technical stuff about diffusion, solar angles and shadowing, but they think the picture was taken in a very narrow slot canyon.

"And one more detail. Again, about the light. The photo is very slightly backlit. There's a natural *unfiltered* light source behind and above Slater. Not a window, but some kind of lateral opening between the wall and the corrugated roof."

He paused. "So we think he's being held in a storage shed, the kind that is used for storing agricultural produce, mostly grains or fruit. It's the kind of structure that is very common in the region where he was posted."

"So you think he's being held close to where he was captured?"

"Yes, and it's the kind of structure that we can easily identify from the air with satellites and drones. They're already mapping the possibilities."

"I want updates on the search every couple of hours."

"Absolutely, and there's more."

"What?"

"The video of the beheading. What we all saw on YouTube is useless to us for technical analysis. But what the sons-of- bitches sent to Yasmin is something that we can subject to all the fancy stuff. And we got something. It's pretty iffy, but —"

"Just tell me."

"The camera and the mike are directional, facing forward, picking up what's in front of them. But our people can intensify the sound – don't ask me how – so it's like making the mike more sensitive to the ambient noises in the general vicinity.

"We think we're picking up the sounds of several people off to both sides, probably Afghan spectators. We know they like to use these executions for the benefit of people *behind* the camera – not operators, but spectators. And one of them says something. A whisper. 'No. Not that. Please.'

"It's very faint. But we think it's Slater."

"Your whiz kids did a great job," Harlan said.

"Yes, they did. But one thing bothers me."

"And that is?"

"What I said before. They've been unusually sloppy. I wonder if it's deliberate?"

"You think they wanted us to discover all these tidbits? Some kind of signaling?"

"It could be. They've never had a hostage like Slater before. Maybe they're open to negotiation. Although I can't see any advantage for them ... giving us information like this."

There was a long silence from the other end of the line, long enough that Harlan prompted him.

"Arthur, I can hear you thinking. Share with me."

"Our counter-insurgency team has been batting around another idea. They think that the ones that grabbed Slater may not be our usual batch of terrorists, and that might explain the sloppiness. They're staging it so that we'll think they're the brutal bunch that likes to publicly decapitate people. But it may be just the local tribal sorts, not the crazies."

"What do we know about the 'local tribal sorts,' as you call them?"

"A very effective and self-contained fighting force, headed by a tribal bigwig figure known only as 'Malik.' A lot closer to the Taliban than to our side. The Russians hated them. For cause: they did more damage than any other mujahedeen group. And they refused to join our coalition in 2001. And you know how much money we offered. Our assessment is that they just want to be left alone – Afghanistan for Afghanis, under Sharia law and with them in charge, of course."

"Keep searching. And keep me informed. And I think we should move the Seals closer."

"I've already got them at Achin Adi. That's as close as we can get at the moment. But, Harlan ..."

I know what he's going to tell me. And I don't want to hear this.

"Yes?"

"If we're looking at this guy Malik's bunch of jihadists? I'm not sure an armed raid will succeed. I'd keep that as a distant – very distant -- last resort."

Slater - Day Twelve

The three days after the beheading went by in an unvarying routine. The Abdul, Badi and Cyrus trio performed the daily food and bucket routine as though operating with a stopwatch. He could predict to the minute when they would appear. And they were as silent and faintly hostile as on the first day of his captivity. He laughed at himself when he realized he was actively resenting their stubborn hostility.

How American of me! Expecting some sort of social relationship based on eleven twice-a-day encounters with people that hate me.

But the amusement quickly soured when he went on to realize that he was getting bored by the sameness of his existence, even with the constant threat of violent death looming over every instant of it.

Islamists of all sorts have been kidnapping foreigners for years now. Some of them held for hundreds of days in places like this ... years even. How did they survive? What did they do with all the time?

He remembered reading the newspaper accounts and his sense of the awfulness of solitary confinement for months and years.

Religion was important, even for those who had not been particularly observant in their earlier life. They prayed a lot. They played chess on imaginary boards, worked out complex anagrams in their head. They worked at remembering specific things in their past, down to the most minute detail. What the wallpaper looked like in their first house. Birthdays of distant cousins. Capitals of states and countries. One Marine colonel replayed his old golf games on famous courses, stroke by stroke.

Given the construction of his hut, he could hear noises from outside and he devoted himself to an intense listening program. Conversations were faint and his Pashto was not good enough to capture all of what he could hear. But there was a definite rhythm to life at the compound. About a dozen men would gather shortly before dawn and be given tasks, usually in other places. Interestingly, there seemed to be a "back door" into what he had thought was a box canyon. He could hear men approaching in the morning from *behind* his structure. Once the men dispersed, there was little activity during daylight hours other than that centered on him.

He thought about escape. The only practical way out of his building was through the only door. And there was an armed guard stationed outside that door on a twenty-four hour basis and a dozen or more others within shouting distance. Even if he managed to get out of the canyon, he was deep in tribal territory and did not know exactly where he was.

And escape to what? To a court martial? Prison sentence? I wonder how Dalkie is dealing with what I left behind. That damn promise to Ali. "I'll take care of this."

He read the Koran, always opening it at random. The language was a serious barrier, but if he worked at it, it could translate whole passages of the more common prose.

The Old Testament one more time – angry old men called prophets with strange hangups about diet and sex.

He exercised three times a day – pushups, situps, stretching. He pushed himself, always counting the reps and going a bit further each time.

He tried not to, but he could not stop his mind from revisiting the question he had asked Malik, "What are you going to do with me?"

He said, "I don't know." But his options are limited. He can ask for ransom. A big number, for sure. He can stage a public execution, perhaps a show trial of some sort. Maybe a prisoner swap. But what he can't do much longer is keep it to himself. There's bound to be a leak.

That thought triggered a vision of his mother. *I've missed two weekly calls and she will know something's wrong. Although Dear Old Dad may come up with some plausible story just for her.*

Malik appeared for his daily chat, always curious about Slater's personal history. After awhile, Slater began to ask Malik what he thought of as "parallel questions." So when Malik asked him why he chose to go to Berkeley, Slater asked him, "Did you go to college?" That led to a long and – Slater thought –

surprisingly nostalgic monologue about London and long-dead parents. He began to look forward to Malik's visits and – although he would not acknowledge it – his subconscious was becoming hopeful that their emerging relationship would work in his favor.

Could he decapitate someone that had shared stories with him about homesickness when they went away to college?

The firing woke him. It was three in the morning. The first shots came from somewhere above and behind him, apparently from a sentry partway up the canyon wall. That seemed to set off a significant firefight. He cracked the door to see outside, but the guard – it was Abdul -- slammed his rifle stock against the frame, barely missing his fingers, and hissed at him to get back inside and away from the door. He moved to a far corner and sat back against the wall.

A rescue attempt? What can I do to help? Stay alive, obviously. The walls will stop the rounds; the door is the vulnerable spot. Stay away from the door. Put on boots. Be ready to go.

He followed the swelling sounds of the fight as well as he could. *Maybe half-a-dozen attackers, spread out across the entry to the canyon, and at least as many defenders. Doesn't sound like a lot of movement. Not good. This needs to be a surprise and over very quick. Neither of those seems to be happening.*

Nearer to him, a man was shouting at Abdul. Something about staying in place, no matter what. Then another voice was approaching from the side of the canyon where the men gathered every morning. He was speaking Pashto, but Slater did not recognize the voice. Abdul shouted back, sounding confused. Then there was some kind of a scuffle and the door opened.

Abdul came through, taking very small steps and unnaturally rigid, as though walking a tightrope. He was holding his rifle by the muzzle with the stock trailing on the ground. The reason for his strange posture was that the man behind him, nudging him into the shed with not-so-gentle pushes, was holding a pistol to the back of his head. The two of them moved to the center of the room and turned to face Slater.

Abdul looked both confused and angry and Slater would later remember being impressed by his lack of fear. Then Abdul's face seemed to explode outward in a red mist. The sound of the shot was exceptionally loud in the confined space. Abdul fell forward and Slater – still sitting in his corner -- instinctively reached out to catch the falling rifle.

The man looked Afghani and was wearing the traditional costume favored by the fighters that had captured him. Slater was startled when he spoke in English.

"I'm a friend. 75th Rangers, out of Kandahar. Came to take you back. We need to go. Right now. Out the back way."

Maybe he is. Maybe not.

The urgency in the man's voice was heightened by the way he was holding the handgun, vaguely pointed in Slater's direction.

As he spoke, the firing from the front of the canyon intensified and Slater realized that a highly organized diversionary attack was in process, that this man standing before him was the only rescue party that he would see unless they moved.

Slater got up quickly, partly because a large blood pool was forming about Abdul's shattered head and about to include his left foot. As he stood, he brought the rifle up with him and moved toward the door.

The man stepped in front of him and took two very quick looks outside, left and then right.

"You ready? No injuries? Able to move quickly and all that? We're going around to the left and then straight back into the canyon. There's a goat path that starts about fifty feet from the back of this hut."

"I'm 100%. You lead. I'll be on your tail."

"Let me have the M16. It'll slow you down."

Oops!

"I'll keep it. Go!"

The man stood still, clearly thinking about options. Then he shrugged, rechecked the outside scene and darted through the door, moving to his left. Slater followed.

The next few seconds were a blur. Once around the corner, they faced an open space about twenty yards across. Except it wasn't quite open. Malik was in the center of it. And he was aiming an M4 rifle – probably the one he had confiscated from Slater at the ambush site – directly at them. Slater's rescuer was about ten feet in front of him and stopped abruptly, holding his hands out in a mute "don't shoot" plea, but still holding the handgun. There was an instant when all three of them were frozen in place, a pause long enough for Slater to think *OK, That didn't work!*

Then the man whirled, ignoring Malik to bring his pistol to bear on Slater, already firing as he spun. Malik started firing as soon as the man moved, on full auto. Even as he died, the man who claimed to be his rescuer managed to fire three rounds in Slater's general direction.

Malik and Slater stood facing one another across the crumpled body.

"You should probably put your rifle down," Malik said gently, gesturing at the weapon that Slater was holding at his side. "You're not going to be rescued tonight." The M4 was centered on Slater's chest.

Slater laid the rifle down very gently. "That was no rescue party. More like a hostile takeover. I think some of your competitors think they can do better with me as hostage than you seem to be doing."

Malik nodded as if Slater had confirmed his own thinking. "Why do you think that?"

"Well. First, he tried to kill me, not you. I'd guess his orders were to bring me back, but if he couldn't …. Then there was the fact that a supposed U.S. Army Ranger speaks English with a strong Afghan accent and couldn't tell the difference between an M16 and an AK47."

The Projects

The call came in on the landline in the San Francisco condo. That bothered Kaz. *It's like they know where I am at any time.*

"Good morning, Mr. Zanker. This is Ollie. You need to be in Kabul, at the Intercontinental next Monday. You should be prepared to stay in Afghanistan for up to a week."

"That will be difficult." *Actually, it's not. But the bastard doesn't own me.*

But apparently he felt that he did. "You have no choice in the matter. We've heard from them. There will be a meeting sometime during that week and they want you within a day's travel by car. And you have to there on June 1 anyway, for your big announcement. That's only six days from now."

"They want me? Who's *they*?"

Ollie cursed himself silently. But his voice didn't change. "Our side. There are several other people involved in this."

"Just be there." And the call ended.

CC was watching him from across the room. She put down the book she was reading and said, "A disagreeable caller?"

"You can't begin to imagine!"

He wanted to say more, much more. But he kept remembering that single page document he had signed in Mundt's office. *I don't think "need to know" fits this circumstance.*

He went to where she was stretched out the length of the sofa, picked up her feet, sat down and replaced her feet in his lap. He began to massage one of them.

"I have to go to Kabul this weekend. Probably be there through June first."

"The World Bank deal? The one you were working on in Paris in between our … vocabulary sessions?" She lifted her free foot and poked him in his ribs.

It's funny. That's another thing that's also highly confidential. But she's already read and commented on the documents. Breach of professional ethics. Client privacy, etc. etc. Water over the dam ... or is it under the bridge?

"Yeah. Gotta visit the short-listed projects." A quick and obvious lie, but it quickly became a plan.

Why not? The only condition is to be within a day's drive. Might as well be working.

CC brightened. "Want some company? I've got some things I need to do in Kabul and nearby. There's no end of NGO's with a focus on Afghan refugees."

Having CC along would be nice, but it's not exactly a tourist trip.

He equivocated. "Go to Kabul? Don't you worry about security? You don't exactly fit in."

She laughed. "And you do? But you'd be surprised at how I can adapt. There won't be a single blonde hair or patch of bare skin in sight when I'm out on the street."

"OK. But I may be unavailable for a few days, depending on how much time I'm on-site at the projects."

"No problem. I've got lots to do myself. But, even with our schedules, there'll be some night-time overlaps that should be interesting."

They landed at the Hamid Karzai International Airport two days later, on a Sunday afternoon. The driver met them as they came out of customs and they were at the hilltop hotel within twenty minutes. Their room provided a magnificent view of the Hindu Kush mountains and much of Kabul.

The message light was blinking when they walked into the room.

"This is Mohamad Durani. You'll recall that we met in Paris. I've arranged for a tour of selected projects. We can do it in three days, I think. As you asked, I have warned everybody that you may be called away at any time. I will pick you up at seven AM tomorrow."

Kaz remembered Durani. He was the sharp-faced under-secretary of something who said almost nothing in Paris. Not someone to be stuck with for three days!

And, as he thought, it was a long three days. Durani served as guide, translator and – in Kaz's view – babysitter. He controlled where they went, who they talked to, and what they saw. When Kaz sought to go beyond the official itinerary, Durani recited the same little speech.

"Security can be a problem in this area. And we do not want to bring undue attention to the project before it is well underway."

According to Durani, his staff had sifted through thirty-nine specific proposals and chosen a third of them for his review and ultimate allocation to the "best" four or five of the lot. The first thing Kaz did was to read through Durani's thirteen files and compare them with the much more objective and professional reports prepared for him by his team of GABI account officers who had evaluated the projects. He had already decided that three of Durani's thirteen finalists did not warrant funding.

They covered the other ten projects in the three days. Durani dictated the order and the schedule, but Kaz was sure that Durani was setting it up so that the ones he wanted would be the last ones visited.... the Day Three Itinerary. *He must believe in the famous recency effect.*

On the third day, they drove to three of the projects so that Kaz could do a physical inspection of the work-in-progress and meet the project managers.

Just outside of Kabul, a team of USAID agronomists was experimenting with drip irrigation systems within a thousand acre orchard of fruit trees. Present Afghan irrigation practices were based on highly inefficient "surface irrigation" methods, leading to wasted water and low crop yields. The proposed grant would be used for the acquisition and installation of equipment at multiple sites across the country.

In a medium-sized village about forty miles south, a local entrepreneur was converting a warehouse into a textile factory that would use modern weaving looms and first-world labor standards to produce rugs and carpets that would be distributed worldwide. This was a pilot that he intended to replicate across the country.

Their longest trip was eighty-five miles due west toward Herat. A regional agricultural cooperative had formed and had plans to build a ten-thousand square-foot refrigerated storage and manufacturing facility with the capacity to produce fruit-packaging materials. It would be supplemented with a fleet of refrigerated delivery trucks. The manager thought they could reduce the spoilage rates to almost nothing and vastly expand the effective marketing zones for local farmers.

Two other projects were still so deep into the planning stage that there was little to look at except documents. They did that in an office building on the outskirts of Kabul.

The business rationale for one of the projects was obvious from their travels to the first three projects. Fifteen years ago, Afghanistan had fifty miles of paved roads. Since then, ten-thousand miles of new roads had been constructed. But they were badly maintained and in serious need of new investment. The owner of the largest construction company in the country showed Kaz a one-hundred-and-eight page document – page-by-painstaking-page – showing the benefits of purchasing specialized highway equipment and applying it to a master plan for comprehensive and ongoing road maintenance.

The final project was simultaneously the most obvious and the least developed. Telecommunication services in Afghanistan were largely controlled by a single government entity that was highly inefficient and hostile to rapid adoption of new technologies. Outside of the few big cities, cell phones and wireless services were virtually unknown. A group of six businessmen, each from a different province, formed a firm to build regional infrastructures for wireless and cell systems, using new and cheap technology that would "leapfrog" the legacy systems in use.

He didn't see CC very much until the morning of their fourth day in Kabul. He got in late the night before and went to bed alone. When he woke up in the king-sized bed at the Intercontinental, he found her next to him, propped up on a pile of pillows and reading through a sheaf of pages that seemed to be nothing except columns of numbers.

"Ugh. Don't you have something that has some nouns and adjectives in it?"

She pushed his hand away. "We leave those to the lawyers and bankers. Besides, we've used up all of the available adjectives trying to describe the refugee problem. Hopeless, dismal, tragic, brutal, catastrophic, apocalyptic, --"

"I get the picture!"

She put the documents down and scooted back down under the covers and up against him.

He turned so as to maximize the amount of skin in direct contact, saying, "Now there's a word not much used in UNHRA circles – 'snuggling.'"

"An adverb, I believe? And a great example of imagery … A word that evokes the action it is describing."

"Like 'oozing' …"

"Or 'getting laid'?"

She pulled back and propped herself on her elbow, looking very serious.

"Something wrong?" he asked. "That's a pretty piercing look."

She reached to play with his ear lobe, clearly thinking about how to respond.

"I've missed you, you know? Quite a lot."

He cleared his throat, stalling for time. *A crossroads? One of those "be very careful what you say next" times. More witty repartee, keep it light? Or respond in kind and see where it goes? But where do you want it to go?*

He split the difference, feeling that it was wrong even as he did it. "I've missed you, too. These days, something seems vaguely off when I'm in a major world city and you're not with me. It's like some new symptom to go with jet lag."

She smiled in a way that told him that she knew of his ambivalence … and that it would have to be dealt with.

She swung her legs out of bed and stood up, stretching in a very feline fashion. When she spoke, it was an ordinary question, but her tone gave away her intense interest in his response.

"So, how do the projects look?"

He looked at her curiously, but she had her back turned, still stretching.

He shrugged. "Mostly like any other infrastructure project in the third or fourth world, but there were a couple of surprises."

"Oh? Like what?"

"First, I've never heard the word 'scalability' used so many times in that space of time. Everything I saw was what you would call a 'pilot' or a 'beta test' or a 'demonstration of feasibility.' They're all in startup phase. In the States or Europe, they'd be pitching the VC's, not the bankers."

"But that's just it. There are no VC's here. The World Bank and the muddled-up Afghan Reconstruction Fund is it as far as these people are concerned."

"I know that. And most of the projects make some economic sense, allowing for the natural amount of imbedded optimism. But the amount of money that they're asking for up front – and we've committed to -- is what they need to cover the whole rollout and fully scaled-up project. The project write-ups we saw in Paris – you read them – implied that we were funding much bigger ventures than what these are at the moment."

"Don't they need more money to cover security? There are some nasty people out there who don't want these things to actually work."

"They do. And that's in all of their budgets. Several of them have pretty heavy up-front spending for what amounts to a private security force -- armed, trained and thoroughly vetted."

She still was turned away, but her stillness, the lines of her back, signaled that she was listening closely.

"You said 'a couple of surprises.' What was the other one?"

"It's pretty vague. And it's still growing on me. All of the projects are private or NGO's, not government sponsored. That's a condition for getting a grant. But some of them are not just private, but almost anti-government. Each of them should logically be supported by some government ministry or other – ag, telecom, transport, export/import – but they don't want the government involved in any way."

"Given the amount of corruption and sectarian favoritism that Karzai built into his government, I'm not surprised."

"He's gone, and Ashraf Ghani is not Hamid Karzai. But I get the feeling that they don't care who's in the presidential palace, that they think they're better off on their own."

"Is that so bad?"

"It is from the World Bank view. They're not big on regime change."

"I thought we called it 'nation building.'"

"That was George Bush. And you saw how well that turned out!"

"So, what will you do?"

Again, Kaz had the impression that she was intensely interested in his response.

He said, "I don't know." And then the phone rang.

"Hello."

"Are you alone?" The voice was unfamiliar to him.

"No."

"Come down to the lobby. It's time to go."

"But, I'm not --"

"Now!" And the line went dead.

He hung up. CC was still standing alongside the bed. The mid-morning sun streamed through the windows behind her, turning her into a silhouette without any distinguishing features other than her perfect shape.

"I've got to meet someone downstairs," he said. "I'll be right back."

To his credit, he believed that to be true.

When he left, CC walked very slowly to her purse and took out her cell phone. She slumped back down onto the bed, staring at the phone like a recovering alcoholic holding a whiskey bottle.

Slowly, very slowly, she touched a single button on the face of the phone.

"It's about time. News?"

"He's back."

"And?"

She did not answer, but sat looking out the window at the distant mountains.

"CC. Speak to me."

She sat up straight and spoke with a clear voice, as though to negate the sensation of the lone tear tracing a slow arc down her cheek.

"We may have a problem."

The Meeting Place

Two ordinary-looking Afghan men that he did not recognize were waiting for Kaz at the elevator. Each took an elbow and steered him toward the side door of the hotel.

His protest was instinctive, but even as he began to say the words, he knew that the old rules would not apply; that he had volunteered for a game without rules. For the first time, he appreciated that he was in over his head.

"Wait! I need some things from my room!" And he planted his feet, actually digging his heels into the deep pile of the carpet beneath him.

Each of his escorts merely tightened the grip on his arm and actually lifted him an inch or so. They kept walking and he found himself being propelled along like a paraplegic at his first physical therapy session.

A black SUV was double-parked at the side door, its engine idling and its rear door open. He was placed in the back seat with a man on either side. As soon as the door was closed, one of them slipped a hood over his head. It was not uncomfortable but he could see nothing. He felt hands going through his pockets, taking his watch, wallet and cell phone. Some kind of electronic scanner with a faint hum was being run lightly over his body, from his hair down to his toes.

They sat for several more minutes. He heard things being loaded into the rear compartment of the SUV. As soon as the rear door slammed shut, they started moving.

The traffic noises did not last long and then they were driving for about three hours on a paved road. *So I'm not going east or we would have had to go through a Pakistani border post by now.* Then they turned onto a much more primitive road and continued for about three more hours. *I can feel the sun on my back, so now we're headed east. Pretty fuzzy about the elapsed time. Never practiced with a blindfold before. But we seem to be climbing quite a lot – thinner air, definitely. So I'm guessing we're headed to the northeast, further into the mountains.*

Definite bandit country. Toward the area where Slater Crosby was last seen.

The last hour or so was at low speeds with frequent S-turns. They finally stopped and he could hear a large and creaky gate being opened and – when they had driven through – closed behind them.

Not a word had been spoken since the lobby of the hotel, so he was startled when the man to his left said, "We are here. Thank you for your cooperation." And he took off the hood and indicated that Kaz should get out of the car.

He found himself standing in late afternoon sunlight in a walled courtyard, apparently a car park for a multistory, rambling villa. It immediately reminded him of the small palaces in Rajahstan that had been converted to high-end tourist hotels. The walls were high, perhaps a dozen feet and quite thick, with doors constructed of heavy wooden beams criss-crossed with bolted-on iron strips. The SUV and two others were parked beneath a ramshackle wooden roof that extended far out from one wall. *Invisible from the air.*

A door opened in the wall opposite the gate where they had entered and an older man approached him. He was dressed simply in the traditional knee-length shirt and baggy trousers. He had a short beard streaked with grey and wore a flat woolen cap. There was nothing to distinguish him from an ordinary farmer or tradesman until he got close.

He has – for lack of a better word – an aura. There's a gentleness about him, but also fierceness. Like someone wise who would be quick to anger. People will want to please him. Whoever or whatever he is, I'll bet he's the one in charge.

The man had stopped and was looking at Kaz with some mild amusement. When he spoke, his English was impeccable. "Are you finished with your inspection? It is very bad manners for a guest in an Afghan home to be so openly skeptical about his host."

"I apologize. But I didn't know I was a guest and thought the usual traditions might not apply."

The look of amusement did not change. "Oh, but you are. A guest. And I was told that you volunteered for the assignment."

I did. But for what? And how am I supposed to behave while waiting to do whatever it is they want me to do?

And then he remembered the obscene video of the beheading that he had watched over and over in his hotel room. He shuddered, thinking, *this could be the man that arranged it.*

It was as if the man could read his mind. He sounded actually sympathetic. "I know this is very strange, but we hope that there will a happy ending for everybody involved."

He took Kaz's arm and turned toward the door where he had entered. "Let me show you to your room. The others will be here shortly and then we can get to know one another better."

It turned out to be three rooms on the second floor with an attached balcony. Within five minutes of the door closing behind his escort, a man delivered all of Kaz's belongings from the Intercontinental Hotel, including all of the documents that had been spread out on the desk.

That was what they were loading in the SUV while we sat there. I wonder what they told CC?

There was a knock at the door and a man entered carrying a bundle. He was about Kaz's age, but shorter and stockier. He bounced rather than walked and he had a half-grin that looked fixed in place. He reminded Kaz of a life insurance salesman during his first few days on the job. And he looked vaguely familiar. *He's related in some way to the older guy. Something about the eyes.*

"Mr. Zanker. Welcome. My name is Abdullah. For now, I am your host. I know you have many questions and I will try to answer them to your satisfaction."

He spoke English as though he had learned it from books or a software program, with a heavy accent and frequent pauses. Even then, he was in motion the entire time, fluttering his hands and shifting from one foot to another.

He's right. I have many questions. Let's see about his willingness to answer them.

"Where am I?"

"This is a special place. We are in a very remote area, perhaps in Afghanistan or maybe Pakistan. The villa was built in 1922 and has served many purposes. You might think of it as … how do you call it … a demilitarized zone… a place that all sides will respect."

"Even the American drones?"

Abdullah beamed. "Of course. And what you call 'the terrorists,' and the Pakistani secret service, and those tribal enemies that want to kill each other. Everybody needs a place to talk every now and then."

"Who is the older man who met me in the carpark?"

"His name is Malik. He is my uncle and what you would call a 'tribal leader.'"

"Am I free to walk around?"

"Yes, but with some restrictions. First, you must wear these garments." He placed the bundle on the bench near the door. The NATO people have many – how do you put it? – 'eyes in the sky,' so we do not want them to see anything unusual if they happen to pass over.

"Second, please put this on your wrist." He handed him what looked like a simple metal bracelet with a complex clasp. "It is a monitoring device, so that we can find you at any time."

Western technology at its best. He snapped it on and checked to confirm that he could not release the clasp once snapped close.

"Third, you cannot go outside the compound."

"Finally, you are in a quite strict Muslim home. As you know, our wives and daughters do not mingle with male guests. So you will find certain areas off-limits."

"Is the American captain – Crosby – here?"

"Not yet."

For the first time in the series of questions and answers, Kaz picked up a slight off-note. And it must have shown in his face, because Abdullah smiled in a slightly embarrassed way and said, "There are some things about the arrangements that only my uncle can talk about."

"What do they expect of me?"

"This is another of those things. I do not know many things about why you are here."

"Are you mujahedeen?"

The smile widened. "Everyone in my family is mujahedeen."

"Then am I not your enemy?"

The question clearly puzzled Abdullah. He looked down at the floor, apparently composing his response.

"For the moment, yes. But …"

Kaz waited for him to continue, but Abdullah was clearly done. He pointed to the bundle of clothing. "Please put on these clothes. If you need anything, a man will be sitting outside your door and can get whatever you need. Either I or my uncle will be back shortly."

There were five items in the bundle: a long tunic, a pair of baggy trousers, a red vest, sandals and a flat cloth cap. He felt quite strange when he had put them on, but — when he looked in the mirror — he realized that he looked like any other Pashtun male from a distance. Up close, his white skin and the lack of a beard would give him away.

He walked out on the second-story balcony, really a tiled patio with a low wall around it, overlooking a central courtyard with fountains and flowering trees. As he watched, a trio of men walked slowly across it, engaged in intense arm-waving conversation. At one end of the patio, he looked down on a second and much smaller courtyard, perhaps twenty feet in either direction and without any ornamentation of any sort other than a black metallic structure at one end. A single wooden door was set into the far wall.

The starkness of the small courtyard, the sunlit empty space, a mono-color cube open to the sky, relieved only by the metal structure, gave him the impression of a modern art exhibit. Then he looked more closely and a coldness settled over him and the small courtyard beneath him became something sinister.

The black metal structure was the tripod for a video camera.

Kaz and Malik

He sat for an hour on the small patio, thinking about the things that he didn't know. It was just getting dark when Malik knocked and entered. He was carrying a gas lantern that he placed on the small table. Another man was carrying a tray with a bottle of water, and a plate with bread, hummus, figs and dolmas that he placed alongside the lantern. When the man left, Malik sat down opposite him. He said nothing, but watched Kaz intently.

Kaz nodded to him and said, "Your nephew, Abdullah, is –"

"A good man. But he could not answer all of your questions."

"I have many. For example, what –"

Again, a quick interruption. "Let me ask you one. What do you know about Sharia law?"

Kaz visualized the camera tripod in the courtyard beneath them, now invisible in the growing darkness.

"Am I at risk if I answer incorrectly?"

Malik was amused. "You are an infidel. Therefore, your understanding will be imperfect. But I am curious."

"OK. We think of it as 'Islamic Law,' derived from the Koran and the teachings of the Prophet. It mandates both the religious and the secular norms for all forms of behavior, often with what we – the so-called West – deem to be harsh and unreasonable penalties for breaches of the law. And I know that there are many disputes within Islam about the application of Sharia, mostly involving fundamentalist vs. modern interpretations."

Kaz watched Malik closely as he was reciting. Malik's expression was impassive throughout. Without understanding why, he found himself becoming passionate about what he was saying.

"Your Taliban government –"

"Not mine!" The interruption was instant and sharp.

Kaz shrugged and began again. "The Taliban – when they were in power -- ruthlessly enforced a medieval, fundamentalist interpretation of Sharia. Mullahs and imams banned listening to music, contacts between men and women, the playing of games and applied stoning, amputations, and public executions for those who offended. Women were set back a hundred years."

Malik pursed his lips and half-closed his eyes, seeming to weigh what Kaz was saying. But his next question was even more of a surprise.

"Do you believe in cultural relativism?"

For god's sake! What is this about? What does he want?

"Yes! And no! I don't know! It depends!"

Malik continued to stare, knowing that Kaz was as bothered by his non-answer as he was.

Kaz took a deep breath. "I am a product of a particular and imperfect culture. I believe in progress and the perfectability of man… that we should strive for it."

"It? What is 'it'?

Kaz raised his voice. "I believe that there are absolutes that any culture should aspire to attain – eastern or western, ancient or modern, American or Pashtun. Things like equality, classlessness, freedom of choice, the elimination of war, hunger, poverty, discrimination. I believe that cultures – no matter where they start from – will gravitate to those states over time and that the purpose of laws and universities and mosques and synagogues and churches and parents and teachers and politicians and media and prophets should be to speed that process."

He sat back, slightly out of breath and amazed at his obvious passion for something that he had not thought about for a long time.

"What about armies?"

"Armies?"

"Armies. You left them out of your list of institutions that should be seeking change. Should they have the same moral duties and aspirations as the synagogues and mosques?"

"You mean like our Marines, or NATO?" After a pause, he added "Or the mujahedeen?"

Malik smiled again, but this time with great sadness.

"I think you were a very good debater. When you were in college in New Mexico, maybe?"

Then the subject shifted, quite dramatically.

"What do you think of Senator Harlan Crosby?"

This time, it was Kaz's turn to sit back and think very carefully about how to respond.

"I think that it would be inappropriate for me to talk about my client."

"Your client? Is Senator Crosby the one who has asked you to risk your life, to meet with terrorists who blindfold you and drive you deep into the mountains where no one knows where you are?"

In London. With Ollie and the other silent man. He said "They asked for you." But he never said who "they" were.

Again, the image of that camera tripod in the blank courtyard came to him.

"Malik, why am I here?"

Malik stood up and looked down at him. The light from the gas lantern left the upper half of his face in shadow and made him seem mysterious.

"Why, to negotiate a ransom, of course? Didn't *they* tell you?"

When Malik closed the door behind him, Kaz sat for an hour on the small patio, thinking about the depth of his ignorance and the strangeness of the man called Malik. A door slammed somewhere in the villa, rousing him. He felt hungry and realized that the food was still on the table, untouched.

Takhar Province

"I know Seals never complain, but I'd like to have a few minutes of quality time alone with whatever intelligence dude did the analysis for this gig."

Lieutenant Chambers smiled at the thought. The speaker was Luther Small, who was a very large black man with a shaved head and prominent facial scars. And Chambers happened to know that "the intelligence dude" he was referring to was a twenty-five year old, one-hundred-pound brunette named Jenny. *And knowing the two of them, I'd bet on Jenny in a faceoff. But Luther does have a point.*

The Seals –two squads of eight men each – had been sitting around Achin Adi for three straight days waiting for a "go" for a very high priority hostage rescue. It was pure dead time. They had no intel as to location, hostile forces or anything else. All they were told was, "The drones are looking."

Then it got worse. A Major Dalkie and Jenny briefed Chambers.

As soon as Dalkie began with "You're not going to like this –," Chambers thought, *That should be the tag line for every mission briefing I've been to. I wonder what particular form of idiocy they're going to inflict on us this time.*

The British major did not have a perceptible sense of humor and gave Chambers the very distinct impression that he didn't agree with the orders he was passing down.

"You're not going to like this. The bad news is that we have four different possible locations. Small farming compounds far away from any real villages. Each of them fits the profile and each of them is the site of human activity. No large units and maybe just normal agricultural operations. But we don't know. We want you to check them out."

"For what? Unsafe agricultural practices?"

The Major was not amused. "A local Taliban group is holding one of our people hostage – an American infantry captain. We think they intend to use him to star in one of their amateur video productions for YouTube. We want you to get him back. Alive."

Chambers had been expecting this, but was depressed just the same. *We've done this hostage rescue drill four times in the last two months. With dismal results. The bad guys killed two of the hostages as soon as they heard the rotors. We killed one of them in a crossfire. The one of the four ... the one that survived our good intentions? He wasn't there; they'd moved him before we got there. You might say he was the lucky one. Except that he was decapitated for a worldwide audience three days later.*

He said, very conversationally, "Sir. You do know the odds of success on this kind of operation, don't you? Especially when we're going in blind."

Dalkie looked at him in a way that Chambers knew well. *The man's passing on orders that he doesn't agree with. Must happen in the British army as well as ours.*

Chambers ignored Dalkie's glare and asked the question that the higher-ups didn't like. "What if we find him, but we can't get him back without risking his life?" *Which is what usually happens.* "Do we push it as far as we can?"

"This particular captain is very important to us ... and to a very special group of people in Washington D.C. Failure is not an option."

They had four hours to prepare. The intel consisted of detailed topo maps and some hand-drawn detail provided by Jenny. A drone with thermal imaging hardware would make a pass an hour before they were on the scene.

They started as soon as it was dark. They went in two helicopters, at extremely low altitudes and landing five miles from the target to preserve the surprise element. Once on the ground, they had continuous air coverage, both Predators and F-15's standing off, but on call. By two AM, they had cleared two of the sites without incident. No hostiles, no shots fired, and no hostage. The farmers were not friendly and definitely did not appreciate the house-to-house search, but – as Luther put it – "They can spit at me all they want. It's those RPGs and 50 caliber rounds that really hurt my feelings."

The third site was different. The thermal imaging drone had come up with half-a-dozen heat signatures. Not moving about, but stationary as though in defensive positions. It was a very narrow slot canyon, so they had limited access and could only approach from the front. The scene was bathed in moonlight, so their objective – the middle one of three windowless storage sheds with a green plastic roof with a man sitting by the entrance -- was clearly visible at the rear of the canyon.

Chambers positioned two snipers, one on either side of the canyon, about a hundred and fifty meters out. Each of them had a clear line of sight to the storage shed. Their instructions were simple.

"From now on, anybody goes near that middle unit – I don't care what age, gender or species he, she or it is – I want you to put them down."

He didn't think about the likelihood that the shed was rigged with explosives that could be detonated from anywhere. Or that they had a man inside with the hostage ready to blow him away at the first inkling of a raid. His conscience was clear on that score.

Dalkie had caught up with Chambers just before they boarded the helicopters. He tugged him away from the group of Seals and out from under the spinning rotor blades. He said, "The question you asked me ... how far to push it?" He handed him a cell phone. "It's one of those very special people in Washington. For your ears only."

"This is Lieutenant Chambers."

The voice was that of a woman, but one accustomed to authority. "I know this is a difficult mission. We want you to do the best you can. If you find him, get him back. But there is one absolute. Whatever happens, the terrorists must be denied further access to Captain Crosby. Do you understand me?"

Why don't you just say it? If you can't extract him, then kill him! He also thought about asking, "Who am I talking to?" but knew that he wouldn't get an answer. *A woman in DC. One who is used to giving orders.*

They got to about a hundred meters when the first shots came from the first mud hut on the left side of the canyon, pinging off the rocks to either side of them. Another four or five rifles joined in. The muzzle flashes marked their positions clearly.

So much for surprise! They've been waiting for us to show up. But they're amateurs at this game. Full automatic. Spray and pray.

No commands were necessary. The team had practiced for this type of combat hundreds of times. Short bursts of suppressive fire as alternating Seals moved forward up either side. Chambers followed, monitoring progress by the terse radio exchanges. It was over within five minutes.

Luther was waiting for him at the middle storage shed. Its door was standing open.

"They bugged out. Probably right after that initial burst. Had a back door. A goat trail up one side of the canyon. The boys are chasing, but they gotta go slow to check for booby traps. My bet is they ain't gonna catch 'em."

Chambers grunted to acknowledge Luther's analysis. "Not much of a defense, was it? Fire and flee?" He gestured at the open door. "And you're going to tell me that's because they had nothing worth defending, aren't you?"

Luther nudged the door open with the muzzle of his weapon. "Well, we got mixed news on that front. Take a look."

Chambers switched on his flash and went in. The space was absolutely bare other than the simple table and stool in the center of the floor. He pivoted in a full circle looking for markings, but saw nothing except bare walls.

"Mixed news, huh?"

"Well. Somebody was here. But they probably wished they weren't." Luther swiveled his light onto the wall to his left. It was flecked with dark spots. "That's blood spatter. About head high. And this —" the light shifted to the dirt floor – "was a serious blood pool. Still slightly tacky."

"Is that the good news or the bad news? Looks more like no news to me. Everything checks with our intel, but we still can't say if the man was here or not. Or if that's his blood."

Luther shook his head. "He was here. And he's still got his sense of humor." He reached down to one of the table legs and lifted the table so that the underside was facing Chambers. There were characters, upper-case block letters traced out in charcoal on the cheap cardboard backing of the table.

It read, "Property of Captain Slater Crosby." And in one corner, in much smaller letters, there was a date -- today's.

A Walk in the Moonlight

It was Day XIII. Slater had started to think of the days as having Roman numerals rather than ordinary numbers. It helped him to differentiate one from another and – much more important – it helped him believe that this would end soon, as if the Roman numerals were more finite.

Day XIII was clearly different for his captors. There was much more activity apparent outside of his shed. More moving around, coming and going, and conversation. The bits and pieces that he could overhear all pointed to a move. And three times late in the afternoon, he picked up the distinctive engine noise of a drone. Not hovering, but making repeated passes along the long axis of the canyon.

They're coming, but not until after dark. No way they'll try a daylight Special Ops this deep in Taliban country.

Badi and Cyrus, his two remaining minders, came for him as soon as the sun touched the horizon. They had him put on the same generic Afghan garb as they were wearing. When Cyrus handed him a pair of sandals, Badi stopped him. "We're going to be moving very fast on some rough trails. It will be easier for you to keep up if you keep your boots."

Malik joined them in the small square. He and the other three men with him were carrying rifles and light packs. Malik greeted him with a small bow.

"You heard the drones?"

"Yes. I was surprised it took them so long."

"Afghanistan is a very big country, with many hiding places. We finally had to give them a hint."

A hint? A memory flashed through, of a game of "Hide and Seek" with him in a very deep closet waiting to be discovered and finally coming out because he was scared by the darkness and the absence of sound.

Malik was talking. " … last part in a truck. But we need to walk for a few hours first. There's something that I want to show you."

They set off, moving at a quite fast pace. Malik led, then Cyrus. They put Slater in third position, closely followed by Badi and someone Slater didn't know. *Abdul's replacement.* Slater found himself slightly exhilarated by being outdoors and moving through a cloudless night with an almost-full moon.

A nice night for a hike through strange country. After hundreds of night patrols in a countryside ruled by insurgents, always waiting for that first sniper shot or trying to tell whether the scuff marks in the dirt road might be concealing an IED, it's nice to be out at night without worrying about what's just around the corner.

The euphoria wore off within the first few miles. He found himself watching the skies and listening intently for engines or rotor blades. They moved through a landscape without people or even any distant lights. The stars were magnificent. He flashed back to that woman on the flight to London, oblivious to war and raving about the quality of light in Afghanistan.

They were moving to the Northeast on a very primitive path, probably formed by goats or other domestic farm animals moving from pasture to village. Although there were no villages or even farms as far as he could tell. Then they turned uphill onto what seemed to have once been a fairly major cart track, but it was badly overgrown with weeds and the winter storms had washed it out in several places. Whatever community it led to was no longer active.

The track topped out on a small rise that overlooked a shallow valley bisected by a dry riverbed. Malik stopped at the crest and the others formed a line looking down into the valley. Each of the four Afghani men were abnormally still and focused on the scene below.

A village. Or what once was a village. Maybe six square blocks. A grid with a couple of cross streets. Thirty or forty structures. A center plaza with a well. Big enough to have a proper mosque with a minaret. Probably a few hundred people. Pashtuns. Farmers with fruit trees, some row crops, livestock.

Probably poppies. The same families for hundreds of years, doing the same things the same ways.

Malik said something in Pashto and the other Afghanis moved off to a grassy area and sat down, clearly taking a break. Even then, their eyes remained focused on the ruins of the village. Malik walked a few more steps up the track to where an ancient stone signpost was imbedded alongside the track. The etched-in characters were so faint as to be illegible in the moonlight.

He gestured with his arm to include the whole of the valley. "This is the village of Cham Kasi. It is where my family comes from. It is my home."

Slater was struck by his use of the present tense. What was spread out in the moonlight before him was a dead civilization, a jumbled and eroded set of ruins without any sign of life, as still and silent as the Egyptian pyramids.

Then he began to notice the details of his trade.

Four craters with concentric rings of rubble. Right down the middle of the village. Must have been a stick of five-hundred pounders. Those walls that are still standing – that's shrapnel. Probably threw in a cluster bomb or two. Trees cut in two ... rocket fire or at least some fifty caliber stuff. Must have had a couple of gunships make a few runs after the bombs. Not a lot of survivors.

He was struck by the *neatness* of the destruction, how the explosions had reduced all of the buildings into smaller pieces, all jumbled together in a chaotic pile of approximately uniform depth, leaving an occasional pockmarked standing wall. This had not been a casual attack; it was the air force version of sending in bulldozers to level a city. The rubble formed a rectangle, enclosed on all sides by what had been cultivated fields, but was now unchecked greenery beginning to encroach into the tumbled blocks of masonry and brick. This attack had happened a long time ago.

On the far side of the riverbed, another rectangle caught his eye. It also stood out for its orderliness and the way it interrupted the greenness of the fields. It was a cemetery.

Malik said nothing, but watched Slater closely. He was easily able to follow the successive realizations as Slater reconstructed the history of what had happened below them.

This is what he wanted me to see. Cham Kasi was his home. This is a mujahedeen shrine, not just any old wiped-out village. He remembered one of their conversations a few days ago, sitting at the table with the Koran between them. How the Russian gunships had killed his family.

"This was brutal. I can understand why you hate the Russians."

Malik just looked at him with a hard-to-read expression. And the other six men had shifted their focus entirely to him. Slater felt like he was missing some essential point, that he had offended them in some way.

Finally, Malik gestured to the men and they formed their line once more, ready to move back down the faded track. As he turned, he said something very softly that Slater did not catch. He stepped alongside Malik, caught his arm and said, "What did you say?"

Malik did not turn or stop walking.

"I said, 'This was not the Russians that did this.'"

Washington D.C.

Madge was waiting in Harlan's office when he got out of the Senate Intelligence Committee meeting.

"I thought about interrupting you, but I don't know how much of this you want to share with your committee colleagues."

"The less they know, the better." *The mantra for the CIA and every other intelligence officer anywhere, any time. Information is power. Shared information gets people killed.*

"So, there's news?"

"The Seals are back. They checked out three sites. The third one was the right one, but they missed Slater. Apparently, they moved him out several hours before the Seals got there and kept a decoy force in place. Some shots fired, but nobody down on either side."

"Damn it! Any intel on where they've moved him to?"

"Not yet. They're reviewing satellite data, but that's a slow process when we're trying to cover that much surface area."

"What have we got for on-the-ground purposes?"

"The Seals are back in Achin Adi and on standby, but ..."

"What's wrong, Madge?"

"The platoon leader is a Lieutenant Chambers. Dalkie told me that he – Chambers – was ambivalent about the mission. Thought it wouldn't work and that we'd wind up with a dead hostage."

"So?"

"I called him – private phone, just before he embarked – and told him to get our hostage back ... but, in any case, to be sure that the terrorists do not have access to him."

Harlan leaned back in his chair and thought about that.

"Does Chambers know who Slater is?"

"I don't think so, but I don't think his ignorance will last for long."

"Does he know who he was talking to on that private phone? That you were on the other end."

"No. But Dalkie may know."

"Christ, Madge! This is a mess! We've got to get containment on this."

"I know. But there are some positives. We've got Zanker in Kabul on a tight leash, ready to go if and when it looks like they're going to make ransom demands. Maybe we can just moneywhip the whole thing. And we've still got Ollie and his team in the zone if we need some off-the-books initiatives."

Madge was clearly uncomfortable about something, a condition that was unfamiliar to both of them.

"Madge? There's more?"

"Someone was probably killed in the place where he was being held. We don't know who."

Harlan sat at his desk drumming his fingertips on its surface. "Maybe we need to move to Kabul? Sounds like we're getting to end-game.... "

"I agree." She held up five fingers. "Here are the possibilities. First, we buy him back. Second, we rescue him. Third, we attempt a rescue but he's killed in the process. Fourth, none of the above work and we're watching another YouTube sensational beheading, or worse."

She paused, but kept staring intently at him. The silence lasted long enough that Harlan looked up at her.

"So? What's the fifth possible outcome?"

"He's already dead."

This is his son we're talking about. And we're discussing it like we're planning a picnic at the beach!

He stared at her like he wanted to debate one of her points, but finally just shrugged.

"OK. Let's not do anything until we get confirmation that Slater is still alive. And then we need to decide which one of those four remaining options is the best one. Then we'll try to make it come true.

"Get us to Kabul. Not the Embassy. Go through Ollie. He's got access to the CIA safe-house system."

"I'll have to clear your schedule. What shall I tell them?"

He thought for a moment. "Tell them we're going to California for another swing of the contractors. That fits with the timetable for the hearings."

She turned to leave. He stopped just short of the door.

"And get me Ollie. I need to talk to him."

The Absence of Neutrality

They walked downhill for two hours. The men were silent and Slater suspected that part of it was the sobering effect of viewing the ruins of Cham Kasi. A very old van was waiting for them where their rude path became a narrow lane with two ruts. Slater and Malik sat in the front, the other Afghans in the truck bed. To his surprise, they did not blindfold him.

Four hours of driving brought them to a very large and rambling walled villa. It was set on a low hill and dominated the landscape in all directions. Based on his reckoning of direction and distance, he judged them to be quite close to the Pakistan border. A cheery stocky fellow named Abdullah met them and it was obvious from the way they greeted one another that he and Malik were either related or close friends. Abdullah escorted him to his room. It had an actual bed and he collapsed onto it and was asleep within a minute.

When he awoke, Malik was sitting in a chair near the window. He said, "Good morning," and went to the door and asked someone outside to bring in tea.

While Malik poured, Slater looked around him. "My accommodations have improved considerably."

"It is a special place. But it may be that your situation will be even more congenial very soon."

That leaves a lot of possibilities, including the afterlife!

"Where is this ... special place? Are we in Pakistan?"

Malik smiled as though pleased. "Your geographic sense is very good. Almost Pashtun."

Then he shook his head. "Let me just say that we are safe here. It is a sanctuary of sorts. For whoever gets here."

"Whoever? Including your enemies?"

"You know the ethnic and tribal history of Afghanistan ... our tendency to kill one another because of different interpretations of what the Prophet said. We needed a place where we could talk about the differences. A place to negotiate cease-fires and alliances and to discuss areas of common interest. This is such a place."

"So, what is to be discussed?"

Malik looked at him closely, as though expecting what he said next to elicit a reaction that needed to be interpreted.

"What is to be done with you."

Another ambiguous phrase – what is to be done with me. So impersonal, as though discussing the placement of a piece of furniture in a new house. So unclear about Malik's own preferences. And so very clear that I shall have no say in the matter.

He did not know why, but what he said seemed natural at the time, having something to do with how the question "what is to be done with you" was decided.

"Tell me about Cham Kasi."

Malik was impassive. He showed no surprise at a hostage that seemed uncurious about his fate.

Then he nodded, and began talking. After a few sentences, Slater realized that he was listening to a story that must not be interrupted; that the narrator was telling him a tale that had a beginning and an end, and that the story contained an important lesson for both of them.

"We are Pashtun. We are not Taliban or al-Qaeda. But we are also not in agreement with the government. We want to be left alone.

"But it is not possible – or wise – to be neutral in Afghanistan. I and my people fought the Russians and their shadow government. And, in 1989, we stood on the hillsides and watched their columns of tanks and troops slinking back to Russia. It took three more years of fighting for the mujahedeen to get rid of the puppet Najibullah and to begin to build a truly Islamic state. Then we went home and watched the Taliban thugs murder their way into power.

"Some of the Northern Alliance – but not us – continued the insurgency, now fighting the Taliban. It was a terrible time – drought, famine and civil war. They left us alone, but only because we could defend ourselves. My tribal region – and Cham Kasi – was like Switzerland … defended by our mountains, our neutrality and a strong militia. Both of them – the Taliban and the insurgents – wanted us to join them, but we kept to ourselves.

"Then Osama bin Laden and what you call 'Nine-Eleven' happened, and Americans were reminded that the world is a smaller and more connected place ... that it is not possible – or wise – to pretend to be neutral. You 'discover' the Taliban, al-Qaeda and Afghanistan and launch your pompous 'Operation Enduring Freedom' to get rid of the Taliban government, destroy al-Qaeda, and find bin Laden.

"Many of the ethnic and tribal militias in the Northern Alliance were already fighting their bloody war with the Taliban, so it was obvious to ally with them.

"In October 2001, all of the major pieces of the Northern Alliance -- Pashtuns, Uzbeks, Tajiks, Hazara –gathered near Mazan Sharif for a meeting with an American who was there to recruit them into a combined force with American and British military units. Their idea was that we Afghans would fight on the ground and they would provide munitions and air support. The tribal leaders, including me, were there, along with many of our fighters. He – the American -- spoke of democracy and human rights, of 'Afghanistan for Afghans,' but it was your modern weapons and your suitcases filled with cash that were the most persuasive for those of us listening.

"We listened and argued among ourselves long into the night. The American and his staff met with the individual tribes and their elders. They offered 'packages' and promises carefully designed to appeal to the biases of each of the warlords. Most of them agreed to continue their war against the Taliban. And I do not criticize them."

"Many Pashtun tribes joined them. The Tani – my people -- did not. He talked for two hours. I had sixty men with me, mujahedeen from Cham Kasi. We listened and we argued about what to do while the American watched and listened. I served as his translator during our meeting. Our elders voted and were unanimous. The American's vision of a westernized Afghanistan was not appealing and their cash seemed poor compensation for more dead mujahedeen fighters. Besides, we had enjoyed our two years of neutrality – a vacation from war – in Cham Kasi. We were with our families, watching our children and grandchildren do the ordinary things that we had done when we were children.

"We finished late at night. But later, early in the morning, the American came to the house where I was staying. I can remember every word of our conversation."

He said, *"I think you made the wrong decision."*

"It was not my decision. It was that of the group. But I agree with it."

"You make it difficult for me. You are not only a leader of your people, but you are admired by the other tribesmen in the Alliance. Your refusal will make them think very hard about whether they will join us."

I said nothing. Everything about this man indicated that there was nothing I could say that would lead to acceptance on his part. He reminded me of an imam exhorting the children to join in the jihad and the killing of foreigners.

"I can double the cash payment. And make sure that you personally receive the 'extra' amount ... "

"Again, I said nothing. I suspect that my contempt was now sufficiently obvious that he saw the futility of more arguments.

"But I was wrong. I stood up and held the door open for him to leave. He stood, but made no move to leave. He stared at me for a long time.

"He spoke softly. I should have listened more closely ... recognized the threat. But I was smug, thinking that I knew Americans and what they were capable of. That they were somehow different than the Russians and the Taliban.

He said, *"You know, don't you, that there is no such thing as 'neutrality' in what's coming? That you are either for us or against us? That Cham Kasi is in a war zone whether it wants to be or not?*

Then I said something very stupid. But the American irritated me with his outrage over a couple of thousand dead New Yorkers.

"Cham Kasi has survived Genghis Khan, the British, the Taliban, the Russians, and our own government. It will be here long after you Americans have finished your vengeful little war!"

"He walked out the door. But before I could close it, he turned and said, *'I still think you're wrong. But you've helped me.'*

"I see now that we need to demonstrate that neutrality is not possible."

"We left Mazan Sharif early that morning. Four hours later, just as we were close enough to see the planes and hear the bombs, Cham Kasi was destroyed. You saw what they left behind. Two hundred and seven people, mostly women and children, were killed."

Malik stopped. After a few seconds, he looked up and seemed surprised by the silence. Slater said nothing, knowing that the lesson was to come.

Malik's voice was very soft and conveyed an immense weariness. "The American? He was your father – Major General Harlan Crosby."

Kaz and Slater

Kaz left his room, mainly to test Abdullah's "feel free to walk around" assurances. After thirty minutes of wandering, he discovered several things.

First, he seemed to have access to about a third of the villa. Sooner or later, he would come to a locked door and be forced to retrace his steps. Second, he was not going to be able to leave the premises. The exterior walls were high, unscalable and the occasional door to the outside was either locked or guarded. Third, within those limits, he could wander around as much as he liked. However, there was always someone whose job seemed to be to know where he was. Every now and then, he seemed to be alone, but then a man would casually stroll by.

So they don't quite trust the monitoring technology. They are a cautious lot.

He wound up in the central patio that he could overlook from his second story balcony. He sat on a tiled bench alongside a fountain in the shade of an overhanging tree and watched a pair of young boys playing with a soccer ball in the far corner. The only other occupant of the area was a lone Pashtun man sitting on another bench about thirty yards away. The man looked perfectly ordinary except that he did not take his eyes off of Kaz.

When he stood and walked purposefully toward him, Kaz noticed that he was wearing boots rather than sandals. And when he sat down at the far end of Kaz's bench, it was apparent that he had a bracelet exactly like the one Kaz was wearing.

So when Kaz raised his eyes and looked directly at the man, he was not surprised.

"Hello, Kaz. They said you'd be here."

"Slater." *Unmistakably Slater. But he looks like one of them. Dark skin, dark eyes, dark hair. Must have grown the beard in what ... now, thirteen days ... Even looks like a member of the extended Malik family.*

"Stranger than fiction, huh? It's a long way from Berkeley. You and me here, in this place. After all this time."

"Seventeen years, I think. Last time we talked, you were thinking about joining ROTC. I guess we can see how that turned out."

"And you were going to be a world-class investigative reporter. And here you are in the middle of a story that you can't even write about …. a 'breaking story' as the breathless TV announcers always say!"

For some reason, Kaz remembered the bugler playing 'Taps' as the two of them left the Little Bighorn National Monument. It was such a clichéd image that, in reaction to it, he was suddenly impatient with their affected calmness. His voice took on an angry undertone.

"So why *am* I here, Slater?"

Not very polite of me. To skip all of the polite chit-chat that goes with college reunions. But my life is turned upside down – and maybe even shortened – because of him. And he's got about a fifty-fifty chance of decapitation. Doesn't seem right to worry about whether we're 'cool' or not.

Slater looked at him with a curious expression, but finally shrugged. "They tell me that they need you to help them work out the details of what they're calling 'the financial arrangements.'"

It was Kaz's turn to stare. He thought back to the meeting with 'Ollie' in Mundt's office and tried to recall the exact wording. *"We" want you to help us get him back. A lot of vague pronouns. But he sure as hell left me with the impression that the Crosby family was doing the asking.*

"You didn't ask for me specifically?"

"Me? Ask for you?" His puzzlement seemed quite real. "I had no idea what you were doing or where you were. I haven't thought of you in ten years. Until yesterday when your name came up. Malik referred to you as 'the banker.'"

Dead end. Let's try another angle.

"This Malik guy … He seems to be the head guy, but he sure doesn't come across as your run-of-the-mill terrorist. What do you know about him?"

The question sent Slater into a long silence. When he started talking, Kaz got the impression that he was organizing his own thoughts and images, as though attempting to make sense of someone that he himself did not understand.

"First, he's not your average terrorist. In fact, I don't think he's a terrorist at all. I think he wants to be left alone, but we won't stop bothering him –"

Kaz broke in. "We sure as hell won't leave him alone if he –"

The pause went on a little too long. Finally, Slater said it for him. "If he beheads the son of a U.S. Senator. It's OK to say it. I've been thinking about it for almost two weeks now. Funny, but you're the first person that actually brought it up directly."

"But it looks like he is willing to sell you back to us. Why else am I here? And why else hasn't he told the world that he's got you?"

"That's easy to answer, I think. Because that would make it much harder for our side to get a ransom deal done? After all, to quote the President of the United States, 'We don't negotiate with terrorists!'"

And then he said something very strange.

"I'm not sure who the terrorists are any more. Us or them."

"Slater, I know war is hell and all that. And I know that you've seen stuff in Iraq and –"

"You were there. In Desert Storm. You saw what we did. They had kids cowering in trenches with bolt-action rifles. We used armored bulldozers and just filled in the trenches ... buried the kids. Panicked soldiers, some of them in caravans of pickup trucks. Others on foot. No formations. Just running to get out of Kuwait and throwing their weapons away so they could run faster. We machine gunned them from helicopters hovering fifty feet over the roadway."

He was inside his own head, seeing images. "It wasn't war. It was slaughter."

"Slater, I think –"

"But at least we were killing soldiers, men with uniforms that wanted to kill us. Then Bush came up with the idea of a "preemptive war" and it got worse, much worse. More personal. IEDs, snipers, booby traps, suicide vests in crowded markets, torture. Prisoners executed.

"I was a young second lieutenant, but I was older than the kids in my platoon. None of us wanted to accidentally shoot a civilian. But that changed after our first IED took out three of the kids. They were nineteen years old. We had to hose them out of the Humvee. It changed the rest of us. Not in a good way."

He stopped and looking directly at Kaz, as if challenging him to see all the ways he had changed for the worse.

"We've been fighting in Afghanistan for fourteen years now. For what?"

Kaz started to protest, but stopped when Slater pulled an iPhone from inside his tunic, partially smeared with a reddish mud. He tapped a couple of buttons and handed it to him.

"Here. Watch this. Then tell me why we're here."

The Patrol

Kaz watched the video and listened to the recorded sounds. He handed the cell phone back to Slater. Neither of them said anything. Then Slater began talking.

I told Ali, "I'll take care of this." The trouble is, I didn't know how I could do that.

Take it up the chain of command? Tell Dalkie? He's got the same problem I do. They're not his troops. All we can do is pass it on to the Afghan commander. And he's an Uzbek who hates the Pashtun and will cover for the fuckers that did this.

There were eight of them. I could identify five of them from Gholam's video. All of them were from Abad's company and he had to know about this. Shit! He was probably one of the eight, giving the orders.

The night recon was already scheduled for that night. I gave Abad the five names and said I wanted them specifically for the patrol. That made him very nervous, but he didn't ask "why?" I figured he knew why. I also figured that my chance of surviving the patrol went to zero when he heard my list of names.

According to some dumbass officer that's never left Kabul, our post is designated a "secure area." That's bullshit, but the good news is that it means that the troops check their weapons when they're not out in the field. We give them M16's. They're not as good as our M4's, but still a good weapon.

Thirty minutes before we left, I went to the armory and stuck a small piece of duct tape on the top of the thirty-round magazine in each of their weapons. Pull the trigger and you'd get an instant jam.

We assembled at the front of the police station. They drew their weapons from the armory and I made a show of inspecting a couple of them, including pulling the magazine and snapping it back in. I briefed them on the route and the objectives – standard stuff – and Abad helped out when my combination of Pashto, Arabic and Uzbek vocabulary wasn't good enough. They were nervous, but not in the usual way. And

I think I knew why – they'd already gotten the real briefing from Abad.

We moved out in the usual order. Three guys on each side of the street, checking windows and rooftops as we moved. I brought up the rear, where we could see the whole scene and I could advise Abad on tactics. Not much real drama. We hadn't drawn any fire within the town for a month or more.

I figured I was safe until we got to the bridge. It was the furthest point, out-of-sight of the town, and by far the logical choice for a Taliban ambush. If you wanted a plausible story to explain how the captain got killed, the bridge was the place.

The dirt track sloped gently downward the last quarter of a mile to the stone bridge and offered no cover. The bridge itself was only about sixty or seventy feet long, without any side railings. It crossed a small stream about fifteen feet below its flat stone surface. The opposite bank was covered with head-high brush that could have concealed a hundred mujahedeen. It didn't matter whether it was bright daylight or a moonless night. We never covered that quarter mile without shriveling up in anticipation of the first shot.

I kept Abad close to me and we stayed behind the five others moving in single file. They walked slower and looked back at us several times as we covered the last hundred yards. As infantry tactics go, it sucked. We were all watching each other rather than the perimeter vectors. It was bright moonlight and we weren't using the night vision gear yet.

When the first soldier was a few yards from the entrance to the bridge, I ordered, "Take a break" in Uzbek. I stopped and Abad continued the few steps to join the others. They huddled and Abad said something I couldn't hear. They spread out into a ragged line facing me. The six rifles were more or less pointed in my direction, but still slanted downward.

Abad's nervousness was gone, replaced by a look of pure hatred and something else. Satisfaction, or maybe even joy. Whatever it was, I knew then that he had been at the massacre. That he had given the order that started the shooting. That he was looking forward to killing me.

"Abad," I said. "Do you know why I'm here? Why I selected you and these men for this patrol?"

I had practiced the Uzbek phrases over and over. It became almost a mantra for me as I thought about my promise to Ali – "I will take care of this."

Abad stared at me, gradually realizing that I was not behaving according to his script.

I said, "Pashtunwali."

The man on the left was the first to react, crouching and raising his rifle. I shot him and the one next to him in the face. By then, the other three were jerking about, cursing at their rifle that wouldn't fire, so I put short bursts into the head and neck. Their body armor was hand-me-down crap, but at that range, it didn't require much marksmanship. That left Abad, but he was already halfway across the bridge, running as fast as he could. It was an easy shot in the moonlight and I took my time, wanting him to feel a little bit of what the villagers must have felt while they stood waiting for the bullets to find them.

But then Abad was amid vague shapes that suddenly filled the far end of the bridge. And other shapes – men with rifles – were around me. They'd been waiting under the bridge and on the other bank.

We'd walked into a classic Taliban ambush, the kind where you leave bodies behind. But they didn't have to fire a single shot. Because I did it for them.

Slater stopped talking and just sat there with an unfocused gaze.

Kaz was silent, not knowing how to respond. He wondered if Slater was Catholic… whether his narrative was a necessary step in some strange quest for understanding if not forgiveness.

Slater sat upright, coming back to the present. He was smiling.

"They think they're rescuing a hero. Won't they be surprised when they find that they've gotten a war criminal, a murderer who kills his own people?

Two Old Men

Above them, the banker stood at the second-floor window, looking down at Kaz and Slater sitting in the courtyard below. He shook his head.

"I'm old and I thought I was beyond surprise. But what has happened in the last two weeks…"

Malik came and stood beside him. "Trust Allah, Abdul-Karim. Your surprise is only insufficient belief."

"You are not my imam, Malik." It was a gentle rebuke.

Malik took a full step back and bowed slightly. "I apologize, old friend. I have become pompous. It comes from being old among all these younger and more impatient people. I find myself constantly cautioning them, reminding them that it is a long war and that our enemies are resourceful and determined."

He gestured at the two men below them. "And you are right. This has the potential to change everything."

Abdul-Karim smiled. "The son of a U.S. senator and his American friend, a prominent banker who happens to have a hundred million dollars to disburse. And a video of Afghan soldiers killing unarmed villagers and then raping their daughters. And then a story about the deranged American who kills his own comrades. So many gifts for us!"

Malik shook his head. "But we cannot have all of those gifts. We must choose some and give up others. Would you rather have money or vengeance? Massive outrage or quiet victories? I think it will be a difficult choice."

And it is not entirely our choice to make. Those two men talking so earnestly together … each of them with their own conflicts to be traded off. A soldier who kills his own men. A civilian who doesn't even know why he's here.

And our enemies. What do they want? The senator wants his war, but he also wants his son back. Or does he? Does a man who killed hundreds at Cham Kasi have normal feelings about his own child? Does he have his Seals and

Rangers planning the raid even now? Does he even want this never-ending war to actually end?

Then there are our "friends." Their preferences are not the same as ours. The fanatics want to behead Slater Crosby and draw the Americans back into this ongoing Armageddon. They no longer care about Afghanistan or money.

Abdul-Karim was looking at him with a troubled expression, as though reading his thoughts. His next words confirmed it.

"And you, Malik? What do you want?"

And me? What do I want? Pashtunwali? A woman in a green silk dress?

Harlan - Kabul

I've been here before. The feeling was very strong as Harlan slowly walked through the sparsely furnished rooms of the CIA safe house. The final confirmation was the door into the kitchen, covered with brightly painted tiles on both sides.

Can't be much of a safe house, in use for fifteen years.

Then the memories came flooding back.

October 2001. Begging and buying. Trying to line up the Northern Alliance tribes to take on the Taliban for us.

Cham Kasi.

It had been a mistake. A show-off stunt for his own ego satisfaction. But then so many mistakes were made in the immediate aftermath of nine-eleven. All the cowboys were let loose as the CIA tried to make up for their massive intelligence failures by trading on the reality that they were the only ones that knew anything about the tribal factions around Osama bin Laden and the Taliban government.

And Oliver was the go-to source! He'd been in-country for six months and knew more about the real players than anybody else. He told Harlan, "Get Malik on your side. The other Pashtun will follow his example." And when Malik stiffed him, it was Ollie that "suggested" a way to make an example of him.

It was easy. We had all this air power sitting around looking for something to bomb or strafe, no questions asked. But we had nobody on the ground to tell the hotshot pilots where the bad guys were. Except the CIA types. So when Ollie asked for a couple of F-15's and helicopter gunships for a sortie against a Taliban hotspot, it didn't take layers of approval. And it was Ollie that showed him the photos and estimated the body count.

Later, when he was CIA Director, he personally oversaw the destruction or modification of the field reports generated during that time. His own "recruiting" efforts and the village of Cham Kasi were as extinct in CIA files as the eroding ruins in the shallow river valley deep within the mountains … the mountains that could not protect the village from attackers who came from the air.

He was tired. They'd left Washington at midnight and he'd been planning to sleep on the plane. But two related and unexpected conversations had kept him awake long after they had ended.

He and Madge were the sole passengers on a G4 that belonged to a very patriotic and elderly gentleman farmer in Utah. He was also a retired Marine Corps brigadier general who made a very nice living serving on boards of several defense contractors when he left the Corps. The plane came in handy for unofficial trips, the kind where somebody needed to be someplace without anyone else knowing of it.

Harlan was surprised to find the plane's owner waiting for him on the plane, sitting on the tarmac at Reagan Airport.

"Nice to see you, Buell. But –"

"Don't worry. I'm getting off here. I hate this goddam city, but I've got some unpleasant people that I have to see. I've told the pilot that you're the man. He'll take you where you want to go and bring you back."

"Thanks, as always."

Buell looked at Madge and then at Harlan with a quizzical expression.

Harlan nodded in the direction of the cockpit. "Madge, why don't you get acquainted with our pilot. Give him some idea of where we're going and a rough timetable."

She nodded and went into the flight deck, closing the door behind her.

"You know who I represent?" Buell asked in a way that signaled it was not really a question.

Harlan nodded. *The military-industrial complex that Eisenhower warned us about. It's quite real. And Buell's their point man for the moment. And they think I'm their patsy. That a few million bucks of political donations buys them access.*

Which it does. And maybe more.

The old man leaned forward, intense. "Harlan, you've seen this from all sides – military, CIA, family, now political. You know the territory better than anyone in this goddam city. We've spent trillions of dollars and thousands of lives getting to this point, and now *they* want to walk away and hand it to Iran and a bunch of seventh-century jihadist fanatics!"

He pronounced *they* with so much bitterness that – for Harlan -- the word symbolized everything that was wrong with what Buell called "this goddam city." Its contempt, racism, polarization ... a provincialism that was as ingrained here as it was among the jihadists that Buell ranted about.

This is not why he's here. We're both far beyond drinking that particular Kool-Aid. He has something specific he needs to tell me.

"Buell. I'm on your side. But we're swimming upstream for the moment. The public is tired of –"

"What if there was another 911? Another terrorist extravaganza that would outrage every American?"

Harlan shook his head. "They've already tried genocide, public executions by beheading, burning, stoning. Mass killings in museums, shopping malls and airports. No end of outrage. But we're still committed to withdrawal, other than a training mission and a few Special Ops types."

Buell hunched forward and motioned for him to come closer. He actually began to whisper.

"You know that some of those people you call 'Special Ops' are contractors. They work for people like you and me."

Oh, oh. I think I know where this is going. And I don't like it.

"I got a call this morning. Can't tell you from who or how he got the info. But there's a rumor going round in raghead circles that the Taliban have what this guy referred to as 'a prominent American' lined up for their next YouTube spectacular."

Harlan focused on keeping his voice skeptical. "C'mon, Buell. Fourth-hand rumors from mercenaries?"

Buell stood up, shaking his head. "I think it's good intel. And I suggest two things you need to think about while you're flying to wherever you're going."

Harlan tried to keep his expression neutral.

"First, take an inventory. Who's missing? And second, be grateful if it's true. This would bring us back into the game. Where we need to be!"

"Buell, are you suggesting –"

"I'm suggesting nothing. But I read in the New York Times that these new crazies want to restore a seventh-century caliphate. I'd be happy to help them. Just give me an excuse to bomb them back to the seventh century!"

He waved and headed for the stairway onto the tarmac. "Have a good flight."

Harlan watched him leave, but his mind was replaying what the man had said.

He knows. And I know how he found out. It's time to have a serious talk with Ollie about his priorities.

The other conversation was a call from Yasmin just after they'd lifted off from Spain. But what she said didn't make sense.

"They want a hundred million dollars."

Then it did. He remembered the photo and video. *They're communicating through Yasmin's personal email. Makes sense. Minimizes the chance of discovery ... until they want to go public.*

"Yasmin. Don't forward anything to anybody. Just tell me what the email says."

"It says, 'One hundred million dollars for Slater.'"

"That's all?"

"No. He asked for your personal phone number. Your cell. And I gave it to him."

"Him?"

"He signed the email 'Malik.'"

The single word "Malik" jarred Harlan. *It's a common Afghani name. Just coincidence.*

But what was definitely not a coincidence was that 'Malik" was the name of the tribal leader and Taliban sympathizer that ruled the countryside around Achin Adi, where Slater was operating.

Yasmin repeated something. Her voice was different, not what he was used to.

"Harlan?"

"Yes, I'm here."

"Pay him."

"I'm not sure I can. I –"

"Harlan. Pay him. You'll find a way." And she disconnected.

Oliver showed up an hour after he got to the house. He laughed when Harlan said, "Not much of a safe house after fifteen years, is it?"

"The Agency hasn't used it for years. I kind of took it off their hands when they decided that I should retire. They said that I had ... how did they phrase it ... 'a tendency to go rogue.' Funny, how I seem to be OK as a contractor."

"We've gotten a ransom demand. A hundred million."

Ollie whistled softly. "A record, I think. Although I seem to recall that the Somalis once asked a hundred million for one of the supertankers that they nabbed."

The callousness jarred Harlan. *We're talking about my son.* But the comment served a purpose: it reminded him that he was dealing with a sociopath, a man without feelings. That could be quite useful. It also reminded him that major geopolitical forces were in play; that the life of one man – even an important one – might not matter very much. He remembered Buell saying, "Just give me an excuse to bomb them back into the seventh century."

Ollie asked, equally casually, "Will you pay it?"

He surprised himself by answering honestly. "I don't know. We haven't heard any of the details yet, so there's a lot we don't know."

Will I pay it? Such a cynical question to ask a father facing a ransom demand for his only son. And my response ... cynicism squared!

He motioned Ollie to one of the two chairs in the barren room. "I need options. What have you got?"

"I assume you mean military assets?"

"Yes, but I'm not interested in your tribal militias or local gangs. Just professionals."

"I've got four three-man teams scattered around. Give me twelve hours and I can have them in one place, fully equipped and ready to go. Ex-rangers, some SAS, everybody with Special Ops experience in the back-country."

"Transport?"

"Humvees – old ones. A couple of Hueys if we need them. Old but very reliable."

"What about intel?"

Ollie didn't answer. Just looked at Harlan with an expression that somehow reminded him of a political donor that he'd just asked for a million dollars for his campaign.

"Ollie. Intel?"

"Better than yours, apparently."

So he knows something I don't. I wouldn't be surprised. I've got the latest and greatest multi-billion dollar satellites and hundreds of geeky Ph.D.'s with computer algorithms sifting billions of phone calls out of the ether. But he's got goat-herders and truck drivers on the ground. No contest there.

Harlan just looked at him until Ollie shrugged and said, "OK. I've got something. But I don't think you're going to like it much."

The Kaz Wrinkle

"I don't think you're going to like it much."

Harlan was not used to hearing that introduction from a subordinate. One of the problems with being first a general officer and then the CIA Director was that it was difficult to get objective advice. To his credit, he recognized that a large part of it was his fault, stemming from his need to intimidate. He knew it to be a personal weakness, but found the habit hard to break.

But Ollie is different. First, he can't be intimidated and, second, I need to know what he knows.

So he adapted. "Ollie, whether I like it or not won't change whatever it is you know. Just tell me."

"OK. There are two new developments. We know that the group holding Slater is headed by this guy named 'Malik.' The not-so-surprising new development is that our old friend Mullah Omar is pushing Malik to hand him over to his team. There are rumors he tried to take him by force two nights ago."

"This Omar, he's –"

"Yep. He's the Mullah Omar we've been chasing since 2001, from Tora Bora on."

"Do we care which one we end up negotiating with – Malik or Omar?"

"Malik is an unknown. But he doesn't seem to be a real fan of the hard-core Taliban. We're guessing that he could be swayed by money. Omar is definitely a fanatic. I'm not even sure he'd be interested in a mega-ransom. It's a pretty easy choice ... if we get to choose."

"You said 'two new developments.' What's the other one? The more surprising one ..."

"In your proverbial nutshell ... the other side is playing Zanker the same way we are. They're going after his hundred million for their own set of projects."

Harlan sat motionless, waiting for the surprise to dissipate so that he could think about it properly.

He's right. I don't like it. It changes the entire game.

"How good is your information?"

"I have what you would call a "very highly placed source" in the office of an Afghan official in their Ministry of Finance. He works for a bureaucrat named Durani –"

Harlan interrupted. "I know the name. Isn't he the gofer who's collecting all of the paperwork for the FARD projects?"

Ollie nodded. "More than a gofer. He's the first filter in the chain of approvals. He's received thirty-nine proposals and has recommended thirteen of them for consideration by Zanker. All five of our projects are in the set of thirteen."

"How did you manage that?"

"As I said, a highly placed source …"

Harlan shrugged. "So? What's the problem? Isn't that what we want?"

"The problem is the other eight projects. My source says that at least four or five of those are outright Taliban fronts and that Durani's job was to be very sure that they were included in the final cut."

Harlan leaned back and thought about it. *Not so surprising. That hundred million bucks and the fast-track approval process outside of ARTF control would look like the honey pot for them … just as it does for us.*

"So they have the same problem we do. The beauty contest. How to get Zanker to pick the right girls. What does your highly placed source say about that?"

"Can't help you there. Clearly, they've got some kind of leverage in mind. I don't think they've made any approach to him yet. As far as we can tell, all Zanker thinks so far is that he's representing our financial interests in a hostage negotiation. I don't think he's made the connection to the "

OK, Plan A is off the table. Getting Zanker to route the hundred million to our set of pet projects, "or else," won't work if the other side has its own list of projects and what Ollie calls 'leverage.' Unless we have even more of it.

To his own surprise Harlan felt a twinge of sympathy for the man. *Poor bastard! A competent and apparently honest man who's going to be forced to choose one of two equally corrupt options. And both sides have really nasty consequences if he doesn't do what they want.*

But does it matter? If the objective is to use the hundred million as ransom, then Malik winds up with it rather than our side regardless of which projects are on the end list.

Ollie sat quietly, watching Crosby think about options and counter-options. *He wants it his way. The money, the projects, his son, NATO troops back in the field ... The man just doesn't like to lose.*

"Zanker's here? In Kabul?" Harlan asked.

"Yes. Touring the final set of projects." *And happily screwing a gorgeous woman in his spare time!* "I've got someone watching him."

Ollie's cell phone rang. He picked it up, glanced at the caller ID and answered, "Yes?" He listened for twenty seconds and hung up without saying anything more.

He looked at Harlan with a speculative expression. "We've got some moving parts."

Harlan raised an eyebrow.

"They've picked up Zanker. We've had him cooling his heels in Kabul. Yesterday morning, two tough-looking Afghans escorted him into an SUV."

"And the SUV went where?"

"It started north, on the Kunduz highway. But we lost it two hours later."

Harlan fixed Ollie with a stare that he had practiced thousands of times on junior officers. Ollie merely looked back at him with an indifferent expression.

"You're right," Harlan said.

When Ollie raised an eyebrow, Harlan said, "About your so-called intel. I don't like it vey much."

Camille & Derek (Kabul)

Kaz had told her, "I've got to meet someone downstairs. I'll be right back."

But it wasn't Kaz that came back to their Kabul hotel room. It was Derek Williams and a local type that she had never seen before. Derek pulled her aside, over by the windows, while the other man began throwing Kaz's clothes into the still partially packed roller bag sitting open on the credenza.

"Derek. What are you doing here? I was just talking with you … I thought you were …" And she showed him her cell phone, still in her hand.

"I was downstairs. Things are moving a little fast right now. In fact, we need to go. Get dressed."

She moved to the closet, her mind racing. *I said, 'we may have a problem.' And he's here in my room three minutes later. What is there that I'm missing about this scene?*

He was standing alongside her, looking at the few items hanging in the closet. "Wear something sexy. We're going to need you to look your best."

"Sexy? In Kabul? I don't think so. Derek, what the hell is going on?"

"Here. This should work." He pulled a pair of black slacks and a bright orange silk blouse from the hangers. The blouse was designed for cleavage. She started to protest, but cut it off when he handed her the all-purpose hooded caftan garment that she used when traveling in Muslim territory.

"You can cover up with this when we're out on the streets. And pack what you need for two or three days. We're going to be on the move for a bit."

She heard the door close behind the man with all of Kaz's things thrown into his suitcase.

Ten minutes later, the two of them left the hotel through the side door. An SUV with a driver was waiting. But when he held the rear door open for her, she stopped. She pushed the door closed and stood facing Derek.

"No more. I'm not getting in this vehicle until you tell me what's going on."

He reached for the door and put his hand on her arm. She shook it off and took two steps backward. "Derek. I mean it. Not until I know where we're going and what we're doing."

He stood and looked at her, the door half open and the driver looking at him, waiting for an order. *Well, you knew this would come. She's smart and independent. And she may not even know it yet, but she's got a thing going with Zanker. It shows.*

"CC. Get in the vehicle. I'll tell you everything, but we need to move."

She glared at him, unmoving. After twenty seconds of the standoff, he sighed and said, "We're going to the same place as Zanker. He'll need you there."

As soon as they were moving, she turned to him and said, "I'm listening."

OK. The best lies are the ones that stay close to the truth.

"It's pretty straightforward. Our firm is retained by the Islamic Republic of Afghanistan to look out for their interests in the U.S. Essentially, for their purposes we're a lobbyist disguised as an economics think tank. This reconstruction grant that Zanker is working on is enormously important to them and they've asked us to help keep it on track. That's where you come in. You're –"

"A lousy spy."

Why so bitter? You've known this since Day One. It doesn't take a genius to figure out your role in this whole sordid business.

Derek tried to look sympathetic. "It got a little too personal. I know that. That's my fault, and I'm sorry. But we're almost done and Zanker is in the dark about us ... and your assignment. A few more days and all the cloak-and-dagger stuff will be over. The two of you can go off into the sunset together, hand-in-hand."

"So where are we going?"

"Near the Pakistan border. It'll take several hours."

"And what am I supposed to do when we get there?"

"Hopefully, nothing. We're reserving you as our last and most persuasive resort. But I promise you that you won't be asked to do anything that is not in your own best interest."

She reclined her seat and turned her head to the window, watching the Kabul street scene unwind before her. She mistrusted happy endings as much as she did Derek Williams. But, for the moment, she had no choice.

Derek pulled some papers from the briefcase at his feet and pretended to study them. But he was replaying what he had said after her "I'm listening" mandate.

Only one real lie. And one slight – well, not so slight really – distortion. All the rest was true.

Photoshopped

The video reminded Kaz of a very bad home movie, filmed in poor light with a single camera in a fixed position, the kind of thing that was the mainstay of the reality cop shows. It featured two men in an office, filmed from directly behind the unidentifiable man sitting at the desk with his back to the camera so that the other man – Kaz – was the center of attention. That effect was enhanced by the way the film was edited so as to blur both the foreground and background, leaving Kaz in sharp relief.

Abdul-Karim's office in Dubai. Ten days ago. What the hell?

Onscreen, the man at the desk spoke; but his voice was disguised by some kind of digital tweaking. No way they were going to identify Abdul-Karim.

"I'm bothered by some rules."

Kaz heard himself reply – his voice, his words. But not all of his words. Just the ones that the editor chose to leave in. He sat back and watched with increasing horror.

He listened to his on-screen version say, "Yes. Rules can be a nuisance."

The blurry man with the distorted voice went on. "Your Foreign Corrupt Practices Act, your money laundering requirements, your sanctions against so many countries for so many reasons! I was wondering if there was any way that you could make it easier for us?"

"I'm sympathetic. I really am. I can make them go away."

"There's just too much risk. I'm hoping that all of these adjustments can be managed without a lot of fuss? Even if they do run into all those "rules" that seem so essential to people in Washington and London …"

"That's easy. Those rules are just guidelines. I have lots of discretion to interpret them in ways that make life easier for the customer. You do what's called for in Syria and Yemen and I'll make sure the bank goes along."

He watched the man in the film hand the package across the desk to his onscreen image, saying, "You have been a good friend to us. This is to indicate how much we value your friendship."

The video froze on the final screen, with Kaz reaching across the desk to accept the package that was exactly the size and shape of a bundle of currency. The expression on his face was one of obvious pleasure.

Malik closed the laptop and looked at Kaz. He actually looked sympathetic, in the manner of a friend playing a practical joke that had gone slightly too far.

There was a long silence. Kaz was remembering the actual meeting with Abdul-Karim. He was surprised by his lack of outrage at what they had done. The sadness was pervasive.

He said, "You got that from –"

"Does it matter where we got it?"

"No. I suppose not."

Then the obvious thought occurred to him. "But why? What is it that you're blackmailing me to do?"

"You have a hundred million dollars to distribute. We want you to give it to us."

"It's not my … I can't just give it to you … What – "

Malik handed him a half sheet of paper. "Here are five projects that are deserving of such reconstruction funds, with suggested amounts for each."

Kaz looked at the list, remembering how the projects seemed so small and vaguely anti-government. Despite himself, he felt a stirring of admiration for such an elaborate scheme.

He shook his head. "It won't work. There are other people in the chain –"

"Yes. A Dr. Obani at the World Bank and a Mr. Durani in the Afghan Ministry of Finance. They have agreed to endorse whatever allocation of funds that you propose."

Kaz's disbelief was quite obvious.

"They are not like you," Malik said. "They can be corrupted by mere money. Although they would say that they do it for their faith, for jihad, that the money is 'to cover expenses.'"

Kaz surprised himself by asking, "Why should I do this? My reputation will be ruined anyway if I dole out money to fake projects."

"They are not fake projects. The Taliban are serious about governing. Even more than our so-called 'government.' I promise you that they will do what they are promising, even if some of the money is diverted to, shall we say, more revolutionary purposes. Five years from now, your FARD program will be deemed visionary."

Maybe. Maybe not.

Another thought startled him. *Abdul-Karim is in on the swindle. That damn video is part of it, but maybe there's more. They could just take the $100 million as soon as it's deposited in his Kabul branch. But if they do that, his bank goes belly up and he's on the run. Seems unlikely.*

Malik broke into his thoughts. "And there's one other benefit. One that I hope will be persuasive."

Kaz waited.

"The money shall serve as ransom for Slater Crosby. You and he can leave together."

Kaz's expression was part exasperation, part puzzlement. "But then, why did you –"

"Alter the video of you and Abdul-Karim?"

Kaz nodded. "You don't need it. You had Crosby. And you already knew that my objective was to get him released by paying a big ransom."

"Because we acquired Captain Crosby – by accident -- long after we had been planning our $100 million swindle. We needed some leverage over you and that seemed the easiest course to follow. Then when Crosby came along, we knew we could use him to convince you to give us the money."

But you could have had both. Blackmail me into giving you the money and keep Crosby for some terrorist decapitation video. Or ransom him in a separate transaction.

Nothing made sense. Rather, all of the individual pieces made sense, but they didn't fit together.

That explains Ollie's approach to me in London. They foresaw that they could reroute the FARD money so as to pay a hefty ransom. They couldn't tell me that – I would have refused – so they made up a need for a negotiator.

For the first time in his life, Kaz felt truly insignificant.

Pashtun Options

"Mullah Omar is here."

Abdullah stood just outside the doorway, as if to distance himself from his announcement. He knew quite well that it was not good news.

Malik was not surprised. "So he's decided to come in person rather than send another raiding party disguised as CIA contractors ..."

Abdullah looked puzzled. "Uncle, I don't –"

"Never mind. It is not important."

I wonder who it is that keeps the Mullah informed? What the Americans call a snitch. Omar knows we have Crosby, where we were keeping him, and where we are at any particular time. There has to be someone in our party that belongs to him. This complicates things.

Characteristically, he did not bother to pursue the question with Abdullah or even in his own mind. It would have been surprising if Omar did *not* have someone feeding him info. There were so many overlapping families and political factions within the Pashtun society that loyalty to a single cause or person was difficult to gauge, particularly if that person – like Malik – was trying hard to remain disengaged from all sides of the long-running insurgency.

"How many men are with him?"

"Six. That was the agreement. The same as for us."

"Weapons?"

"Checked and under my control. Those are the rules."

"Put them in the same wing. We need to be reminded that we are all Pashtun."

Abdullah took a step into the room. "But they –"

Malik raised his hand. "Give me five minutes. Then ask Omar to visit me here, in this room."

Abdullah turned to leave, but Malik said, "And, Abdullah ... keep Crosby and Zanker in their rooms. It would not be good for them to be seen while Omar is here." *Although he probably already knows that they are here ... and why.*

Malik remained seated. The late afternoon sun bisected the room, creating well-defined zones of light and darkness.

A suitable setting. One of those times where the choices are clearly defined. But how to make that choice? And if I can't even decide for myself, how can I hope to convince Omar?

Omar entered, followed immediately by a servant with an elaborate tea service. He was a tall man, well over six feet, who seemed to be constantly in motion. Even standing still, his hands were fluttering and his feet constantly shifting. His head seemed too large, partly because of the fullness of his beard streaked with gray. He walked with a limp because he lacked three toes on his right foot, thanks to a Russian Colonel with a pair of lawn shears.

Malik stood and they faced each other in silence. Omar bowed slightly, placing his right hand over his heart. Malik did the same. Only another Pashtun would have noticed the very slight hesitation.

So. We shall drink tea and make small talk. We shall ask about each other's families, although most of them are either dead or living in caves or refugee camps. I shall inquire about his health, although he is one of the most wanted 'terrorists' in the world and has no future. We will share what we know of our common acquaintances, even though some of them will have died since we last met.

But he was wrong. As soon as the servant left the room, Omar ignored the tea, leaning back against the cushions and lighting an American cigarette. He did not offer one to Malik.

So. We have become like our enemies. We shall discuss business rather than drink tea and talk of our families.

The thought caused an instant and pervasive depression to come over him. And he knew that he was at a disadvantage, that this man's hardness would overcome his own uncertainty. That he was old and tired of war.

The thought became words. But even as he spoke them, he knew that, in Omar's eyes, he would be displaying weakness and that, in doing so, he would cause Omar to despise him.

But I must try.

"We are old friends, Omar. We were children together. We fought the Russians together, and their Afghan stooges. We have forced the Americans and British to go home. We have watched our family members die."

Omar watched him through the smoke curling between them, seeming to look for motive, or insincerity or some other marker that would tell him how to respond.

"Old friends? Yes. But newer enemies. We do not agree on many things."

"Not enemies. We want the same things. And we are close to getting them."

Omar leaned forward and became quite still. He spoke in tones of reasonableness. "You cannot ransom him. It is the wrong thing to do. And the Americans cannot be seen to negotiate with terrorists."

"I have a way. We will get the money and the Americans will not lose face."

"How much money?"

"One hundred million dollars. All for your cause. I want none of it."

Malik watched his eyes. They told him that Omar thought about it for about three seconds. Then he leaned back in his chair and looked at him as if he was evaluating the sincerity level of a new convert to his cause.

When he spoke, the reasonableness was gone. "You have become one of them. It began when you went off to university in England. You became soft. Content to be left alone. To open a school for girls. To stay in your mountains in comfort. To forgive those who have insulted your religion and your honor."

It is hopeless. I said that "we want the same things." But we don't. He wants Sharia, enforced by Taliban thugs. A perpetual dark ages with the mullahs and imams as our moral leaders. He is wrong. But his extremism gives him strength. Doubt makes one tired, open to compromise.

He sighed, "What do you want, Omar?"

"Crosby, of course. He is a gift from Allah."

"I agree. But for what purpose? Such gifts are rare, not to be wasted."

Omar stared, his scorn barely hidden. Malik wasn't sure if he would even bother to respond.

"Shock and awe, Malik. Shock and awe. The Americans think it comes from columns of tanks, cruise missiles and stealth bombers. They shall learn of it from watching the torture and execution of one man. One insignificant man who happens to be a symbol for American power. Like their pretentious 'twin towers'!"

So. We need no longer speak in riddles. As the Americans say, the cards are on the table.

When Malik spoke, his voice was different. The weariness was gone, along with the talk of 'old friends' and the conciliatory tones. "Two days ago, a Pashtun raiding party tried to kidnap and then kill a guest in my home. They were pretending to be American Special Ops forces on a rescue mission. I think you know them, Omar."

Omar did not even pretend. "They would have taken Crosby. If you had not interfered. You have become an enemy to jihad!"

Time to end this.

"You can't have him. He is mine."

Omar's expression did not change. He leaned forward and very gently dropped his cigarette into his untouched tea. Then he stood and stared down at him. Again, he seemed to be looking for cues.

"We shall see."

And he left.

Mujahedeen Reflections

Abdullah entered the room as Omar was leaving. He stood silently near the door. Malik sat in the late afternoon shadows, replaying their conversation, as well as what was not said between them. Finally, he sighed. "Watch him closely. I think he and his men will leave shortly. Let me know when they do."

Abdullah did not leave, but stood looking at Malik with concern. He spoke softly with a questioning note, "We have come a long way. This business with Crosby... Perhaps it would be best if –"

"Come a long way?" Malik's tone surprised both of them with its sharpness. "Really? I started out when I was your age, fighting against our own government because they were greedy and corrupt. And now, forty years later, we are still fighting our own government because they are greedy and corrupt. And along the way, we have lost brothers, wives, children, and turned against other Pashtun! And you say, 'We have come a long way!'"

The onrush of bitterness surprised him and left him feeling exhausted. He waved his hand at his nephew. "Go! It is not your fault. Leave me alone to reflect on how far we have come."

Abdullah stood, clearly wanting to say more. The ten seconds of silence before he turned and left the room was an eloquent expression of his concern.

Is Omar right? Have I become soft?

No, not soft, just empty. I can no longer want what he wants – revenge, a pure Islam, Pashtunwali, a sense of honor derived from blood and arrogance. That lack of wanting makes me weak, and he can see that.

The English and Americans are right about many things. One of them is their infuriating belief that exposure to their societies will make us want to be like them. Not just desire to have what they have, but to share their values ... to become "civilized" in ways that require us to reject what we once were.

For the first time in years, he thought of his father on the rooftop in Ankara in 1973, saying, "There will always be fighting in Afghanistan. It's what we do."

Four days later, he was dead. And when he died, I was in bed with Yasmin, with her injured shoulder and the green silk dress lying on the floor. Dishonoring my religion and everything that I once thought was important. But it seemed so right, so inevitable. Then I deserted her too. Brave enough to fight Russian Spetznaz but too cowardly to tell her that I was leaving.

So a boy named Ali goes home again, to a country that didn't want him and that he no longer knew how to fit into. But there was fighting, and he discovered that he was good at it. And, much more importantly, that he reveled in the violence and anarchy; in a place where strength of will counted for more than blood lines or education or what your name was.

So Ali became 'Khalid' and a leader of men and a reconstituted Muslim with a wife and son that he sacrificed to a Russian gunship for the sake of his personal jihad against himself. A son that I intended to send off to English schools as soon as he was old enough.

If I had not gone to Istanbul in 1980 ...? I probably would have become another Omar, relentless and pure. A walking container of rage. No one and certainly not me could have foreseen what would happen to me. And the American Stinger missiles that were my reason for going did turn the tide against the Soviet helicopters. Perhaps even killing the one who murdered my wife and son as they sat eating their ice cream and laughing.

But Allah ordains all things. So, incredibly, Yasmin was there, in Istanbul, now the unhappy wife of Harlan Crosby, with her own memories of that green silk dress and three days that should never have been. This time, there was no talk of marriage or the future. Neither of us believed that we had a future. We made love frantically. And I returned her to her husband, another cowardly act.

But Afghanistan is a good place for a man who is lonely and bitter, angry about his fate and wanting things that he cannot have. The landscape absorbs such feelings and the fighting offers an alternative that is strangely comforting. There were Russians to kill and then the Taliban. So 'Khalid' becomes

'Malik,' a feared and reclusive warlord whose only loyalty is to his own people.

Then the world shifts once again. A small group of ordinary-looking young men armed with box cutters and a mandate from an obscure fanatic named Osama bin Laden carry out the most dramatic act of 'irregular warfare' ever conceived. The horrified Americans lash out – and Afghanistan is their first target.

I do not care about bin Laden and I am content to let the Taliban govern Kabul as long as they leave my people and me alone in our mountains. But Allah moves in mysterious ways. He sent Harlan Crosby to me once again. The Americans are not like Afghans – they delegate their wars to others. And as my father told me, "fighting is what we do." So the CIA and the war planners come to us with their suitcases filled with cash and false promises of what they will do for us. Another fifteen years of war, mostly Afghans killing other Afghans.

I should have seen what was coming. Crosby even told me, "You know, don't you, that there is no such thing as 'neutrality' in what's coming? That you are either for us or against us? That Cham Kasi is in a war zone whether it wants to be or not?"

So Harlan Crosby gets his revenge for what Yasmin and I did to him in Istanbul twenty years ago. His honor is reclaimed. Cham Kasi and hundreds of my friends and relatives are taken as reparations for those three days of frantic lovemaking.

I wonder if he knew who I was or what we had done to him? No matter. All is ordained.

But to what end? Why has Allah given me Yasmin's son? And what shall I do with him?

Ransom Details

Harlan's cell phone rang at four in the afternoon in the Kabul house. The caption said "private caller." He put it on speakerphone so that Madge could listen.

"This is Harlan Crosby."

"My name is Malik. I have your son."

"I've been expecting your call. But there is something I need to know before you tell me what you expect from me."

"I *expect* nothing from you except your compliance. What is it that you think you need to know?"

"It's a simple question. Have we met before? Should I know you?"

"We met in Istanbul a long time ago. And again in Masan-Sharif, more recently."

There was a silence on both ends of the call, finally broken by Harlan.

"What do you want?"

"One hundred million dollars.... and your continued silence about this transaction."

"And in return?"

"I shall release Slater Crosby ... and be equally silent about this transaction ... and the aftermath of Masan-Sharif."

"I want –"

"*What you want* is irrelevant. There are no other terms to be negotiated."

"How?"

"You know how. The mechanism for paying us is already established. You will tell your *negotiator* – Zanker – to approve certain projects that we will designate and disburse the $100 million accordingly."

"I cannot control Zanker."

"You are lying. You have made some *arrangements* and you think you can control him. But you cannot. And you do not need to. That is our problem, not yours. What is required of you is silence, both now and after he chooses."

"I need to know that Slater is still alive."

"Of course. I will arrange that immediately after this call."

"And what if I cannot agree to our terms? You know that it is our government's stated policy not to pay ransom to terrorists."

Malik's sarcasm was thick. "Your country will pay billions of dollars to kill a few innocent shepherds thousands of miles from your shores. And yet nothing to save one of your own citizens? The son of an eminent American? I do not understand either your moral or economic reasoning."

Harlan did not bother to respond, merely waiting for Malik to say what he already knew.

"Slater Crosby will die in a horrible and public way. And the world will be told of Cham Kasi and of your participation in this negotiation. And we will get the hundred million dollars in another way."

There was silence on the line, as though Crosby was weighing the pros and cons of his various choices.

Malik added, "And he will not die as a war hero. There are things you do not know about your son."

"If you kill him –"

"He will be exposed as a murderer. An officer who killed five of his own men. We have a video and a confession from a certain Captain Abad of the Afghan Army."

There was no response, and the silence told Malik that Crosby was not surprised; that he somehow knew the accusation was true.

"Senator, I know that you want your war. You want your troops to come back. "Boots on the ground!" We both know that. You've lost, but can't admit it. But will you sacrifice your son to that objective?"

Then he ended the call.

Ten minutes later, the cell phone rang again.

"Hello."

"Senator Crosby? This is Kendall Zanker. I've been–"

"Yes, I know who you are. Where are you?"

"I'm not permitted to say. But Malik asked me to call you and verify that Slater is in good health. I saw him and talked to him about an hour ago. He's fine."

"Zanker, I need to know –"

"I'll see you in Kabul tomorrow. At the FARD ceremony."

And the line went dead.

A Starring Role for CC

Kaz hung up the phone under Malik's watchful gaze.

"What now?"

"We wait."

"For …?"

"I do not trust our Senator. I think he will be looking for another alternative."

"Rather than ransom his son?"

Malik considered how much to tell Zanker. *He is an honorable man. And practical. But I do not think this is the right time to disillusion him. It will happen soon enough.*

"He cannot stop fighting his lost war." *And he has other demons that will make this a hard choice for him.*

"In the end, he will do what we ask. It requires nothing of him except his silence."

Kaz's premonitions were queuing up, clamoring for his attention. *It's about time, stupid. Everybody wants a piece of you. And they all have ways of getting even if you're not compliant.*

"Malik, am I at risk? What happens to me if the Senator doesn't cooperate? Or even if he does?"

"You have safe passage. And you are not a captive. You'll be leaving here within the hour, back to Kabul for your grand public ceremony tomorrow. Beyond, that, we need you alive and well to maintain confidence in our newly-funded projects."

"A lot of things could go wrong." *For example, I could refuse to do what you ask.*

"No matter. You are protected by Pashtunwali. There is *melmastia* – hospitality – that says that guests in one's home must be protected. And *nanwatay* – asylum – which must be granted if requested."

Kaz thought, *so reassuring, except for the exceptions.* He said, "But that applies only among Pashtuns, doesn't it?" He spread his arms as if to display a new set of clothing. "As you can see, I am not a Pashtun."

Malik smiled, pleased by this westerner who understood the nuances of tribal law. "Choose the projects that we have listed. And go home to London or San Francisco safely. Slater Crosby will be released and all of Afghanistan will benefit."

Several hours later, Kaz was back in Kabul, in his room at the Intercontinental. They did not blindfold him on the return trip. But it would not have mattered because he was totally focused on his tumbling thoughts, not on the passing scenery.

My meeting with Abdul-Karim in Dubai – the "sting" -- was weeks ago. Long before Slater was taken. So they've been setting this up for months, ever since the FARD grants were announced. So why throw in the release of the single most important hostage they've ever had? Just for more leverage on me?

Even stranger, what was the object of "Ollie's" visit in London? Why would the CIA or Crosby recruit a "negotiator" that they're not going to use? Did they anticipate that Malik's ransom arrangements would involve FARD?

The answer to that question was obvious. And it depressed him. *Because they have their own set of projects they would ask ... tell ... me to approve. But why would I do that? Unless they had their own video or its scary equivalent to hold over my head.*

He'd tried questioning Abdullah during the long drive back to Kabul. His role was apparently to serve as Malik's guarantee of compliance with his end of the hostage release. Abdullah would be released simultaneously with Slater, the assurance that Malik would honor the terms of the arrangement.

Abdullah was quite comfortable with his hostage role. Kaz asked him, "Aren't you a little bit offended to be used as a sacrificial lamb? And why you?"

He was amused by the question. "Why me? Because I am family. The National Directorate of Security will know that Malik values me as highly as he does his own freedom."

I announce the awards. The $100 million is sent to Abdul-Karim's bank and the insurgency gets a large financial injection. Slater and Abdullah are released simultaneously. And the world goes on, unaware of what's just happened.

"Abdullah? There are some things I don't understand–"

"I cannot help you. I do not know any of the details."

"But you are Malik's nephew. And you live in the place where –"

"Yes, but as soon as we get to Kabul, I am also a hostage. Malik would not share information with me if he is sending me into the hands of the Afghan counter-intelligence service."

After a pause, he added, "My uncle is a very complex man. I am like you: I do not understand why he is doing what he is doing."

"Yet you are willing to serve as hostage."

"I do not understand him, but I trust him. We are family. All will be well. En'shallah."

Abdullah handed Kaz his briefcase with his laptop and cell phone when the SUV stopped at the front entrance to the hotel. "Here are your things. If anyone asks, I am in room 2612 and will remain there until everybody is satisfied with the arrangements."

CC was not in the room and there was no note from her. Most of her clothes were still in the closet, so he assumed she would be returning soon. There was a large envelope on the desk that turned out to contain a briefing document for the participants in tomorrow's FARD announcements. He opened it and thumbed through the material. As he expected, it was going to be staged as a major PR effort. TV and other media would be well-represented.

He looked at the one-page agenda. *A brief introduction by the World Bank representative for Afghanistan, then a short speech by President Ashraf Ghani (transcript included) and then I come on and announce the winners and push a prominent "send" command on a keyboard that transmits $100 million into Abdul-Karim's Kabul branch, to be disbursed as soon as the selected projects establish an account.*

What he thought of as "Malik's list" was in his pocket. Of the designated five projects, none were on his own list of winning project proposals. Malik's projects were alike in that they had all submitted project budgets well in excess of their needs. *But they sound plausible, the sort of investments that the country needs.*

What are the optics? Can I do this without looking stupid or – worse – corrupt? I'm covered on the Afghan side of things. Durani and his cronies have enough skin in the game to make sure of that. The IMF and World Bank will grumble about the choices no matter what, but we've kept them at arm's length and everybody that matters will treat their complaining as sour grapes because they've been left out of the process. The U.S. side? The sad truth is that no one much cares. The program will be declared a great success and promptly forgotten.

I could pick five projects at random. It wouldn't matter!

The thought made him tremendously sad.

He opened his laptop to check email. Not surprisingly, given that he'd been off-line for three days, his inbox contained a couple of hundred emails. He scanned the "subject" lines quickly and found one labeled "From CC" that had been sent just twenty minutes earlier. He opened it and saw that it had no text, just a video to be downloaded. He transferred it to his hard drive and then opened the video.

It was just three minutes long, but those minutes were interminable. The opening scene was like a stage set -- a sunlit space, a small courtyard of sorts, completely empty and without any distinguishing features other than a crude wooden door in the wall facing the camera. As he watched, the door opened and two masked tribesmen entered with a third and smaller person between them. The center figure was hooded and obviously struggling against his two captors. He was completely covered by a loose cloak, but his arms and legs were clearly bound, so that the two men had to drag and semi-carry him across the courtyard. They forced him to his knees facing the camera and stood one on either side of him.

Kaz could not turn away.

It's like stumbling across hard-core pornography when you're flipping through the cable channels in a hotel room looking for CNN. I know what's coming and I don't – I really don't – want to see this.

But the subject line on the email, "From CC," and his certainty that this had something to do with Slater Crosby kept him fixated on the stark scene with a growing sense of horror.

The now-familiar executioner came through the door and positioned himself directly behind the kneeling figure. It was the masked and black-clad figure that Kaz expected, complete with the naked blade held close against his chest. The camera operator zoomed in on the blade before panning back to show the entire tableau.

There was no sound, making it seem even more unreal. Then the two men alongside the prisoner moved in unison. One removed the hood with a quick jerk and the other pulled the cloak off of the kneeling figure.

The long blond hair and the startlingly orange blouse leapt out of the monochromatic scene at Kaz. He jerked back from the screen as though struck by a physical blow. The distant street noises stopped, along with his breathing and any sense of his surroundings. He shouted, or perhaps only breathed, the single word "No" and then leaned forward, only inches from the screen to see CC more closely.

As if aware of his need, the camera operator zoomed the lens once more, this time focusing on CC's face. The small screen was filled with her tear-streaked features. Her eyes were enormous, filled with terror and rage and pleading, all at the same time.

Then the screen went dark.

The phone call came five minutes later.

"Mr. Zanker? This is Ollie. We met in your London office."

Of course. Who else? The people that needed a negotiator. And a banker. But they didn't. They only told me one thing that was true: that Slater Crosby had been kidnapped. Now they're going to tell me what they really want.

He did not trust himself to respond and just held the phone, breathing heavily.

"You saw the video?"

"Yes." The single word somehow came through his clenched teeth.

He stopped himself before he could plead with them to let CC go or before he could promise them whatever they wanted, no matter what. *It wouldn't be any use. They've got their own timetable and script and nothing that I can do or say will make them deviate from it.*

"At tomorrow's FARD ceremony, we want you to announce five particular winning projects and corresponding dollar amounts."

"Which ones?"

"We'll tell you just before the ceremony. You don't need to know until then."

"You do know, don't you, that Malik will release Slater Crosby if I select *his* five particular projects? That's his ransom demand. The one that you wanted me to *negotiate*."

Ollie ignored the question. "Perhaps our list and his list will be the same. Then you will not have any conflict. Unless you have your own list, based upon whatever economic criteria you would apply to such a competitive allocation process."

There was a long pause and then he added. "But that would be foolish – to not choose the ones we tell you to choose."

"Are we done?" Kaz tried to put as much contempt into his tone as he could manage.

"Yes, for now. But if you do not do what we ask, then we will reenact the video you just saw. But, next time, there will be a much more dramatic ending. You can watch it on YouTube, along with millions of others."

Arrangements for a Swap

Abdullah stayed in Room 2612 at the Intercontinental Hotel only long enough to place two phone calls. The first was to a journalist for Al Jazeera.

"I am here. Do you know what you have to do?"

"Yes. And what not to do. But I do not like this idea of protecting our enemies."

"Then pray that you don't have to."

The second call was even briefer. "I'm leaving now to call on the Senator."

He walked through the lobby and took the first taxi in the queue in the outside. He gave an address in the suburbs and sat back to observe the passing street scene. He had not been in Kabul since the Northern Alliance had finally chased the Taliban out in late 2001. The changes were substantial and he spent the thirty minutes of travel time trying to decide if they were improvements.

The taxi left him outside a walled villa, one of several on a narrow cul-de-sac. He rang the recessed bell alongside the door and stared serenely up at the camera mounted atop the wall. The door was opened by a man in faded military fatigues who simply stared at him. He was holding a large handgun in his right hand, vaguely pointed in Abdullah's direction

"I am Abdullah, nephew of Malik. I am here to present the details of Slater Crosby's release."

Ollie continued to stare. Finally, he shrugged and stood aside, motioning with the gun for Abdullah to enter. They walked together across the courtyard and into the house. Harlan Crosby was waiting for them in the main room.

"This is Malik's nephew. He says his name is Abdullah and that he wants to discuss how to make the exchange."

Harlan was quite obviously controlling his temper. "Some safe house, Ollie. Apparently, the Taliban is familiar with the address too."

Ollie was patting down Abdullah. When he found nothing, he turned to Harlan. There was a noticeable edge to his voice. "Sloppy of me. I'm getting lazy in my old age. We'll move to another location as soon as we get what we need from Abdullah here."

"What else have you gotten sloppy about?"

"Senator, I don't –"

Abdullah cut them off. "There is no such thing as a 'safe house' in Afghanistan. Your drones have seen to that. We have no drones, but we do have ways – old-fashioned ways -- of finding people and places that are not supposed to be visible. And I am not Taliban. But I am not your friend. And, finally, I am not here to 'discuss' anything. I am here to tell you what Malik expects of you."

Ollie stepped in front of Abdullah, no more than six inches separating them. He said, "Taliban, not Taliban. al Qaeda, not al Qaeda. Maybe Daeash? But you kill friends of mine! I know what you are."

"Like you know how to choose 'safe' houses?"

There was a long silence. Then Ollie raised the pistol and placed the muzzle against Abdullah's temple.

Abdullah ignored Ollie. He spoke directly to the Senator. "This man is a fool. Shooting me would be unwise. I have information you need. And Slater will die."

The gun stayed where it was.

"Ollie." Harlan spoke the single word very softly.

And again, "Ollie."

"Okay," breathed Ollie, lowering the gun. He stepped back, leaned against the wall and crossed his arms. He did not stop staring at Abdullah.

Harlan took over. "Ollie, why don't you round up a couple of your friends and have them meet us here? We're going to need a couple of experienced babysitters for our friend here for the next 24 hours or so. And you – Abdullah? – what exactly does Malik 'expect' of us?"

Abdullah handed him a half-sheet of note-paper. "First, that you call Zanker and tell him that these are the projects he should choose. And tell him that Slater's release depends on him doing that.

"Second, while the Zanker show is going on and Ashraf Ghani is speaking, you and I will be in an SUV that I will provide, heading north on the Kunduz highway. Once underway, you will be given additional directions to the location where Slater and I will be exchanged, assuming that the $100 million is sent to the right projects."

Harlan laughed. "You expect me – a U.S. Senator – to drive with you, alone in a vehicle of your choice, to some isolated spot deep in your territory –"

"Malik is not interested in you. Bring as many Seals, Rangers or Afghan troops as you need to feel safe. But they must travel with you in a convoy. No helicopters. No drones."

Harlan and Ollie exchanged a long look. Ollie finally nodded.

"And then?" Harlan asked.

"Then? We all go home and resume doing what we've always done … try to kill one another. But we do it in silence. This transaction … these last three weeks …. Cham Kasi …. Never happened."

As Abdullah spoke, Harlan became increasingly agitated, clenching and unclenching his fists, the tendons in his neck standing out. He took a step closer and his words came out one word at a time, as though drawn from him with great force.

"And Istanbul. In 1980? Did that never happen?"

Abdullah and Ollie looked at one another, equally puzzled.

War Games

Two hours later, Harlan, Madge and Ollie were sitting in a badly lit and small room in another house. The walls were water stained and pocked with fist-sized holes. Abdullah and his two minders were next door.

"What do you think?" Harlan asked.

Ollie slouched lower into his chair and put both of his booted feet onto the low table in front of him, as though he viewed the question as the start of a lengthy session. "First," he said, "it's pretty obvious that Malik has something on Zanker, some leverage he can use to persuade Zanker to do what he wants him to do –"

Harlan broke in, recalling Garrison's summary of Zanker -- *We've got a problem with Zanker. He's like an adult Eagle Scout. Nothing to work with that I can find.* "He doesn't need 'something on Zanker,' as you put it. He's got Slater and he's giving Zanker the chance to save him from public decapitation."

" I think he *almost* trusts Zanker to do as he's told for Slater's sake," Ollie nodded. "But he wants insurance. So he wants you to endorse the ransom scheme as well."

When Harlan didn't respond, Ollie's impatience surfaced. "Look, Senator. This is why I called on Zanker ten days ago in London – because we thought we could use him as a covert channel to ransom Slater. And that's how it's coming down, other than it's Malik who had the same idea and got to him first. What's your problem?"

And the man doesn't know – or want to know – that we've got our own leverage working on Zanker, just in case. Hell! The man doesn't even know what he wants, let alone how to get it!

Harlan was off on another tack. "What do you think about this man Abdullah and their demands for conducting the exchange?"

"So far, it all checks out. Abdullah is legitimate. He's the only son of Malik's only living brother. Believe it or not, as a hostage, he's about the same weight as Slater. From Malik's Pashtun perspective, Abdullah is easily the equivalent of the son of a U.S. Senator. Malik will honor his end of the deal to get him back in one piece."

"Is Abdullah a high-value Taliban target for us?"

"Nope. Not even on the list. Keeping him – or killing him -- does us no good. And it would infuriate Malik."

"How about the swap arrangements? The details?"

Ollie smiled, shaking his head. "Malik's being cute. He's really been quite creative."

"Ollie! Tell me what you think. Never mind all that 'respect your enemy' shit!"

Ollie's irritability ratcheted up one more notch.

He thinks he's still in DC, sitting in his office with his view of the monuments. I wonder when – or if – he will realize how dependent he is on people that are not afraid of him?

Ollie kept his thoughts to himself, shrugged and went on. "Until Abdullah showed up, we were facing the classic kidnap dilemma. Finding a way for two parties who really don't trust one another to *simultaneously* swap two physical objects: a bundle of cash in exchange for a live hostage and then walk away. I haven't seen any stats, but I'll bet the usual outcome is either a dead hostage and/or a dead kidnapper.

"Malik's turned it into a two stage operation. First, we pay the ransom – that's Zanker's button push. Once that's done and the hundred million is beyond our control, then we exchange our respective hostages. We've already paid the hundred million, so our only incentive is to get Slater back alive. And Malik wants Abdullah back, so –"

"But Slater is still just as valuable to him. What's stopping him from --"

Ollie shook his head. "Aside from wanting Abdullah back, everything we know about Malik indicates that he wants to be left alone. He's not Taliban and has no connection with al Qaeda or the extremists who are cutting off heads in Syria and Iraq. He'll probably use the hundred million bucks to buy them off. And he knows the kind of heat we'll bring if he welshes on our deal."

Harlan was still running scenarios in his head. "So, the money's on the way and we're driving around in their SUV. What then?"

"I'm guessing, of course. We're dealing with experts and they've got the home field advantage. My guess is that they'll run us around for a while in the outback, then send us on two minutes notice to some really isolated spot with thousand-yard visibility and no cover for snipers on either side. I'll bet that we'll park the SUV's a hundred yards apart and turn Slater and Abdullah loose at the same time."

After a short pause, he added, "That's how I would do it … if I was playing it straight."

Harlan sat very quietly and Ollie knew what he was thinking through in his head.

"You're wondering if we can take them out *after* the exchange, aren't you?"

Harlan nodded. "It's been done."

"We don't know the time, place, or terrain. We're on their turf and they're calling the shots. They're not even worried about us bringing along our own private army. And they're not stupid."

"What about a Predator drone just below the horizon with a Hellfire missile or two?"

"They'd still have a four or five minute window. But even if it works, all we're able to do is to kill Abdullah and a couple of goons that drove Slater to the rendezvous. What's the point?"

"How many people do we need for security?"

"No more than your usual VIP contingent. And only for the return trip. But by the time we've done the deal, we can have a dozen gunships overhead for support. Or, even better, you and Slater can just helo out. But remember: the bigger the escort, the greater the chance of leakage. And so far, no one even knows you're in Afghanistan."

Harlan nodded. "Let's keep it that way. No satellites, Predators, or anything else we need permission for."

He looked at Madge. "Who's that Seal lieutenant who got there a day late?"

"A Lieutenant Chambers. He and his team are still on call."

"They already know something's going on. Get them here. They can be my security detachment. And Ollie? I want your contractors – you said a dozen of them – along as well. But keep them separate from the Seal team.   I do not want them and the Seals to share vehicles or communications with one another."

Madge and Ollie both nodded, but exchanged a quizzical look.

Harlan withdrew into yet another protracted silence. Ollie got up, went to a half-size refrigerator in the corner of the room, took out a bottle of beer, and went back to his slouched position with his feet on the table.

What Harlan said next made him sit bolt upright, wondering if he'd heard correctly.

"What if we tell Zanker to choose *our* projects, not the ones that Malik has designated?"

Players in Motion

Kaz sat on a small stage in a large room at the Presidential Palace. The Arg, translated as "citadel" in Duri and Pashtun, has been the residence and offices of kings and presidents since 1880. It was a place that Kaz had always wanted to see the inside of, but he had gotten to this point without being aware of the rooms or history that he was passing through. It was as if all of his senses had shut down so that he could channel all of his attention to the bitterness and uncertainty.

The world's all time patsy! Anybody promises you anything and you fall in line. They didn't even need the promises. Hints were sufficient in my case.

CC had me nailed. From that first encounter "I pick you" line in Starbucks. Tell him he's special. That the smartest, most beautiful woman in San Francisco can't wait to jump into bed with him and follow him all over the world just to bask in his presence.

Abdul-Karim covered the professional angle. Tell him that he's a master of the financial universe, but one who can still appreciate ancient Persian poetry. A man who can be trusted with a hundred million dollars. Even got me to recite my lines from a script I didn't even know I was reading.

Oliver – whoever he is – handled the patriotism angle. Really just a naked appeal to the subconscious boy. Do this for the good of your country. Be a hero. Rescue hostages. Dazzle the terrorists with your negotiating ability.

A sudden stir in the audience of fifty or sixty people got through to him and he stood to shake the hands of the World Bank EVP and Ashraf Ghani, the President of Afghanistan, as they mounted the stage and stood before the three chairs in the center of the stage. The other objects included a podium with several microphones and a small table with a laptop computer.

Maybe thirty minutes. Forty if Ghani runs on a bit. Then I choose. Who lives? And who doesn't.

He looked down at the thin, black leather portfolio on his lap. Four sheets of papers. Some notes for a three-minute speech. His own list of five projects, Malik's list, and the list he had been handed as he entered the press room. The man handed him the single folded sheet, saying "From Ollie. Remember the video." That man now sat watching him from the third row. He was a very military-looking western guy with multiple pieces of camera equipment strapped around him.

Kaz had looked at the three lists, each with five names. No one name was repeated across the three lists.

A reporter from Al Jazeera sat behind the man with all the cameras, with an open tablet on his lap. He stood out from his the other reporters in the same row because he had not taken his eyes off of Kaz since he entered the room, as if he knew of the awful choice he had to make.

A bank of TV cameras was at the back of the room and the podium had four separate microphones. Whatever he decided would be known by anyone who cared as soon as he said the words.

Three choices, maybe only two. Forget about my list. That leaves two choices, maybe only one. Go with Malik's list and Slater and Abdullah stay alive. Go with Ollie's list and CC stays alive… I think. Pretty simple … Who do I want to kill?

The Al Jazeera journalist – he actually was one – sat through the two political speeches without bothering to listen. He had the transcripts and had already identified the few sound bites he needed for the five-hundred-word article that would be published in Dari, Pashto and English. All he needed was the names of the actual projects.

He watched Zanker, who was obviously in some kind of distress. He was inattentive to the speakers, fidgeting in his chair, and – once – half-rose as if about to walk off the stage. When his turn came, he rushed through a handful of clichés about the future of Afghanistan and then announced his five selections in a strangled voice. By the time he pushed the large button to send the $100 million to Abdul-Karim's bank, he looked like a man teetering on the edge of a breakdown.

Two hours earlier and a few miles away, a dark green and battered SUV stopped at the entrance to an ordinary looking house in the outskirts of Kabul. Abdullah, Harlan and Ollie stood watching while three uniformed Seals went over the inside, outside, engine compartment and undercarriage of the SUV. When they gave the signal, Abdullah got in the driver's seat and the two Americans in the rear seat. When the SUV pulled away, four unmarked Humvees fell in immediately behind them, each of them with a four-man crew.

Two minutes later and a half-mile away, three more strange looking vehicles started their engines and entered into the heavy Kabul traffic. They had started out as early-edition Humvees, but each of them had been modified in distinctive ways, as though a Rolls Royce had been acquired by an East LA gang member and reconfigured as a low rider suitable for Saturday night promenades on Ventura Boulevard.

Madge sat alongside the driver of the first Humvee dressed in fatigues without insignia of any sort, with an M4 rifle clasped between her knees. She gave directions to the driver based on a red dot moving across the face of the electronic map on the iPad on her lap. The tracking device was in Harlan's cell phone. A backup signal was being emitted by another device Ollie carried in a concealed pocket of his military jacket.

There were eleven of Ollie's contractors with her. They were an assorted lot of seemingly mismatched characters, some in a semblance of a uniform and others looking like Afghan farmers. But they had some things in common. They were all veterans of irregular warfare, most of it in Iraq and Afghanistan. They didn't like being assembled into a single unit and they really didn't like the idea of Madge being in charge. Most of all, they didn't like carting the other woman with them.

The woman was an impossible complication to manage, but Ollie had said to bring her along. He told Madge, as if to compensate for the inconvenience, "But she won't be with you on the return trip."

Fifty miles to the north of Kabul, four helicopter pilots sat and wondered what their mission was. Those who flew the three fully armed Apache Longbows were told, "We may have a target for you. Be ready to go." The other copter – a Pave Hawk with a search & rescue team was told, "Follow the Apaches. There may be passengers to pick up."

CC sat on the floor in a corner of the Humvee's cargo compartment, compressed into the smallest possible bundle that she could make of herself, her head down and her arms wrapped tightly around her, pulling her legs back against her chest.

None of the men paid any attention to her, even the three that had staged the execution video.

It had taken a long time for the trembling to stop. It seemed that every muscle and tendon in her body was vibrating of its own volition. And she couldn't get enough air, taking in great gasping breaths.

Derek! That son of a bitch! I will fucking kill him!

Her rage was so intense, so all-consuming, that it was several minutes before the other questions began to crowd in.

What's he doing? Who's he working for? What could push him to this kind of monstrous behavior? What's he going to do with the video? Or me, for that matter? Why am I being dragged around with this ragtag bunch of mercenaries?

OK, girl. Use that famous brain of yours. First, it's obvious that they're using you to get at Kaz. He's been your assigned target the whole time; all they've done is to apply pressure in a way that you did not anticipate. Second, what they want from him is equally obvious – the $100 million he's about to hand out.

Third, they ...

Her certainty and her internal monologue stopped there, and she was left to consider the mostly horrific possibilities.

Does he care enough about me to override his professional obligations? That's pretty easy, I think.

But that was reassuring for no more than a second, the time it took for the more important question. *How can they leave the two of us alive once they've got their money? There's nothing to stop us from blowing the whistle. Derek goes to jail, the so-called projects get shut down, and we become regulars on the talk-show circuit! They can't let that happen.*

The trembling started again.

Decisions

Slater was in motion again, crammed into the rear seat of a crew cab Toyota Tacoma pickup truck between Cyrus and Badi. Malik was in the front passenger seat. Six sheep were in the truck bed behind them. They'd been driving for about two hours before Malik said, "The ransom is due to be delivered in the next hour or so. Then we'll be done with all this."

"Are you sure they'll pay it?"

He could see the uncertainty in Malik. Not in the words he spoke but in the very slight hesitation and the careful neutrality of his voice.

"You're his only son. Of course he'll pay."

Slater wasn't sure.

OK. You're like a death row inmate on the eve of his execution. Your attorneys have made a last minute appeal for a pardon by the governor. The clock is ticking.

Slater sat in the truck trying not to think about the future. The easiest way to do that was to concentrate on the past.

It was easy not to think about the immediate future. He had no control over that and no information as to what was unfolding.

And beyond the next few hours, there were so many possibilities – most of them bad – that he found it difficult to plan … *No, not "plan," that's not the right word. Maybe "react." It's like a firefight. Where time and distance are measured in feet and seconds.*

He sat back, trying to stop thinking about the five Afghan soldiers he had killed, so neatly lying side-by-side at the entrance to the bridge.

Malik wanted to ask Slater some of his many unanswered questions, but respected the young man's inner battles. *Besides, his answers – if there are any – would simply lead to more questions.*

How did we get to this point? Where no matter what happens, there are only victims? Where revenge is more important than stopping the killing? Qur'an says, "Hell is for the proud people." And it's true.

Mullah Omar had come to his room early this morning.

"We are leaving. I am asking once more. Will you give me Slater Crosby?"

"No."

"Then what happens is on your head."

"Yes." *Just as it would be if I did as you asked.*

Omar seemed to puff up and he stood glaring at Malik, clearly wanting to say more. Finally, he spun around and stomped out.

Thirty minutes later, Malik's best friend came to his room. His name was Sahid and he had been with Malik since he had returned from London more than forty years ago. They had intended that Malik's son would marry Sahid's daughter, a union that would insure them many grandchildren. But then, the Russians had killed his son, and the Taliban had shot Sahid's daughter because she dared to go to school.

Sahid said, "Omar and his men have left. And they were joined by more fighters. I do not think they have gone very far away."

"You know what he wants?"

"Of course."

"Do you think that I should –"

Sahid held up his hand, signaling 'stop.' He shook his head in a way that Malik accepted as a reproachment.

"I'm sorry. It is a sign of weakness to even ask."

"I have known you since you were called 'Ali,' and then 'Khalid,' and now 'Malik.' But it is only the names that changed. You have always been our leader. The one who makes the hard choices. It shall be as you say. Whatever you decide."

Malik placed his hand over his heart and bowed slightly. The gesture was a poor substitute for his feelings at the moment.

"We leave shortly. Are the others ready?"

"I have sent three of them ahead. They need to place the explosives and can use the extra time. Badi and Cyrus will be with us."

"I hope we will not need the explosives. If we do, then some one has been stupid."

"And dishonorable. They deserve what they will get."

Ollie looked at Harlan. "How long before Zanker's announcement?"

Harlan didn't need to look at his watch. He was intensely aware of the passage of time. "Sometime in the next few minutes. Depends on how long the speeches run."

Harlan's satellite phone buzzed when they were about an hour out of Kabul, traveling west.

The caller spoke only a single sentence. "Zanker went with the list we gave him."

"Then you know what to do next."

Harlan ended the call and waited, hoping that Abdullah's phone would ring within the next few minutes.

If not, I've killed Slater.

The call came ten minutes later. Harlan was holding Abdullah's phone and answered immediately. "This is Harlan Crosby."

"You didn't do what you were supposed to do." The voice was Malik's.

"No, but I still want to go through with the exchange of hostages."

"Without paying me my hundred million dollars?"

"It can still happen. I control the money. They are my projects and I can insure that it is spent in certain ways."

"And Slater's life?' Malik asked mildly. "This is to be bargained with too?"

Harlan held the phone away from him, looking at it with real curiosity. *There's no outrage. No negotiation. No interest in how I will pay, or how much or even when. Only his transparent contempt that I would risk my son's life.* Once again, it occurred to Harlan that he might not understand what they were engaged in.

"His life? It's been on the line since you kidnapped him. And it will be until this deal is done. No matter what I do or don't do."

He paused and then said, "And so is Abdullah's."

A silence set in. Harlan could hear the faint sound of the man breathing. Finally, he said, "Let me talk to Abdullah."

Harlan handed the phone forward. Abdullah said only "Yes?" He listened for about ten seconds, said, "I understand," and then ended the call.

Harlan literally held his breath, until it became impossible not to breathe. Finally, Abdullah said, "Another forty minutes to the exchange point."

Tactical Arrangements

They'd been driving for ten minutes after the call, at first due west and then in a northwesterly direction. Two Humvees with the Seals were in the lead, following Abdullah's directions. Their SUV came next, followed by the last two Humvees. Abdullah clearly had a prearranged route in mind. He had his satellite phone in a cradle on the dashboard, but had talked to no one, except for the communication about Zanker. Ollie was in the front passenger seat with a book of topographical maps open on his lap, tracing their route and looking ahead.

"They're taking us to Bamyan Province." Ollie watched Abdullah closely as he spoke, but could not detect any reaction.

"Is that a surprise?" Harlan asked.

Ollie shook his head, inclining his head to indicate Abdullah. He said only, "Hazara territory. Lots of mountains."

Abdullah here knows where we're going. Maybe not the last mile or so. That's what the sat phone is for. Bamyan is famous for its caves. And where there's caves, there's tunnels. That's Malik's escape route. Predator drones don't go into caves, and they could pop out anywhere. Booby trap the entrance just in case we try to follow with the Seals.

The only flaw? It puts us at risk. He could hide twenty men with sniper rifles in that terrain. Why would we go along with that? But I'll bet he's got a way to keep us happy.

Abdullah's satellite phone buzzed when they were passing through the village of Bamyan, a place made famous because of the gigantic statues of Buddha that overlooked the village until the Taliban destroyed them.

Ollie picked up the phone, saying only, "Yes?"

"Once you leave the village, follow the river to the west."

"Who is this?"

"My name is Sahid. That's all you need to know."

"Where are we – "

But the phone was dead.

Ollie picked up the tactical radio and said, "Chambers?"

"On the point. What's up?"

"Go west on the river road. That's all we know at the moment."

"OK," Chambers said. "By the way, Bamyan Province has been reasonably quiet for some time, but I spent some hard time around here. It's nasty terrain. Riddled with caves and tunnels. We lost some good troops there."

"Let's not lose any today. A walk in the park."

"Roger that."

The phone rang eight minutes later.

"You'll see a boulder with a splash of white paint on it within the next mile. Turn right fifty meters past that point, away from the river. There's no road, but you'll see tracks."

Ollie checked the topo map. "Once we turn, there's a straight two thousand meter run that dead ends into *that*." He pointed to his right, where what seemed to be an unbroken sheer wall of stone rose hundreds of feet straight up.

The tracks were very faint, probably made by no more than two vehicles. The landscape was barren. Mostly sand and gravel studded with short twisted trees. The convoy came to a halt just short of a slight rise. Chambers radioed back, "Time for a huddle. Once we crest this hill, we're exposed to whatever and whoever is waiting for us at the base of that wall."

Harlan, Ollie and Chambers met in the shadow of the first Humvee. Ollie carried the tac radio with the "transmit" switch in the "open" position, and what they said was easily picked up by Madge in the shadowing convoy.

Chambers drew a diagram in the gravelly soil with a stick. "We're here." An 'X' in the dirt. "We have another eight hundred meters ..." A wavy straight line ..."before we hit the wall." A perpendicular across the straight line in the dirt. "The track between us has a lot of dips, but it's basically pretty flat until it dead ends at the cliff face."

Harlan took the stick from Chambers and jabbed at the crude drawing in the dirt. "So why don't we get to the top of the hill and see what we're facing. We're blind here!"

Chambers was careful to keep his voice respectful. "Well, sir. Once we top this rise in front of us, we'll be exposed to fire from the cliff face. I suggest –"

The sat phone buzzed, startling all three of them.

Ollie answered. "Sahid, we're here. But we don't like driving over that hill blind."

"Your Seal team carries a small observational drone with them. For close battlefield observation. Get it up and take a look."

Chambers was already moving. Within three minutes, they were viewing live feed video of the ground between them and the cliff face.

The drone hovered a hundred feet in the air over the group standing around the pickup truck. The picture was remarkably clear, showing Slater Crosby and three other men with rifles. One of the weapons was quite clearly a long-range sniper rifle. Another man was sitting in deep shadow in the cab of the truck. Six sheep were tightly bunched in the bed of the truck. The camera also showed a narrow cleft in the rock behind the truck. It looked barely big enough for an ordinary-sized vehicle. Humvees wouldn't fit.

Chambers ordered, "Dobbs, show me the face of the cliff and what's on top. For one thousand meters on either side of those people." The Seal operator used his toggle switches to redirect the drone and show them a wider perspective.

Sahid spoke as though he was standing with them looking at the scrolling video. "Your technology is very good, so you will know that we are alone. And that we have an exit route planned. One where you cannot follow unless you want to be buried alive. And I have someone that wants to speak with you."

Then another voice. "This is Crosby. Sahid is being straight with you. The exchange is structured such that neither side is at risk if they play by the rules."

Harlan snatched the phone away from Ollie. "Slater, are you –"

"I'm fine. I didn't expect –"

"This is Sahid. Put Abdullah on."

Ollie gestured to Abdullah, who was standing nearby, and Harlan handed him the phone., saying "Our man Crosby said that Sahid is playing fair. I think he expects the same kind of reassurance from you."

Abdullah watched the three of them as he spoke. "Sahid. All seems ordinary here. There are four Humvees with Seals, but they're all in place here. We have the video from the drone."

He handed the phone back to Ollie, who took it and said, "Hold for one minute."

He turned to Chambers. "Anything new from the video?"

Chambers shook his head. "It's like the man said. All clear in all directions. It's a good setup for an exchange. Once we top that rise, there's no cover between us and them. Neither side is going to be able to get close without being spotted. And the only live objects on the other side of that hill are your man, his three minders and six sheep. And whoever's sitting in the cab of that truck."

"What about that opening in the cliff?" Ollie asked Chambers.

"Drone can't help us much there. But I'll bet it leads to several possible exits. Those cliffs are like an ant farm."

Ollie smiled. "It's refreshing to be dealing with professionals again."

He spoke into the phone. "OK Sahid, how do we finish the deal?"

"Drive the SUV to the top of the rise, to where you can see us. Just Abdullah, you and no more than two Seals. The senator can come along if he likes, but no Humvees. Stop there, wait one minute and then you – you personally -- will drive the SUV to us. You alone. No weapons. I will bring you our vehicle, the truck you see in your video. Then Abdullah and I will drive our truck back to us, and you and Crosby will drive the SUV back to your position. We will time the drive so as to reach each end at the same time."

Neat. An exact balance of forces. Each side will have the hostage targeted with sniper rifles until the very last second. And the exchange of vehicles eliminates the chance of tracking devices or even booby-trapping the vehicle so that it blows up after the exchange.

Looks like I'll get to meet the mysterious Sahid.

"OK. Sounds good. We'll be on the top of that rise and ready to execute in five minutes."

Ollie turned to Chambers. "I'll need your two best snipers."

The tac radio squawked at him. *Madge's channel.* He walked away from the other men and spoke softly. "The arrangements are –"

"Never mind that. I need Harlan. We've got another issue to deal with."

Ollie gestured to Harlan and handed him the radio when he joined him. Chambers looked at the two of them curiously.

"Tell me."

"We're half a mile behind you. Just off the river road. About thirty seconds ago, four pickups went by – Toyota technicals moving fast. Classic Taliban party. I don't think they saw us, but I can't be sure. They sure as hell didn't slow down. Two of them had mounted 50 calibers. Probably about twenty fighters."

"Moving in broad daylight. In a semi-pacified zone. Sounds like they have a serious need to be somewhere." Harlan was talking to himself as much as to Madge.

"That's what I thought. I also thought that they might be interested in the same transaction that we are. Lots of local folks might not like the outcome we're working on. Then again, maybe they're Malik's people and he's running some kind of scam on us. "

Harlan thought about the options. *None of them good.*

"Where are the Apaches?"

"Eight or nine minutes away. They're on the ground, but spooled up and ready."

He said, "Get them in the air and close by. And for god's sake, keep them out of sight and hearing of our little group. In the meantime, you stay on the tail of that bunch that just passed you until we know they're not part of this deal."

He gave her a quick overview of Sahid's requirements for the exchange. She listened and asked no questions.

"Madge. Keep that bunch away from the exchange. Do whatever you have to do."

There was a long silence, then Madge said, "The woman is still with us."

"Nothing's changed."

Harlan waited. Long seconds went by.

Madge broke the silence. "I understand. But I don't like it."

"Just do it. Over and out."

Loose Ends

Kaz walked off the stage in a daze. Half-a-dozen TV reporters and cameramen, including a couple of Anglo types, were waiting for him, already shouting questions as he approached. But he walked through them unseeing. It was as if his vacant gaze had the power to silence and part the tangle of reporters with their outstretched microphones. Two of the men followed at his heels as he stumbled through a smaller briefing room and then into a vast hallway that seemed to lead to an ornate reception area of sorts.

He had no destination in mind and no idea where he was, driven by the image of CC on her knees in the dirt and accompanied by the voice that began when he pushed that damned button to transmit the hundred million to Abdul-Karim's bank. *What have you done? But she was so alone. What have you done? She was so alone.* Halfway down the dark tunnel that was the hallway, he whirled around, waving wildly at the reporter still pursuing him.

"Leave me alone! I have nothing to say –"

The rest of his protest went away along with all of the breath in his body. The man's fist was buried deep in his abdomen, leaving him doubled over, held up solely by his attacker's other arm. Three shuffling steps brought them into a small alcove with two garish brocaded chairs facing one another. He was pushed down into one of the chairs, unable to breathe or even sit upright. The man stood opposite him, swaddled in cameras. It was Ollie's messenger, the one who gave him the sheet of paper with those goddamned names. The man kept his left hand on Kaz's shoulder as though consoling some distraught, gasping person.

The man lifted one of the camera straps over his head and moved behind Kaz. He was almost gentle as he slid the leather strap around his neck and pulled him upright in the chair. He leaned down and whispered, "Relax. This will be very quick. Watch for the white light."

Then he crossed his hands and pulled the strap tight, yanking Kaz's head and shoulders back into the softness of the chair.

Christ! That hurts!

Instinctively, he clawed at the strap, but it was already imbedded in his flesh. He reached further back but all he could do was to scratch at the hands that were killing him. Within seconds, both his consciousness and vision were fading.

I'm dead! What a stupid fucking waste!

There was a noise behind him, a "whuff," about like the sound of the blow to his stomach, and the man said "ah" as though mildly surprised at some unexpected discovery. The ungodly pressure around his neck suddenly eased, enabling a huge gasping intake of precious air. The darkness at the edges of his vision began to recede. He lurched forward out of the chair, falling onto his knees and taking great rasping breaths.

Seconds passed before fear took control again. He stumbled to his feet and turned to face the man. But he was lying face first, doubled over the back of the chair that Kaz had just fallen from. The haft of a knife protruded prominently from the middle of his back. Even as he looked, a hand reached out and pulled the knife out, seemingly without any effort. It was an extremely thin and long blade, a stiletto of sorts.

The man holding the instrument was small, thick and dark, wearing blue jeans and a sport coat. A large white badge on his lapel said "Al Jazeera." He was looking at Kaz as if he was an extremely annoying panhandler who had interrupted him on his way to an important meeting.

"We need to go. Security is very tight when Ghani is in residence." He stepped into the hallway and looked intently in either direction.

Kaz looked at the man lying across the chair. A very thin trickle of blood was coming from the corner of his mouth. He pointed to him and asked the other man, "Who is he? And who are you? And why is any of this happening?"

The small man was amused. "I am the journalist – the one to ask so many questions." He started to walk away, but stopped after a few steps.

"Who was he? An assassin, of course. Hired to kill you. Who am I? A friend of a friend. Your other question – why is this happening – would make a wonderful story for my newspaper, but I don't think it will ever be told."

Again, he turned away. Kaz put his hand on his arm and said, "Thank you. You saved my life. And I don't even know why."

"That's easy. Malik promised you safe passage."

If You Are Not My Friend

Sahid walked back to the truck where Malik sat in the passenger seat. He was just putting down the hand held radio, looking at it with an expression of strong distaste.

Malik grimaced at Sahid. "I think Mullah Omar is here. Our watcher in Bamyan tells me that four vehicles with Taliban just went through. Converted Toyotas with mounted weapons."

Sahid shook his head. "That's crazy. The NATO satellites will love it. They'll have Predators or F-16's all over them."

Malik wasn't listening. *They know we're here and what we're doing. So Omar's informant is still at work. And it must be someone in this small group. Well, I know who it isn't ...*

"Who knows where we are at this moment?"

Sahid was startled by the question and looked intently at Malik before answering. "The two of us. Abdullah, of course. Badi and Cyrus." He inclined his head toward the two men standing nearby with Slater. "And the three men who prepared the tunnel behind us."

He shook his head. "They have all been with us for a long time." But, even as he uttered the automatic denial, his mind was running through the possibilities.

Omar is a hero to many Pashtun. The leader of the Taliban. The man on the American's 'most wanted' list, with a bounty of a million dollars. The successor to bin Laden. It would not be hard for him to recruit a spy among us.

"The question is," said Malik, "whether Omar requires only information from his informant. Or perhaps something more action-oriented?"

Assassination? Of Crosby? Or Malik himself?

Sahid said, "The three men who mined the tunnel are gone. There's nothing to be done about them now."

His reluctance to continue was so obvious that Malik felt sorry for him. *But it is the very words you do not say that speak as clearly as if you had shouted them.*

"Which one?"

Sahid answered immediately, knowing that Malik would already have made the same calculations. "Cyrus, I think. He is carrying a cell phone, and I know that his son – he is seventeen -- has joined the Islamic State fighters in Syria. And I have often heard Cyrus speak of his admiration for the Taliban."

"We shall watch him. Perhaps we are wrong."

Neither of them believed that to be true.

"Bring Crosby to me."

When Slater came to the truck, Malik asked him, "That night that the so-called Ranger tried to rescue you, how did he get control of Abdul?"

Slater closed his eyes, trying to recreate the sounds he had heard. "The shooting woke me. Then I heard voices talking to Abdul, telling him to stay in place."

"Voices? More than one?"

"One was the guy you shot. He's the only one I saw."

"But you heard the other?"

Slater looked closely at Malik, sensing that this was important to him. "I think it was Cyrus. But I'm not sure."

Malik looked past Slater, at Sahid, whose answering expression was a pure question mark. Malik said to him, "It is my problem. I shall handle it. Soon."

Sahid nodded and said. "So. We are ready to make the exchange?"

"There's one more complication," Malik said. "Our watcher also reports that there are three more Humvee's following Harlan Crosby at a distance. Probably some of this man Ollie's contractors."

"Do we care? They've already got a Seal team. More numbers can't help them."

The question reminded Malik of why he loved Sahid. *He is not distracted by the irrelevant detail. Or perhaps it is only that he has so little left to care about. Except for me.*

He did not answer the question, but asked instead, "What do we know about this man 'Ollie'? Why is Harlan Crosby allowing him to make the decisions?"

"He is ex-CIA. Been in Afghanistan since 2001 running paramilitary operations of all sorts for both official and unofficial sponsors. Works for money and has become very rich. Crosby *thinks* that he works exclusively for him, but we know that he also has other clients. I think he is one of those people who like wars and what they permit him to do."

After a few seconds, he added, "He will die in Afghanistan...or somewhere just like Afghanistan, with its own dirty little war."

"Can we trust him to follow the rules?"

Sahid thought for a few seconds before responding. "If following the rules will get him what he wants."

"Isn't Slater Crosby what he wants?"

"Perhaps."

The single ambiguous word saddened Malik. *How long has it been since I dealt with someone whose agenda was both simple and transparent?* And he knew the answer to the rhetorical question.

It was 1980, in Istanbul, with Yasmin.

Sahid's question brought him back to the present. "What are we going to do about Mullah Omar's people?"

"We can't fight them with the few of us. And they will not go away. So we shall tell the Americans to deal with them. But only if – when -- they move against us."

The sat phone buzzed. "Changing the rules?" Ollie asked.

"No," Sahid answered. "Just making sure you know who's who. There's a group of four Toyotas – you call them 'technicals' -- with Taliban fighters somewhere west of us on the river road. They are not any part of this deal, but they might try to take Crosby away from us."

"So?"

"If they move this way, you'll have to protect us. We don't have enough men or weapons."

It surprised Ollie. And then it seemed natural. *That's why he was so willing to let us show up in force. He's running a con on his own side. Christ! Wheels within wheels!*

He stalled, trying to think through the options. "Four vehicles, huh? Probably twenty or more people. They'll outnumber us as well as you."

"Not if you count those three 'extra' Humvees that are tailing you at a discreet distance," said Sahid with an amused tone.

Of course he knows. They'll have watchers set up in Bamyan.

"What about air support?"

"Bring your gunships closer if you like," said Sahid. "But keep them away from us. And why don't you use your drone to find and track our Taliban party instead of hovering over us and our sheep?"

"Thanks for the tactical advice. I'll take it into consideration."

Ollie beckoned to Chambers. "Task the drone to cover the ground to our west. There's apparently a Taliban group – four technicals, maybe twenty men – out there somewhere."

Chambers didn't move, just stared at Ollie, thinking. *Great. The mission was to cover for the Senator and get the hostage back. Now I've got to fight a pitched battle with the Taliban on their turf. And this guy is not exactly forthcoming about what he knows.*

"Getting intelligence from our friends over there?" He gestured at the screen, showing the men clustered around the white pickup truck in the distance.

When Ollie just stared at him, Chambers shrugged and then spoke quickly into his headset mike. He turned back to Ollie and said, "Done. When do we move up to the hilltop?"

"Three minutes. But only the SUV, with two Seals and a good long range gun."

"That'll be me and Luther. He's a multipurpose kinda guy."

Half a mile away, Madge held a quick briefing with the men. She didn't know what Ollie had told them about her, but – from their expressions – it can't have been too reassuring. It was hard for her to distinguish their skepticism from not-so-covert hostility. She spent the first sixty seconds by looking directly at each of them long enough to make them uncomfortable.

She started by saying, "Ollie told me that you were good at your job. We're about to find out. We've got maybe twenty or so Taliban out there somewhere. You saw them go by a few minutes ago. We're going to bird dog them and make sure they don't get involved in the main event."

One of the men – a barrel-shaped and bearded gnome-like figure with the most faded set of fatigues she had ever seen, wearing a red-checked keffiyeh – he looked like Yasir Arafat – said, "Twenty, huh? And there's how many of us?"

"Twelve, counting me. Did you want to stay behind? Make the fight a little less one-sided?"

That brought out a scattering of smiles from the men. After about ten seconds, she said, "There's three Apache Longbows on the way, maybe five minutes out *if* we need them." She put a lot of emphasis on the word 'if.'

"Oh, yeah. And a Seal team. *If* we need them."

Less than a mile away, the Taliban commander finished positioning his four vehicles and twenty-three fighters. For the first time since this crazy outing started, he began to feel hopeful about the outcome.

He was an ignorant man, an imam in rural Afghanistan who viewed the Koran as a license to kill infidels, including other Muslims of insufficient purity. For Mullah Omar to call upon him for a mission that he called "a chance to rid Afghanistan of the American scum once and for all" caused a surge of joy. Only when he learned that Mullah Omar expected him to travel in an armed convoy in daylight hours to prevent "a hostage exchange" did he begin to regret his chosen status.

They had assembled in Bamyan to minimize their exposure from the air, but even their brief time on the road left his neck muscles aching from his 360 degree scanning of the – thankfully, praise Allah – empty skies. Even crazier, Mullah Omar gave him the discretion to attack whichever side of the exchange he came across, whether American or Muslim.

"But do not kill the hostage to be exchanged. We must have him alive."

One does not question the Mullah, but the commander wondered *how do I do that?*

So when they spotted the three Humvees parked off the road, his choice was made for him. *At least I can kill Americans rather than misguided Muslims.*

Lethal Skirmishes

Madge made two radio calls. The first was to Ollie. "Can you have the Seal drone make a sweep down river? Give us some intel."

"Chambers has got it covering the ground west of us. We figure that's where they'll come from if they're coming. I'll have him send it your way."

The second call was to the lead Apache pilot. She gave him the GPS coordinates and described the Taliban force. She also stressed the need to avoid coming within sight of Sahid's party near the cliff.

The pilot was eager to go. "Sounds like fun. Four trucks in open country against three Apaches. They must be suicidal."

"Let's just say there's a lot at stake. We're moving out now. What's your ETA?"

"Six or seven minutes."

That was two minutes too long. Several lifetimes for the eleven men and two women in the hand-me-down, under-armored Humvees.

Just as Madge in the lead Humvee pulled out onto the river road, the radio went frantic. Harlan was shouting. "Madge! Abort! The drone is showing … You're driving into an ambush! Go back!"

The imam was an ignorant man, but he was a master of irregular warfare. The truck-mounted 50 caliber heavy machine guns concentrated on the two lead vehicles. The exposed gunners on the 30 mm turret guns were killed instantly. The rounds did not penetrate the side armor but wrecked the engines and deafened the men in the passenger compartment.

The third Humvee never had a chance. A shoulder-fired Javelin anti-tank rocket struck it from behind, leaving the vehicle a burning hulk in the middle of the road, a crematorium for the shredded remains of the four man crew.

Madge and the five survivors of the initial assault scrambled out of the other two vehicles on the side shielded from the machine gun fire and into a shallow ditch alongside the road. Which is exactly what the imam wanted them to do.

Two of the men went down in the storm of small arms fire from behind them. Madge was hit twice in the left leg and twice in her lower back, but she crawled to a trough that gave her some protection and started firing blindly in the direction of the incoming rounds.

You're going to die in this stupid fucking ditch! And it's your own stupid fucking fault!

Then there was a fury of new sounds. First, the "whup, whup" of rotors, then the explosions as Hellfire missiles took out three of the trucks. One of the Apaches used its M30 chain gun on the dozen or so tightly-bunched Taliban that were on foot in the patch of scrub trees about a hundred meters behind Madge and the three men still alive.

The imam was in the lone surviving Toyota, careening onto the road. A sixteen-year-old boy – his nephew and acolyte – was standing braced in the bed of the pickup, wildly firing the fifty caliber into the sky, nowhere near the Apache that was stalking them as calmly as a leopard circling a staked goat. The imam saw the Hellfire missile fall free from its hard mount beneath the Apache, screamed when the rocket motor flared, and watched in terror as the faint contrail stretched in a straight line from the Apache to him. He actually put his hands up to shield himself as the missile came through the windshield.

Chambers, Ollie and Harlan Crosby watched the action from start to finish on the laptop screen with the video feed from the drone. They even had a soundtrack as the firefight was only a mile from where they stood. The fireballs from the Hellfires were easily visible over the crest of the small hills between them and the carnage.

"Luther! Take Gillespie and Spotts and check out the scene. I'll keep the Apaches handy if you need them, but from what I can see, it's mostly a job for the body collectors." Chambers barked out the orders while keeping Ollie and Harlan fixed in his glare.

He turned to Harlan. "OK, *sir,* " – the word was heavily inflected – "exactly what in the living hell are we doing here? And who are – were – those people in those three Humvees?"

Harlan looked at Ollie, but he was still staring at the screen, his fists clenched and tendons standing out on his neck.

They were his people. And he just watched them die.

Then he remembered Madge. *She made it out of the Humvee. Into the ditch. Maybe ....* He looked blankly at Chambers. He didn't answer his question. Just turned away and stared off into the distance, where the smoke was still rising from the burning vehicles.

Chambers watched Luther head over the hill with the other two Seals and thought about all that he didn't know. *It's the stuff you don't know you don't know that kills you out here. Time to do something about that. Too many good men hung out here for target practice.*

Ollie was still looking at the screen. The drone was filming from a static position, just beginning to pick up the three-man Seal team coming into the picture in the upper right quadrant. They were spread out and moving quickly. Chambers reached past Ollie and closed the laptop.

"I don't care if you're CIA, NSA or the PTA! I want to know what we're really supposed to be doing here and who else is hanging around –"

Ollie wheeled and fixed Chambers with a look that made him step back and disengage the safety on his M4.

"Fuck you and what you want to know, Lieutenant! Those are my people out there" – he gestured vaguely toward the smoke – "and it was me that put them into that shit storm! I could care less what you think you need to know."

He drew his sidearm from the holster on his belt and headed for the SUV.

"It's time to bring a little reality into this affair."

Abdullah was sitting in the driver's seat, staring straight ahead, his hands fingering his prayer beads and his lips moving as he recited the ninety-nine names of Allah.

Ollie leaned against the door and spoke through the open window, the pistol dangling loosely from his right hand. His tone was even, conversational. Unless one listened carefully and caught the slight pauses between each word, the careful enunciation required for the suppression of a consuming rage.

"Eleven men, Abdullah. Eleven. Friends of mine. Because of you and your uncle."

Abdullah turned and looked at him, knowing that this moment had been coming for some time and that nothing he could say would alter the outcome. He focused on reciting his prayer.

"Ollie. Let it go." The senator was standing about ten feet away, near the rear bumper of the SUV.

"Can't. Not this time. Not after that. Not even for Slater. I'm done. Just this one more thing."

He brought his pistol up and rested it on the door frame. It was a Beretta M9.

"Ollie. We need him."

"You're right about that, Senator. But we need him in different ways." He lifted the Beretta and placed the muzzle against Abdullah's temple.

The shot was incredibly loud in the silence. Ollie's head snapped sideways, as if to follow the instant cloud of blood and brain matter that seemed to hang in the air. The Beretta fired as he collapsed, the bullet going through the roof of the SUV.

Harlan lowered the gun he was holding and looked at Ollie's sprawled figure in a trancelike way. After a few seconds, he stared at the gun in his hand and then at Chambers.

"Any problem, Lieutenant?"

To his credit, Chambers thought for a brief couple of seconds before answering, "No sir."

Now is not the time for a lengthy discussion of the finer points of the military justice system.

Luther's voice came through his headset. "Lieutenant? What's the shooting about?"

"All's cool here, Luther. What have you got for me?"

"No Taliban except the best kind -- dead ones. The Apaches really tore 'em up."

"What about the people in the Humvees?"

"A small traveling circus, I think. Four dead for sure, plus however many are in the middle of a bonfire that used to be an early model Humvee. I've got three ragtag-looking live white guys. Civilian contractors, right out of the 'Soldier of Fortune' want ads. They want to talk to our man Ollie."

"That's not gonna happen. What else?"

"One badly wounded. A very angry ex-U.S. Army colonel, with leg and back wounds. Wants to talk with the Senator. Happens to be black and a woman. Kinda makes me wonder if the world is passing me by."

"She gonna make it?"

"Ask me, anybody that mean is not gonna die from a mere couple of bullets. But it's gonna be close. She needs serious help."

"OK, come on in – I'm sending down a Humvee."

"But I haven't told you the best part. There's another woman. Just crawled out of one of the Humvees. Dressed for a cocktail party. Looks a lot like a Playboy centerfold before silicone was discovered."

Prelude to an Exchange

Harlan, Abdullah, Chambers and Luther stood in front of the SUV at the crest of the hill. In the distance – six-hundred and seventeen meters according to Luther's rangefinder – Sahid, Slater and two other armed Afghans were lined up in front of the pickup truck. Faint tire tracks connected the two clusters of individuals. The drone was at the approximate midpoint, sending video to the Seal team behind them just below the crest in the road.

It had taken about ten hectic minutes to get to this point. Once the three Seals returned with Madge, CC and the three surviving contractors, Chambers had deployed two men a thousand meters in either direction as observation posts on the river road, telling them, "I want to know what's headed our way, even if it's a kid on a skateboard!" The remaining men in the team were in two Humvees with the engines idling, ready to go on Chambers' order.

The Pave Hawk copter was called in and was now headed for Kabul at max speed, carrying Madge and CC. The medic on the search and rescue team had already used CPR on Madge once and he was not optimistic.

The three Apache helicopters were on the ground, parked about a hundred meters away. Sahid had insisted on that. The engines were shut down and the six crewmen had hiked back to join the Seals. It would take ten to fifteen minutes to bring them into action.

There was one more exchange of reassurances by the respective hostages, Abdullah first.

"All is well on this end, Sahid. But the man Ollie will not be driving the SUV to you. It will be a Lieutenant Chambers. He will be unarmed."

Sahid was clearly uneasy. "I do not trust this Ollie. I would like to have him where I can see him."

"He is dead," said Abdullah. After a pause, he added, "A side effect from the skirmish with Mullah Omar's fighters. The senator shot him."

Slater was next. "Nothing has changed here. Let's get this done."

The sun was low, nearing the western horizon. The angled light transformed the bleak landscape, adding shadows and depth to what had been a two-dimensional featureless plain. A very slight breeze was blowing.

"OK. Step one," said Sahid. "First, we exchange vehicles. I'm ready. I'll start when you do."

Chambers nodded to Luther, who dropped a small sandbag onto the ground and stretched out behind it, propping the tripod of his sniper rifle onto it. "Good to go, boss. I'll have you covered."

But when Chambers moved toward the SUV, he was stopped by Harlan's hand on his arm. "You're staying here, Lieutenant. I'll make this leg of the trip and come back with Slater."

"Sir. I don't think that's a good idea. You're the most valuable hostage they could hope to have. A U.S. senator would —"

Harlan slid into the driver's seat, saying, "He still wants his nephew Abdullah. I have a feeling that – in Malik's eyes – I'm not nearly as valuable as he is."

He grinned. "Kinda restores some perspective about what's important, doesn't it? In any case, I'm going. And you don't have a choice. I outrank you. And I've got this if things get squirrelly." He held out the semi-automatic pistol that he'd used on Ollie.

Chambers shook his head. "OK, but at least take this radio headset so that I can talk to you. And keep the channel open so that I know what's going on with you." It took ten seconds to clip it on and insert the ear bud.

Harlan engaged low gear and started out, moving at a steady ten miles per hour and heading straight for the pickup truck already underway and headed for them.

What are you doing? You really don't know, do you? You're jet-lagged and exhausted. You've just murdered a man you've known and worked with for twenty years. Maybe killed the only woman you've really cared about. Committed treason. You've become more of a terrorist than the people you're fighting. And then you do this colossally stupid thing ... For what?

The New York Times has prewritten obituaries. They call them "advances" and they're for the VIPs – including ex-CIA heads and serving Senators. They leave the "when," "where" and "how" to be filled in. I wonder how they'll spin this ending? Heroic gesture? Atonement via suicide? A tragic miscalculation by someone who's been behind a desk too long? Probably all of the above.

Buell and his right wing friends will appreciate what I'm doing. Shake their heads at the stupidity of it. Maybe even impute motives to me that would enable them to make sense of it.

The truth is that I just want to see and talk to the man.

He's there. I can feel it. The man sitting in the cab of the truck.

Chambers' voice came through the ear bud. "Sir?"

"Yep."

There was a slight hesitation, just long enough that Harlan knew that he was about to be told something he didn't want to hear.

"Your aide. Colonel Prentis? She didn't make it. I'm sorry."

His vision clouded and he forgot about the mechanics of driving. The SUV coasted to a stop. Harlan leaned forward, his arms resting on the steering wheel, watching the battered pickup truck slowly approach. The truck stopped alongside the forest green SUV.

The two men looked intently at one another across the six feet of space separating them, as though expecting to learn something significant from a prolonged visual inspection. As if the decades of impersonal antagonism that had existed between them would somehow be visible in some way.

Sahid recognized him immediately and was puzzled by his own lack of surprise. *He looks more like the soldier he once was rather than a U.S. senator. And nothing like his son. Curious, that he would put himself at risk like this. This is not an ordinary man ... and I don't think he's a particularly good man.*

"Senator Crosby. It's a long way from Washington DC."

"Salaam, Sahid. Nice looking sheep."

Each of the men felt the need to say something more, to commemorate in some way this unlikely encounter. But neither of them had the necessary words. Perhaps they sensed that in each other and deemed it sufficient. Or perhaps they recognized that they shared a bone deep calmness. A calmness based on acceptance and an indifference to consequences. For Sahid, it stemmed from the combination of religious certitude and the sheer weariness that sets in after decades of guerilla warfare. For Crosby, it was the sheer accumulation of omens, leading to – for the first time in his life – a sense that he was no longer in control.

Harlan sat back, ready to drive on. He said, "I'll be glad when this is over."

Sahid said nothing. *I wonder what "this" he has in mind. The exchange of hostages? The never ending war? Or something else?*

The pickup moved away first. The SUV started up after a few seconds, toward the reunion of father and son, its slowness of pace seeming to convey a reluctance to reach its destination.

The Meeting

Sahid stopped alongside Chambers, making sure to stay out of the line-of-fire of the rifleman lying prone next to him. He made a circling motion with his left hand and Chambers nodded. He made a wide circle and left the truck aimed back down the rude track that it had just traversed. Chambers motioned him out of the truck and patted him down for weapons.

When Chambers climbed into the truck bed among the sheep, Sahid said, "They're not armed either."

A low growl came from the very large black man lying next to him with the rifle in firing position. "The man just likes animals. You might wanna count 'em before you head back." He did not take his eye away from the scope, nor did the rifle waver an inch.

Strange. How much alike we are. But we will try to kill each other just the same. It was so much easier when we could still hate them.

Chambers stood among the sheep and did a slow three-sixty scan of the horizon from his elevated position in the truckbed. He spoke into his headset. "Dobbsie. Run that drone around our perimeter. A thousand meter radius. And one more time along the top of that cliff face."

He jumped down and stood alongside Sahid. Both of them stared intently at the four figures standing in a row five hundred meters along the track, watching the green SUV as it approached.

"Anything unusual, Luther?"

Luther swung the muzzle of his rifle a few inches in either direction, keeping his right eye fixed to the high-powered scope. "We've got an extra player. The guy who was in the cab of the pickup. No apparent weapon. Older guy, Afghan. Going by the body language of Mutt and Jeff, I would pick him as the boss."

As they watched, the tallest of the four moved to the side and assumed a prone firing position. Luther chuckled. "And the sniper? He's aiming at you. I guess you must look like the boss on this end."

"What about the other one?"

"He's keeping his rifle pointed at our hostage. But he could easily take out our heroic senator if he wanted to."

They watched the SUV do as Sahid had done– stop and then circle behind the group to finally come to a halt alongside them and facing back the way it had come. A lone figure got out and merged with the other figures.

"Oops!" Luther said. "Our sniper is now vertical again."

Chambers swore violently. "Crosby! Damn him! He's turned off the headset!"

He lifted his M4, centered on Sahid's chest. "If there's any surprise, I will –"

Sahid spoke mildly, "It is your side that seems to be having all the surprises. We are doing what we said we would do."

"Man's got a point, Lieutenant." Luther's tone was carefully neutral.

Sahid said nothing, but he was thinking furiously. *This is what Malik wanted. This is why he came along, put himself needlessly at risk. Defied Omar. To get the man face-to-face. And he knew he would come. For what? What does he expect to get, or learn?*

He had no answers. *So I shall do as he asked. Play this strange game with no rules, to whatever end it has.*

His final thought was a premonition. *This is not going to end well.*

He realized Chambers was talking to him.

"I'm sorry. What did you say?"

"Step one … exchange of vehicles …. It's done. What next?"

Sahid looked at the five figures in the distance. "It's up to him."

Six-hundred and seventeen meters away, five men were coping with serious uncertainty, made worse by the need to conceal it from one another.

Cyrus was lying prone, mostly keeping the crosshairs in his scope on the name tag that said "Chambers." Every twenty seconds or so, he would check out the other Seal, but all he could see of him was half of his face. The other half was behind the sights of his sniper rifle. Cyrus noted that it was the same model he was using – the 300 Winchester Magnum. Twice in the last couple of minutes, the rifle was sighted on him and each time Cyrus experienced an immobilizing fear for about three seconds, waiting to see the muzzle flash. He wondered if it was possible that he could move quickly enough to dodge a bullet fired from six hundred meters; however, he knew nothing of muzzle velocities, nor was his arithmetic equal to the task even if he did.

His other problem was his need to kill the men he was watching through his scope; a need so intense and visceral that he did not trust himself to put his finger inside the trigger guard. He was like a boy who'd been given a kite on a windblown day and told to stay inside. *Seals! In the open. I will kill the sniper first, then the man Chambers.*

Wait for the Taliban fighters. They must be close by now. Then!

He began practicing, simulating the head shot to the sniper, then a quick traverse to Chambers, going for the body as the man would almost certainly be moving.

He was so engrossed in his rehearsal that the voice in his ear did not register for a few seconds.

"Cyrus. Leave the rifle and help Badi. Suddenly we have two Crosby's to worry about."

"But Malik –"

"Leave the rifle. We will not need it until Slater is on his way back to them."

Harlan stopped the SUV and turned off the engine. The four men standing and waiting for him wore various expressions.

His son was a mixture of surprise and uncertainty. *It's like the time I dropped in on him in his Berkeley rooming house. That didn't turn out very well at all.*

The two Afghans flanking Slater and holding their rifles across their chests looked both curious and hostile. They had been expecting a soldier, not a fairly distinguished looking elder statesman. But he was still an American.

But it was the older Afghan that Harlan looked at first, hoping to see surprise and uncertainty. Instead, the man looked back at him with an unreadable expression.

He got out of the SUV, closed the door and stood facing the others.

"Hello, Slater. Glad to see you're well. Your mother has been worried about you."

Christ! A dramatic battlefield confrontation and that's what you come up with? That has to be the worst piece of dialogue ever uttered!

Slater was even more unemotional. He said nothing, maybe a faint nod, but Harlan wasn't even sure of that.

Malik – he was sure that's who it was – gestured at the shorter man. "Badi?" He pointed at Harlan. The man leaned his rifle against the SUV and ran his hands over Harlan's torso. He took the pistol that was tucked inside his belt at the small of his back and handed it to Malik. Then he stepped back and picked up his rifle and went back to stand alongside his taller companion.

Malik looked at the pistol that he'd been handed, then at Harlan with a disappointed expression. "The driver was to be unarmed," he said. He sounded neither surprised nor offended.

Harlan shrugged. "I was a last minute substitution. I didn't know the rules."

"Yes. A substitution. Because you killed your friend Oliver."

"It was necessary. He was about to --"

Malik held up his hand. "You do not need to explain. I understand."

He turned slightly, bringing Harlan's pistol up. He fired one shot, striking Cyrus in the left temple.

Chambers heard the shot and saw one of the five figures fall to the ground. "Luther! What the hell's going on over there?"

"Damned if I know! They took the handgun off of Crosby – no surprise there -- handed it to the old guy and he turned around and shot the tall guy – the one with the long gun. I think we just witnessed an execution."

Chambers looked at the two Afghans standing with them. They were a contrast in emotions. Abdullah was shocked, wide-eyed and uncertain. Sahid looked merely sad, like someone attending a funeral for a friend who'd been waiting to die.

The Conversation

Harlan's first wild thought was *he's going to kill all of us!* But Malik lowered the gun, letting it dangle loosely from his index finger. He leaned down to pick up the rifle lying next to Cyrus' crumpled body. He handed it to Badi and said, almost gently, "Here. Take this and aim it at those two Seals who are watching us. I'll watch these two."

Malik moved so that both Crosbys were between him and the Seal with the sniper rifle. *I don't think the shooter will risk a shot with Badi in place, but this will make his choice easier for him.*

Harlan said, "About the hundred million –"

"I do not care about that."

Harlan could not conceal his surprise. *Not care? About a hundred million dollars?* Then there was a surge of resentment. *All that scheming and setting up all those people ... and you don't care!* Finally, and for the first time in a long time, he felt the beginnings of fear. *Is this about vengeance?*

Malik spoke to Slater. "Sit down and stay put. I need to talk with Senator Crosby about the final arrangements." He brandished the Beretta to make it clear that compliance was not optional.

He led Harlan behind the SUV, keeping the vehicle and Harlan between him and the Seals.

Slater sat in the dirt, facing the last six hundred meters between him and his apparent freedom. But the image he was seeing was that of the two men behind him and his thoughts were not about his freedom, but rather the nature of the negotiation they were conducting.

The two men stood facing one another, separated by about six feet of space. And by culture, their personal histories, and a war that had gone on far too long at much too high a cost for either of them. Each of them was aware that this was an encounter they had been seeking, but neither of them fully understood what they wanted from the other, or from themselves. It made them strangely inarticulate.

Harlan broke the silence. "I want my son with me."

"He's not your son. He's mine."

As soon as he spoke the words, Malik knew that this was the reason for him being here. To say what he had always needed to say. To this man, in this way. The six simple words also had a profound effect on Harlan. He took in several huge intakes of breath, each time letting it all out slowly, closing his eyes as if trying to sense the rate of outflow. He turned his head and looked toward the sun, now low in the sky.

He said, "He's not your son." But the words and even his posture lacked conviction. As if he sensed that, he added, "You don't know that he's your son."

Malik said, "But you do, don't you? That he's not yours?"

But Harlan was no longer listening. He was back in Washington DC and the summer of 1980.

I was watching the news. Jimmy Carter had been re-nominated and Richard Pryor had suffered serious burns from free-basing cocaine.

Then Yasmin said, "I'm pregnant."

He remembered the sequence of his reactions. *First, disbelief, then anger at the betrayal. I never thought of the word 'infidelity.' It was always 'disloyalty.' Never lessened by his own deceptions. His certain knowledge that he was physically unable to father children, a fact carefully concealed from everyone except Madge. Then came irritation, fed by his omnipresent concern for his career. In his script, Yasmin's role was that of "the general's wife," not that of 'mother.' And the idea of divorce with hints of sexual scandal was unimaginable. Last, there was a simple curiosity. A poor substitute for jealousy perhaps. Who was it? The real father?*

Given even the little he knew about gestation cycles, it wasn't hard to reconstruct. Istanbul. Three days on her own while he worked eighteen hours a day. The month-long, almost clinical, depression that set in after they returned.

Khalid. Now Malik.

Slater confirmed it with his birth. There was no part of me to be seen. Yasmin was there, the eyes and mouth, the long legs...and someone else ... but nothing of him.

He looked at Slater, sitting in the dirt twenty feet away. Then at Malik in front of him. *Slater is his descendant. Color of skin. Dark and curly hair. Even the posture, the way they hold their head and their expression when they're listening intently.*

Yasmin knew, of course. Who the father was. But she never said anything. Slater was always "our son." But the marriage became a stage play, the two of us playing roles for one another and the various circles within which we moved. The two of them – Yasmin and Slater – were always close. I was the outsider.

Only then did the obvious question occur to him. *Did she tell him? Slater?*

Until this minute, he had always assumed that Slater believed that he was the natural-born and only son of Harlan Crosby, a career military officer and now a senator. There had never been the slightest hint that he thought otherwise, even in the worst of his teenage acting out.

But she taught him Arabic. At first at home, and then special classes. And they worked together on Pashto before and after his first tour in Afghanistan. When did she learn the Pashto phrases that they rehearsed together? And she would join in the discussions about Afghanistan – the escalating arguments that he and Slater would fall into so often since 2001.

Malik broke in. It was as though he'd been listening to Harlan's self-doubts.

"He thinks he is your son. I have said nothing to him."

"What do you want? *Really* want? Why are we here?" asked Harlan, intending indignation, but only sounding incredibly weary.

The question depressed Malik. *What do I want? Why these elaborate arrangements to have this conversation? Vengeance? For Cham Kasi? For all the evils this man has caused for me? Is that what this all comes down to?*

The flurry of questions in Malik's own mind seemed the answer to Crosby's question: *I don't know what I want.* But then he realized that Crosby himself had provided the answer. The flicker of emotions that came and went as he was forced to confront the reality of Slater's creation was evidence that he and Harlan shared the same need. Wanted the same things that all men want late in their lives.

"What do I want? I want to know my son. To sit and talk with him. To tell him about me, who I really am. To learn who he is and what he wants and how he thinks. To tell him that I loved ... love ... his mother."

Harlan listened and envied Malik, realizing that he himself had forfeited the chance to have the same things.

He heard his own voice, surprisingly harsh. "You can't have him. He's coming with me."

Malik smiled, an incredibly sad smile.

"Of course he is. He's an American. With American parents and values. He believes in freedom, equality for women, democracy, due process instead of summary executions. Wine bars, rock music, baseball, mixed-race marriage and two-car garages. Afghanistan is no place for such a person."

Maybe someday, but not for a long time.

"Besides, I want Abdullah and Sahid back. They are my best, last and only friends."

The two men turned and looked at Slater, sitting cross-legged in the middle of the faint tire tracks that connected the two groups of men, each of them with a rifleman lying in a prone firing position. The sun was just above the horizon, about to merge with low-hanging cirrus clouds, long strips of white turning gray. It was going to be one of those spectacular sunsets, the kind that causes Western tourists to rave about the quality of light in Afghanistan.

Harlan turned on the switch for the small mike dangling loosely around his neck. "Chambers? You there?"

"Yes." Relief was quite apparent in the single word.

"We're coming back. Send Abdullah and Sahid."

"Yes sir."

"And Chambers? Have Luther stand down. No more killing today."

Epilog

The failure of the United Commercial Bank of the Emirates did not threaten the global banking system, but it did cause considerable disruption and scandal within the Middle Eastern countries where it operated. It was both instantaneous and unexpected. One day UCBE was perfectly sound and highly respected; the next day it failed to open its doors. And when the authorities arrived, the vaults were empty of cash and the owner – Abdul-Karim, one of the most respected bankers in the region – was equally absent. The bank's branch in Kabul apparently triggered the collapse. It had just received a prominent $100 million deposit, which had disappeared into an electronic maze that examiners despaired of unwinding.

Kendall Avery Zanker, known as "Kaz" to his friends, heard of the UCBE failure within minutes of its discovery. As the person responsible for all of Global American's European financial relationships, he worked furiously to ascertain the amount of his bank's exposure to UCBE. To his surprise, he found that GABI had lost almost nothing. The assets and liabilities netted very close to zero. When he looked at the account histories, he noted that UCBE had engaged in a series of repayments and other transactions in the last day before its failure to effectively zero out the relationship.

It seems that Malik's 'safe passage' extends to corporations as well as individuals.

He was sitting in his London office thinking of Abdul-Karim and where he might be when he had a visitor.

"Hello Kaz."

She's still the most beautiful woman I've ever seen. And then he remembered the last time he had seen her. On a video screen, kneeling in the dirt, terrified.

"Hello CC. I'm glad you're OK."

"Thanks to you. You paid a hundred million bucks for me. Puts me in a league with Helen of Troy."

Technically, that's true, I guess. But we both know that they were going to kill both of us regardless of whether or not I complied with their demands. I wonder if she had an Al Jazeera guardian tailing her as well?

He said nothing. He did not want to think any more about that dais in the Presidential Palace or his agonizing choice. CC or Slater? He wondered if his decision to sacrifice Slater Crosby would ever stop haunting him. *Or her?*

He asked, "You heard about UCBE?"

"Yeah. They suckered us every which way, didn't they?"

He couldn't help himself. He said, "They?"

The single word seemed to turn her from a confident, assertive and beautiful woman into an abject and powerless supplicant, here in his office to ask for something; something that would be trivial for him to give, but overwhelmingly difficult for her to ask for.

"Kaz, I … I didn't want … mean … they told me …"

She turned to the window, as if the elusive words would appear somehow in the air. She had thought about – and discarded -- a hundred different ways to say what she needed to say. As she listened to herself stammering, she recognized her problem.

You want sympathy, not forgiveness. Because you were sniveling in the dirt, waiting for that knife to start sawing at your throat. Because you sat in that Humvee, feeling the bullets drumming against the steel wall next to you and blood dripping onto you from the turret over your head. Because to ask for forgiveness would be like saying you did something wrong.

"They. And me. That's why I came here today. To tell you that I'm sorry. That some of what happened to you is my fault."

There's more, but it's too much like begging. I can't do that. Even for him.

Kaz heard the words, including the ones she couldn't bring herself to say. He was still dealing with his first reaction when she walked into his office. *She's alive. I didn't kill her. She's alive. And here!* The first tendrils of relief began to penetrate his senses.

He was silent for a long time and CC took a step backward and felt for the door handle. That seemed to jar him.

He stood up from his desk chair and said, "There's a coffee bar downstairs. It's not a Starbucks, but perhaps we could go there and start again."

Harlan Crosby had just finished interviewing the sixth candidate for his personal assistant and chief of staff. This one was a man. He was working on a theory that he had a subconscious need to replace Madge in kind, and that hiring a man rather than a woman would redirect that need.

Her memorial service was very discreet, attended by a small number of close friends and other staffers. The official story was that she'd gotten caught in a crossfire while on a very hush-hush fact-finding mission in Iraq's Ambar Province.

The Seals were easy to contain. They were quite used to CIA operations where the most important line in the post-action debriefing was, "This operation never took place." Harlan saw to it that Chambers and Luther received official but vague commendations; the kind that would lead to promotions down the line.

Major Dalkie was more difficult, having lost several Afghan soldiers in a mysterious fashion. But Slater's unpublicized return after three weeks of detention as a prisoner enabled him to overcome both his curiosity and resentment at being ordered around by the Americans. It helped that a *very* high-ranking British officer called him and personally "requested" his cooperation in keeping Slater's absence out of the press.

Harlan's most difficult sales pitch was to Buell, the gentleman farmer from Utah with the handy G4 and the need for ongoing warfare. It started with a very testy phone call.

Buell was upset. "I've lost most of my contractors in Afghanistan. And the single man there that I trusted most. I don't like it."

He knows that I was there. And I'll bet that Ollie kept him updated on what I was doing there. But he needs me ... the access I give him.

"Afghanistan is old news, Buell. Downgraded from a war to a training mission. I just came from the Central Intelligence Oversight Committee and I can tell you that all of our attention is focused on the Islamic State bunch in Iraq and

Syria. They're getting traction now in Yemen and Somalia as well."

Buell growled, "I still don't like the idea of quitting a war just because we haven't won it yet."

"Don't worry. I promise you that there will always be fighting in Afghanistan. That's what Afghans do. They fight. They always have and they always will."

Yasmin Crosby had just returned from her monthly visit to Walter Reed, seeing the newly arrived casualties from Iraq and Afghanistan. There were fewer of them lately, a trickle compared to the pre-withdrawal period. When she turned on her laptop, she found the usual twenty or thirty emails, but two of them occupied all of her attention.

One was from the law firm that she had engaged to manage her divorce from Harlan. He had promised to cooperate and she halfway believed that he meant it. But he was so steeped by now in his clandestine mindset that she didn't think he could avoid looking for ways to subvert the process.

The other was from "A aka K aka M," a pseudonym that at first seemed Arabic, and then – when she pronounced it – Hawaiian. The message was brief, and cryptic.

I met S. I didn't tell him, but I think he knows. He reminds me of you. I still think of you.

Malik celebrated his sixty-eighth birthday by having an extra cup of sweetened tea with Abdullah, Sahid and Abdul-Karim. It was an unusual party, in that most Afghans did not celebrate birthdays, did not know their date of birth, or even how old they were. He could not help marveling at the unlikelihood that he was still alive.

He did not expect to see his sixty-ninth birthday. He was living in a village near his original home in Cham Kasi. His main activity was running a school for girls from the surrounding countryside. He told the Taliban to stay away, that he was "neutral," but he knew that they would eventually come. If not them, then the government troops. No matter which side visited, they would not believe that he was not aiding their opponent. They would say something like, "If you are not my friend, then you are my enemy." And they would kill him to make the point.

He waited for them to come. And was content.

Six months had elapsed since the withdrawal of combat troops and the formal handoff from the NATO forces to the Afghan National Security Forces. There was no commemoration of that event.

It was another ordinary day in Afghanistan.

A car bomb in Heart killed forty-seven men, women and children waiting in line at a theatre putting on a children's play. Three different groups – ISIS, al Qaeda and the Taliban – each claimed responsibility.

A bank was robbed in Kunduz by a group of heavily armed men claiming to be ISIS fighters. They beheaded the seven employees in the bank and posted the video on the internet. Government officials denied that the jihadist group had any operations in the region and blamed local bandits.

A series of coordinated drone strikes was conducted against suspected Taliban gathering points along the Afghanistan/Pakistan border. No information was released as to the specific targets or whether there were any casualties. Pakistan officially protested the incursions into their air space.

Ashraf Ghani, President of Afghanistan, appointed a panel of twenty tribal leaders to recommend ways whereby the central government could achieve, as Ghani put it, "an Afghan society based on the respect of all people for all people."

At dawn, a U.S. Army infantry captain left Achin Adi alone in a Jeep. The Jeep was discovered three hours later, bullet-riddled and overturned in a stream. The captain was declared missing-in-action. Later that same day, a single man walked east, headed directly into mountainous tribal lands. He was tall, dark skinned and dressed in traditional tribal costume, other than the boots he was wearing. He walked with surprising speed despite a pronounced limp. His backpack contained a dozen copies of a book – the story about Alice in Wonderland, translated into Dari and Pashto -- and a silver-framed portrait of his mother when she was a young woman. She was wearing a green silk dress.

About the Author

Thomas Hofstedt is engaged in approximately his fourth career, each of which is partially reflected in this book. He has worked as a professor, an international banking consultant and finally as advisor and board member for not-for-profit organizations. He is the author of four other books: *A Conspiracy of Patriots, A Convergence of Evils, Once Upon a Time in LA,* and *The Hundred Year Storm.* He lives in San Carlos, California with his wife and most diligent critic, Sharon.